*Praise for Dead Fish . . .*

"Debbie Ann Ice achieves the impossible with this wildly compelling story about a woman obsessed with saving a collapsing world. Mixing politics and environmental activism, Ice creates a dark but all-too-believable future, managing to infuse it with hope and humor. It's stunning!" — Ellen Meister, author of *Love Sold Separately*


"This is a smart and important and wonderfully funny book from the point of view of the daughter of a woman obsessed by the environmental disasters around her. It takes place sometime in the future but I hope all young people read it right now while there's still time to grow up and do something about it. And on the way, hand the book to your mother and tell her to get busy saving the planet for you." — Barbara Milton, award-winning author, environmental activist, former Director of Connecticut Audubon in Milford

# DEAD FISH

# DEAD FISH

and

# What the Blue Jays Know

# DEBBIE ANN ICE

*Bink Books*
Bedazzled Ink Publishing Company • Fairfield, California

paperback 978-1-949290-56-1

Cover Design
by

Bink Books
a division of
Bedazzled Ink Publishing, LLC
Fairfield, California
http://www.bedazzledink.com

*To: Carman Goldsmith, who taught me to love animals.*

# Acknowledgements

My story was imagined with the help of wildlife friends who visit me in my back yard. Blue jays, in particular, have been engaging with me for quite a while. I did, however, reach out to other sources, because sometimes one needs more than observations and conversations with bird friends.

I was inspired and informed by many blogs and books. I was particularly informed by the book, *Dirty Waters* by Bill Sharpsteen, University of California Press. Other books: *Saving Jemima* by Julie Zickefoose, about her experience raising a blue jay. It was so wonderful to find a professional wildlife writer who, like me, loves blue jays! *The Bird Way*, by Jennifer Ackerman. Terrific book about all kinds of birds. I was also informed by Cornell Labs and the National Audubon Society. (Please support these organizations. They do much good.) Notable blogs—climaterealityproject.org, juliezickefoose.com, and the YouTube site, lesleythebirdnerd, were all very informative. Lesleythebirdnerd has wonderful videos on blue jays. She is a blue jay whisperer.

Saving the planet and protecting our wild life is not political, but there is a clear connection between authoritarianism and environmental corruption and disregard. Anne Applebaum and Timothy Snyder have written about the road to tyranny and the impacts upon the souls of nations. *On Tyranny* by Timothy Snyder and *Twilight of Democracy* by Anne Applebaum were particularly enlightening.

OK, thank yous . . .

My novel is a big thank you to all the activists who have inspired me and collectively have succeeded in changing our world.

Thank you, Bart, my husband, who's a devoted fisherman and was patient enough to answer questions—or tell me where to go to find answers to questions. He also reads my first drafts. Anyone who reads first drafts deserves more than I can ever give. But I'll give him a book and my love.

And of course, thank you Bedazzled Ink—particularly C.A. Casey, Liz Gibson, and Claudia Wilde—for not only publishing this novel, but also encouraging and supporting me.

And, as always, thank you Thomas and Jimmy for being exactly who you are.

"Ordinary people with extraordinary vision can redeem the soul of America by getting in what I call good trouble, necessary trouble . . ."
— John R. Lewis

"In yourself right now is all the place you've got."
— Flannery O'Connor, *Wise Blood*

# Book 1
## Haley

# Prologue

Hey Mom,

I'm not the letter writer in the family, I know this. I used to be the reader of your letters. We all were. We had to be. I miss your writing, actually. I bet you miss writing.

You did love your letters didn't you, Mom? Our life was filled with your letters. Complaints zipped through the cyber universe to anyone of importance—editors, public officials, bloggers, publishers. I think about those letters often, but I don't believe the community is nostalgic for your writing days.

Anyway, I thought you may appreciate my very long letter to you about what you already know but what others may not. I'm hoping it will pique someone else's interest and jolt a memory, eventually leading to that one clue that slipped by me. Also, perhaps it can generate some Mom guilt. I'm confident you'll find this; I know you'll read it. Probably five times.

So, here goes, a story in letters. Your story, my voice, because, of course, you have no voice. You're voiceless not because you can't talk or are incapable of expressing your concerns, passions, world views, ideas. There's not one thing in the world you have not considered and expressed an opinion about. No, you can't write this, because for once in your life, your story has gone silent. But don't worry, I know your story, I even know what you say and do when I'm not there.

You insisted on that activist march. Off you went by yourself, because there was no one to go with you, due to your alienation of everyone in town. I had to stay home to take care of our bulldog. Remember how you insisted I stay home? I think about that now. Your casual flip of the wrist. "No, no, Haley, you hate these things. And Lolly's anxiety disorder cannot survive a strange babysitter." I was so naïve. I watched you step on that train, alone with your poster board shouting the one thing you want everyone to know—"Fish Are Dead."

At first, when you didn't return, I was terrified. We submitted a missing person's report, contacted the New York City Police Department and the FBI. I called your sisters down in Alabama—Honee and Mary Louise—who told me they hadn't heard from you in months. I traveled the route of the march, knocked on doors, wrote a letter to all the papers, even the *New York Times* and *Daily News*. I interviewed everyone who had any connection to you. Nothing.

No one found you. No one found a body. I cringe typing that, because I cannot imagine another body that once was my parent and now is something we have to bury. We suspected there could be a body because there was some sort of disturbance at the march, an explosion of sorts that caused mass hysteria. A few people were taken to the hospital. But not you. We checked everywhere.

Lydia Russo, your dog friend, suggested you probably hit your head and developed amnesia. But, I said, wouldn't someone find her? She said, "No, they could find normal people, but not your mother. Your mother would become a homeless activist. She will organize homeless marches, advocate for better housing, feed pigeons in the park, investigate dead fish in Central Park Reservoir."

So far, we've found no homeless marches. But it's not been that long.

People in town treat me like an orphan. You'd be appalled at the pity showered upon me. That's because they assume something horrible happened to you. But you're not dead. If you were dead, I'd feel a small part of my heart vanish. That's what happened when Dad died.

When I later found out you sold our house, my terror turned to something else. Anger is not really the word because I miss you so much and you did at least find me a great place to live. The lawyer—or sleazebag who arranged everything—showed up at our door and told me not to worry, everything had been taken care of. I did a little research, looked into the real estate deal, and, indeed, his story was true. You taught me well. I do not trust a soul. I reported all my research to our wonderful deputy lieutenant at the police department, who misses you, by the way. Louis shook his head and said, "We're all here for you, Haley."

Oh, and you have to know the birds are beyond despondent. How could you leave your birds? Particularly the blue jays, your best friends.

I remember returning home early one day, and after calling out to you and getting no response, assumed you were upstairs, earbuds in, reading, or—God forbid!—posting another complaint on some blog comment section. I dropped my handbag and headed for the kitchen. Right when I opened the refrigerator door, I caught a flash of red in my peripheral vision. I looked out the bay window. You were wearing that red t-shirt with "Red's Not a Color, it's an Attitude" in black letters dancing over your small breasts. It was one of your old t-shirts. You had worn it to my graduation party, which mortified me but also resulted in an upgrade in my social standing.

You were tossing peanuts to maybe twenty-five blue jays hopping around you. I watched them snatch their treats, a few flying toward the distant conifers as you talked with those left behind. We all talk to ourselves, Mom, it's no big deal. It's just that you seemed to *really* talk to them, as if there was a real connection. And maybe there was one. Remember when you told me that only the blue jays get you? You said they were the only ones who knew all your transgressions.

So, why did you leave them?

I believe I know why you are where you are. I just want to know where you are. The story I tell myself is imagined in some places, factual in other places. I have a great memory, and, like I said, I certainly understand you better than anyone else.

Except blue jays, of course. But since blue jays can't write, you're stuck with me.

# Blue Jays Memo

What? She said what?
We can't write.
Said who?
Can't write?
Who?
Pay attention!
We dictate. Same thing.
Shut up!
Why?
Come back!
Stay on limb!
Shut uuuuuup! Listen!

OK. So, look, we dictate. We perch mostly. Perch, perch, perch, perch most days, but we can dictate a memo. We collect data when we focus. We focus when we aren't not focusing.

Who's focusing?
Shut up!
What?
Pay attention.
No.
Stop.
Shut uuup! Listen!

Where were we? We collect facts, then we dictate. We use Google song translation, even though it sucks because everything has come to a standstill down there. Nothing moves forward in human world. It used to change and improve, according to elders. Now? Nothing.

Hold on!
Where you going?
What's going on?
No. Look over here!

*Hawk!Hawk!Hawk!*
*Hawk!Hawk!Hawk!*
*Hawk!Hawk!Hawk!*
*Hawk!Hawk!Hawk!*

*Hawk gone*

Sorry about that. Look, we'll explain ourselves. A small introduction is in order, right? Quickly. We're the Corvidaes. We come by way of eastern North American Blue Jay migration path—one of many, mind you. Ours extends from latitude 44.3592, longitude 67.8412 to latitude 24.3921, longitude 80.1519. OK, that's how humans would find the path. We find it with stars, land markings, a deep place in our souls attached to a deep place inside the earth (Details would confuse humans. And, frankly, we don't want them to know). Many of us leave our path permanently, remaining with extended family members and close friends at various drop-off locations.

*Why can't we all talk?*
*Shut up!*
*Where you going?*
*No, not over there.*
*Here!*
*Shut uuuuup! Listen!*

Where were we? See, most of us choose family and community over, say, adventure. We're family oriented. We build nests, create rules, regulations and ultimately become, whatcha call it? A tribe? Yeah, that's it. (Humans refer to us as a "party." What the hell?) We name our tribes because names for tribes give us that team spirit. Our particular tribal name is Great Hawk Watcher tribe of eastern Connecticut. Pretty good name, right? See, that name reflects our job. We watch out for hawks. We hate those assholes.

*Hawks?*
*Where?*
*Where're those fuckers?*
*Where you going?*
*Stop!*
*Shut uuuuuup! Listen!*

Many of us live around friendly humans. Those of us who're bored—usually the kids, juveniles, two-year-olds—join the other Great Hawk Watcher tribe members before cold days return and travel on the migration path. Then, when the cold goes away, these gypsy kids return. Only twenty percent of us go south. Sure, it's hotter there, but every place is hotter now, and humans down there shoot metal into the sky often. Not exactly receptive.

When they come back, we sing to them and others. "Come have sex." "Come have sex." Every year, same thing, same song.

Sex? Did someone say sex?
What?
Who?
Where you going?
Shut up! Listen!

Our tribes consist of many families. Our particular family—which includes sons, daughters, grandchildren, great grandchildren, cousins, uncles, aunts, nephews, nieces, great nieces, great nephews, and so on—is called Children of Athena, after our great, great, elder who moved here years ago.

Our family is at a New England female human nest located approximately ten miles southeast of the North American migration path. Our late cousins—may they all rest in peace—the Honorable Crows, who could decipher human song—told our elders many years ago that other humans refer to this female human as "Lorraine."

Who's that?
The human.
Where you going?
Come back!
Pat attention!

For crows' sake!

Anyways, we don't call the female Lorraine. We just call her female host. A name infers a type of intimacy we don't reserve for human-bird interaction. Our female host is our primary feeder. We like to eat.

We notice things. Little things. Major things. Like, for example, the destruction of female host's original home nest a long while ago. She destroys her nest! Then, as if that's not bad enough, she gets male humans with baggy lower appendage covering to rebuild nest in a strange configuration. This was after her mate died. Oh yeah, we noticed that, or our elders did. We know all the details.

Her what?
Mate.
Elders saw the death.
Yeah, they said . . .
Shut up!
No discussion of death!

So, OK. Look, we draw no conclusions. We simply see what we see. And know what we know. And what we know? Is more than humans know.

# Chapter 1

*When death comes in waves*

IT HAPPENS IN those moments when you stop and look beyond the air in front of you, in the direction of something that does not exist in our immediate world, only the wild world that surrounds us. When you stop and look this way, you always notice. And when you notice, things happen.

You usually notice what's up, not down. Up in the pine branches shimmering with wind and life. That's how you discovered the crow problem many years ago. Oh, dear, remember the crow problem? The beginning of your extreme state of anxiety. Well, the Great Transition sparked it, but the crows added the gasoline. You've always taught me to pay attention to the societies above us. I guess you think why ignore them when they don't ignore us.

You ride your bicycle everywhere because it's what one does when one doesn't work. Dad's life insurance and investments cover more than you need. And, really, who would hire you? Sorry, Mom. I love you, but, really, who would hire you?

Your bicycle route is usually far away from our neighborhood. You poke down Lamont Avenue, which takes you by neat, square houses behind tiny green lawns with no trees. Lamont crosses Main Street and heads south two miles until it finds water at Shoreline Road which hugs the coast a few miles, heading west toward Suffolk.

This morning traffic is light and only two cars pass you, one so close you almost leave the road. When you reach Shoreline, you slow down to enjoy the bright day. I can picture it so clearly—your long athletic legs pumping the pedals, your thinning hair loose down your back, those alert green eyes looking down at the road before you. You are quite lovely looking for your age, particularly when you're in your element.

To your right, houses retreat up hills, spreading out to announce their wealth. To your left an expanse of gray—slightly undulating water, barely licking the rocky land—connects the WASPY Connecticut communities to the Italian, Jewish, and Irish non-WASPY communities of Long Island. You told me once that to the birds flying over us, the Long Island Sound resembles a bladder swollen with salt water squirted in from the Atlantic Ocean. "That's the true metaphor," you said. Whatever that means.

You do not like looking at mansions. Instead, you look in the direction of the water and notice glitters of light reflecting off the surface. You pull off the road, shield your eyes with your hands. You leave your bike and walk close to the underbrush that separates grass from mud and water. Thousands of fish bellies cover the water. You step through the underbrush, slide down the steep bank into the mud, and there before you lie layer upon layer of dead and dying fish.

You consider this extraordinary event. Dead fish blanket the mud. Fish bellies undulate across the Sound. A noxious smell in the air. You decide to take a closer look. To your right, a wooden walkway juts out a hundred feet and connects to a floating dock, where a Whaler is parked. The boat of course inspires a thought—something you always have, a thought, that is. You're very proud of your thought generation. You've been told on numerous occasions that having a thought does not mean one has to act upon the thought. Dad used to tell you to breathe for a while after a thought emerged. You said, "Do you think I hold my breath to generate thoughts? I'm already breathing."

My advice to anyone who lives near water and builds a dock would be this: do not buy a boat, unless it will be chained to the dock. I feel very strongly about this. Chain the boat to a dock, particularly if the motor is left on it. If one does not do this, and there is a gas tank in a chest on the dock platform? Someone could reach into the chest, remove the gas tank, place it in the boat, start the motor, and drive the boat away.

You sit confident and stiff-backed in the boat, hand on the throttle, as it cuts through the water filled with dead fish. A complicated array of emotions washes over you. You're repulsed by the death. You're shocked and saddened by the loss of life. You're amazed at the tragedy. And of course, you're angry. I suspect the anger pushes other emotions into a corner of your brain, or maybe it kills the other emotions.

Because dead fish swirl near the propeller, threatening to stall it, you turn off the engine and tilt the motor out of the water. The boat drifts. You spend several moments fuming about the tragedy, then try to count the fish, which is like counting grains of sand on the beach. You stop counting. You take a paddle, touch a few fish. Two do nothing but float, one appears to flip its tail weakly.

You pull out your phone and take pictures, but since you have closed all your social media accounts, you can't post pictures for public viewing. You tap a neighborhood app and search. Surely others have noticed this and have posted comments online. But you find nothing. Before you Google, you glance back at the coastline—greensward, rocky banks, six thousand square feet Tudors, a few three-story colonials with fluted columns. Only one lawn has human life—landscapers blowing leaves and detritus.

You stand and yell.

Nothing.

You wave frantically.

Nothing.

You yell again, wave again, yell again, wave again.

Finally, they both look up, pause briefly—without turning off the blowers—stare back but don't yell or wave back.

You sit and type into your Google box, "Fish problems Long Island Sound." Several links to fishing blogs appear. You type "dead fish Long Island Sound." Links to articles about gutting and filleting striped bass appear. You type, "Death on the Sound." A few short stories.

You sit in your borrowed boat, dead fish surrounding you, and do nothing for a moment. You decide to call environmental advocate friends. No one answers. You text a few, but the messages turn green with an exclamation mark, indicating they are unsendable.

Reluctantly, you tap in the phone number for Westbrook Town Hall, hoping no one will recognize your cell phone number or voice, although it's been a while since the gas company conflict.

Ellen, the town hall receptionist and town secretary, answers.

"Hi, can you direct me to the person who handles fish in the Sound. Particularly dead fish."

Ellen says she doesn't know anything about dead fish people. "Sometimes brackish water doesn't have oxygen for large schools. Although it's a little early for bunker. It's been a very hot April, though."

"There's a greenish hue to some of these fish. And black spots. I don't think I'm looking at bunker. A few may be bunker, but truly April is not a bunker month. And if lack of oxygen killed them, there's no oxygen because they're dead everywhere."

"May I ask who's calling? You sound familiar."

"I need to talk with someone who monitors water quality."

"You will have to call the state environmental department."

"I hate talking to voicemails."

"Just leave a message."

"So, how about Game and Fishing Department? Is there a Game and Fishing Department? I'll take that."

She tells you to call the state and insists you leave your name, and of course you are not going to leave your name since they all know you there and all you want to do is inform someone somewhere about "millions of dead fish, a sea of dead fish." Ellen does not transfer you, only keeps asking questions, all personal, so you threaten to call the state and leave a message about Ellen. Ellen laughs and soon you are talking to some man from some wildlife department who listens to you talk about dead fish for one minute before interrupting and asking if this is about a fishing license.

"I don't need a fishing license mainly because I can reach down and grab a fish. I don't need to entice them, then kill them. They're all dead. They're floating on top of the water. Hasn't this raised alarms with anyone else?" He transfers you back to Ellen.

So here we go. Conversations always go this way with you. It's why it's so easy recreating them.

"Can I have your name," Ellen now demands. "You sound familiar."

"I sound familiar? Or am I saying something familiar?"

"Oh for heaven's sakes. Lorraine Mulderon. Is that you? Are you still living in that house?"

"The one I still own? Yes."

"Every time you walk across that center, you're trespassing on gas company property." She laughs. You do not. "Have fish died in your culvert?"

"No, Ellen."

"203-666-8976. That is the number for someone in Fish . . ." You don't hear the name because you drop the phone accidentally. You pick it up, make sure it isn't wet, then put it to your ear.

"You still there?" Ellen says.

"Yes."

"That's a division of the department. Again, it's 203-666-8976. Do you want me to text it to you?"

"No, my texting doesn't work out here in the water for some reason."

"Where are you? You have a boat now?"

"I don't own one, but, yes, at this very moment, I'm in a boat. I borrowed it."

"Where are you?"

"I'm in the water off Shoreline Road, amongst dead fish."

"Where'd you get the boat?"

"That was 8976 right? Bye, Ellen."

You sit a moment and stew about Ellen, someone you think gets too involved with everyone who has an issue with the town and state. Ellen was right there in the audience when you filed your petition to stop the easement for the gas line on our property. She was always right there in the audience when anything happened. She had to be. She was the town secretary. She was also the first at our house when Dad died, stepping into our foyer, holding onto her homemade chicken stew, her eyes puffy and red. "They're nice for exactly two years," you told me. "Then they go back to where they were before the wife becomes a widow and daughter a half-orphan."

You start calling Fish and Game something or other. You expect a voice mail, so you prepare. You always prepare for voicemails. "Lack of preparation always results in an overflow of verbiage unedited as it comes out, which requires numerous start-overs and 'never minds.'" This was a problem back during the petition days, when the gas folks dropped by to check on their pipeline, interrupting your day, resulting in more complaint calls to the gas company. The biggest complaint was about our cut-in-half house. Life's complicated, isn't it, Mom?

You sit in the boat with the phone to your ear, listening to the rings. You count seven rings. You hang up. You look online for other organizations, find something with land in the title and tap its number.

"Department of Energy and Land Services."

"Hello?"

"Department of Energy and Land Services."

"Hello?"

"Department of Energy and Land Services."

"Are you a human being?"

"Yes."

"Wow. Thank you for answering the phone."

"You're welcome."

"This is great, because I'm not organized enough right now to talk to a recording. Look, I was riding my bike on Shoreline Road. I'm not there now, as I have borrowed a boat and am floating amongst a zillion dead fish. And here I am at the point of this call. See how fast I get to the point with a human? There're a zillion dead fish in the water and I think someone should know."

"In what water? Have you called the state environmental department?"

"There're a zillion dead fish."

"OK, we're not the right department, but now I'm curious. A zillion dead fish where?"

"I just told you. On Shoreline Road in Westbrook. I was riding my bicycle and looked out over the water, which is of course the Long Island Sound, and there they were, belly up, a zillion dead fish."

"Do you need a fishing license? Because that's Fish and . . ."

"For dead fish?'

"Well, that's what Fish and Gaming does. Fishing licenses."

"Who do I call about dead fish."

"It's probably bunker."

"Bunker in April? They look like alewife but what do I know?"

"They get chased up those tributaries by bigger fish and die," he continues, not listening anymore. "Can't survive brackish water. No need to panic. You can call the environmental agency, make sure they're on top of it. Let me find you a number . . . 203-654-2309."

The next number is the usual robot everyone gets because the EPA now has only three people working there. You leave a long message, the first part describing your bike ride, the second part describing the dead fish, the third part describing how you borrowed the boat. There is a beep, then click. You call back. You mention your last message, then quickly move to the dead fish again. You end with a reference to our house split in two and the gas pipeline running through the middle but emphasizing that gas probably has nothing to do with the dead fish as you do not live near water. You then suggest they simply forget you mentioned the gas pipeline, as it is irrelevant, and not to say anything to anyone about the "borrowed" boat. Beep, it's over.

You then attempt to call again but stop because you note activity on the dock where the boat was parked before your borrowed it. You start the motor and head back. As you approach the dock, you recognize the patrol car. Louis is walking down the dock.

He stands patiently because Louis is always restrained.

"Hey, Louis. You look particularly sharp today."

"I was at a police brotherhood breakfast. I didn't get to finish. Why don't you lock that bike up and come with me?"

# Blue Jays Memo

*Come have sex with me!*
*Come have sex with me!*
*Come have sex with me!*

*Where's female host?*
*There she goes.*
*Who's following her today?*
*Not now, we're having sex.*
*Gotta follow female host.*
*Shut uuuup.*
*Listen!*

Female host does same thing most mornings. She takes out manual mobile perch[1] and travels a route we've memorized.

Here's the deal. We could fly to the destination in a few minutes because bird routes actually make sense. But humans route paths around trees, other human nests, over other travel paths, which makes their travel distance twice as long as it should be. But we do it, OK? She feeds us!

*Hey, come back.*
*Where you going?*
*No, not over there.*
*Follow her. Follow her. Follow her.*
*HAWK, HAWK, HAWK.*
*HAWK, HAWK, HAWK.*
*HAWK, HAWK, HAWK.*
*Hawk gone.*

OK. So. The designated followers today are trailing her now. Her first stop is the land of tablets.[2] This is a large plot of land with many, many tablets. Female

---

1       bicycle
2       graveyard

host perches by one tablet which is where we assume they place her dead mate's remains. Humans always bury remains of beloved humans underground, then plop a tablet there to remind them where they buried it. Bad memories. Poor fools can't recall where they bury things. Sad!

She's leaving!
Pay attention!
Get back here.
Where'd he go?
Hey, come back!
She's leaving!
Shut uuuup. Listen.

Oh, for crows' sake! Where were we?

Oh, yeah, we follow her after she leaves land of tablets. Again, it's around nests, other paths, other trees. Boring. Boring. Boring. She ends up on path by water. We observe female host notice dead fish.

We of course have noticed dead fish. Everyone has noticed dead fish. Humans are always the last ones to notice.

Female host touches dead fish. Stares at fish. Female host becomes overcome with emotions. How do we know this? Easy. There's a certain arrangement of fur above eyes and coloration of face that accompanies extreme emotions. We're experts. Trust us.

Conflict!
Conflict!
Conflict!
Shut uuup! She's OK.
Conflict!

Female host engages in usual activities she engages in when overcome with emotions. Conflict behavior we call it. Human conflict is annoying.

There she goes—waving appendages, singing loud songs into communication enhancer—a device we believe transmits songs to other humans at distant locations.

*I'm out of here!*
*Can't take this noise.*
*Come back!*
*Nope, nope. See ya!*
*Back. Come back, now!*

*Oh, owl pellet! These guys!*

OK, so, female is now in motorized mobile water nest[3] which makes collateral annoyance. Collateral annoyance is noise with no melody, no meaning, no purpose.

*Shut up!*
*This is important.*
*Come back.*
*Pay attention!*
*There he is again!*
*Again!*
*Stay on limb!*
*Go away!*
*No, quiet!*
*Shut uup.*

*We've exhausted ourselves!*

So here's the deal. We now see male human with white head fur and red human beak who travels in orange motorized mobile nest.[4] He arrives and observes.

We know this guy, OK? We've seen him on other occasions. He perambulates to her home with his dog often. Once he arrives near her nest path, he stands before it. On occasion, if female host is on nest grounds, he stands behind large maple tree. This male human sings no song, only observes her and house. Viewing whilst wishing not to be viewed. We don't know why male does this. That's not our job—to know why, OK? Our job is to see. To remember. To write memos.

Anyways, he, as usual, views whilst wishing not to be viewed. He leaves.

*What're you doing?*
*Everybody stay on limb.*

3       boat
4       car

ON LIMB NOW.

For crows' sake! OK, let's do some imitation chirps to calm down. (We like to imitate. Our favorite is Hawk scream. That's funny because it scares the hell out of the critters. We also like imitating robins. Robins are assholes, though.)

Human protector arrives. Protectors are like us, they protect humans from human predators. Like what we do with Hawks. We've seen this one protector many times. Also, sometimes he sits in motorized mobile nest in front of female host's home nest and views whilst not wishing to be viewed.

This viewing whilst not wishing to be viewed may be a human male trait. We don't know. Again, that's not our job, OK? Who can figure out a human? Impossible! We observe and take notes. That's what we do.

She's coming back in motorized mobile water nest.
Oh, for screeching out loud!
The collateral annoyance!
We're gone!
No, come back.
Come here! Now!
On Limb!

OK, we're observing again. Human protector invites our female host into his motorized mobile nest. They travel away.

We follow because she feeds us.

# Chapter 2

*One outrage deserves another*

YOU RIDE UP front with Louis and try your best to control your words. You are alarmed and appalled at the nonchalance of a world that is losing its fish, but it's the way things have been for a while and you've been through so much, you're trying to allow everything to just be. This is hard because you can't imagine you're seeing the world more hysterically than everyone *should* see the world. There are dead fish everywhere and it's only April. You insisted Louis note this unusual event and become as upset as you. But he simply stared at the fish, shook his head, and led you to his patrol car.

Why isn't anyone ever moved by events like you? You ponder this as you look out the car window and regard the scenery scrolling by. One-acre yards still covered with large brown spots that landscapers are now trying to heal with their fertilizer, aerators, bags of grass seeds, and stacks of hay. After the yard wounds are patched, everyone will turn on automatic sprinkler systems and waste gallons of water to make sure their small territories appear healthy. The town is heading for another drought. Everyone knows this. Water is becoming a scarce commodity all over the globe. Everyone knows this. They do nothing.

And yet, they're all so fucking decent.

It's this decency that gets to you. You want to hate them, but when you're in the front seat of a patrol car with one of them and he asks if you'd like some coffee as he pulls into Dan's coffee shop, you look over at his kind face and say, "No coffee but I'd love some chamomile tea please." You want to continue to lecture him, shake him up, but there he is, with his Roman nose, slightly pockmarked face, receding hairline, thick fingers grabbing the steering wheel, so swollen his wedding ring will have to be sawed off one day.

"How's Alice?" you ask. "Better now?"

"Doing great, Lorraine. The last chemo about did her in, but she's terrific now. Remission. We don't eat sugar anymore and I'm getting sick of all the vegetables. But she's a trooper." You're glad you asked. You're glad his wife has more years. Louis lives in a town forty minutes away, because of course no police officers, even deputy lieutenants, can possibly afford the one-acre homes in this community. Westbrook labor commutes from lower rent towns that aren't really low rent, because affordable housing shortage is beyond a crisis, it's a tragedy. You wonder how he's paying his bills and mortgage now that his wife quit her teaching job. His struggle to pay mortgage, her survival, occupies your mind and you control your words. Sometimes you can do it.


YOU SIT AT a desk with a woman in a tight uniform who mumbles a greeting and continues to type, ignoring you momentarily, which allows your mind to drift. Your eyes skirt about the station. It hasn't really changed much since you were arrested six years ago. Most of the desks for regular police officers are surrounded by low dividers, which barely hide interviews and don't mute conversations. Beyond the cubicles, large glass enclosed offices line the periphery. These, you assume, are for those who are higher in rank. You suspect the most important personnel are hidden upstairs in larger offices. Importance is always out of sight.

You notice most of the offices and desks are now empty, and for some reason this bothers you. Where are they? Westbrook is fairly small, although not as small as the Connecticut towns with two-acre zoning and even more concentration of wealth. At least there are a few quarter and half-acre zones in Westbrook, due to zoning law amendments—pinholes allowing a small slither of middle class. You wonder how many police are employed in this town and what they're doing. Are they researching traffic violations?

Louis's voice interrupts your brief reverie, reminding you why you're here. Fish. Dead fish returns to your brain.

"Margaret, this is Lorraine. Lorraine, Margaret. Margaret is new so be nice," Louis says as he walks up to the desk. "Margaret, Bob MacAroy's neighbor witnessed Lorraine stealing his boat. Lorraine was bothered by some dead fish and wanted to get a closer look. MacAroy is in New York on the trading floor and can't be bothered now." Margaret continues to type. "I'm sure he won't press charges but just get information." Louis walks back to his office, a fairly large one behind a wall of glass, giving him full view of the administrative personnel. You watch him read the paper as Margaret asks questions.

"Your address?"

"There are a million dead fish in the sea."

"Address please."

"Do you care?"

"Yes, I care. Address please."

"We're also having another drought. There's a big problem with water, and I notice people still turn their sprinklers on."

"Just contact someone in that environmental department. They still have something like that, yes? I really need to get this information. You get one phone call, by the way."

"Do I have to answer your questions first? You already have my address, by the way. I haven't moved in six years. I have a record."

Margaret stares at you a moment, looks at her smart phone to check the time. "Oh, go ahead. Call first. I'll give you a bit of privacy. Just one person, OK?"

And guess who that person is?

I'm at the bank, working on a car loan. That's what I do, as you know, work at the local bank, putting together ordinary car loans and opening checking accounts. You've told me I've failed you, not necessarily because I have a rather unimportant job, but because I have a conservative job and am probably now aligned with our One Party. I am not aligned with any party. I don't like politics. You have caused me to have bad dreams about politics. You also think I am way overqualified for this job, but I will remind you again, there're not many jobs in a small town like this. You're thinking, ACLU again, yes? But I have no law degree, don't plan to obtain one, because, Mom, I do not want to be a lawyer. OK?

Do you see this? See how I digress?

Anyway, when I get the call, you tell me you've been arrested but that's all you'll say until I arrive. "Don't worry. As usual, it's more a problem with our society than with me." Then you tap off. I cannot immediately drop everything and come down to the police station, so I call back and talk to Louis's receptionist. She tells me you "borrowed" a boat to look at dead fish in Long Island Sound. You have managed to explain this to everyone at the station. She asks me to hurry because they are now having to listen to all kinds of lectures on the fish and our doomed human condition. "Please, Haley, we beg you, hurry."

After your quick conversation with me, you answer Margaret's questions in between your continued pontifications about fish and the dying world. You eventually tire of yourself and so does Margaret, who leaves to take a break.

When you're forced into silence after complaining, I think you start to feel slightly regretful. You have moments of guilt and self-introspection. Should you have called your daughter, bothered her at work? Perhaps you should have called someone else. Who? You then feel not only slightly guilty but also depressed because you cannot think of anyone else who would pick you up at the police department. You don't like these feelings, so you glance around the room in search of a distraction.

A lithe Latino woman in handcuffs is escorted to a small open desk tucked in the corner, near the lavatory. She sits, the officer sits. No one removes her handcuffs.

A new thought replaces the dead fish, guilt, and depressing self-introspection. It's another societal problem.

Margaret returns and tells you she is sorry, but you have to wait here until your daughter arrives because while you will be allowed to leave with no bail, they do need for the daughter to sign for you.

"You know where I should be? I should be in town hall demanding action, but tell me something, should she be here like that, handcuffed?" You point at the Latino woman. "Let's say that woman borrowed the boat. Would you allow her to sip tea? Would the officer allow her to sit nicely in the front seat without handcuffing her?"

"You want me to handcuff you?"

"No. Do I look like someone who's going to run down the street? Although, yes, I could. I'm fifty-two years old, yes, but I ride my bike and I'm in shape."

Margaret shakes her head, shuffles through some papers, excuses herself, and walks off again.

The Latino woman sits with her head down. The thought of this woman being treated worse than your privileged white self competes with the dead fish, non-responsive EPA, lazy legislators, insular town, guilt, and depressing introspection. Thoughts fight each other in your brain and the one about the woman wins. You stand and head toward the lavatory, pausing at the desk to listen to the interrogation.

The woman speaks broken English and has a hard time answering questions. The officer asks the woman if she is aware of the charge of possession of illegal substance.

You step up to the desk. "Is this marijuana? Because it's medically legal in this state, only a misdemeanour if possessed for recreation. And was there a search of her car?"

"Ma'am, are you her lawyer?"

"I'm her friend. She has a right to have a friend here, right?"

"No."

"Si," the Latino woman says to Mom. "Pertenecio a una amigo."

"Does anyone speak Spanish?" you ask.

"I think she's saying the pot belonged to a friend. It doesn't matter."

"It does matter, and there shouldn't have been a search."

"Lorraine." Margaret is now by you. She gently grabs your upper arm to lead you away. "This's really none of your business. Stick with the dead fish."

"Can you at least take the handcuffs off? They did an illegal search."

"She was driving without a license," Margaret says.

You turn to walk back to the desk and talk to the woman again.

"This is a warning, Mrs. Mulderon. I will put you back there in the jail."

"Put me in the jail. I've been there before. I don't mind."

YOU CANNOT SPEAK Spanish but manage to communicate with the woman who sits across from you in the jail cell, using your Google translation application. Apparently, the woman did not come to a complete stop at a four-way stop intersection and was pulled over. Four-way intersections are another big issue with you. You've almost wrecked your car at least a dozen times at four-way intersections. You feel they only exist because everyone is too lazy to put up stoplights. So now you are infuriated by everything. The dead fish. The borrowed boat. The non-handcuffed privileged experience. The Latino woman arrested after an illegal search at a four-way intersection that should have been a stoplight intersection to begin with. You have decided the woman simply has to learn English to survive in this horrible country that is intent on shipping her back to whatever more horrible place she has come from. You Google translate these thoughts to her.

When I walk through the door, Louis stands and says, "Be my guest." He swoops his arms toward the door in the corner where the jail cells are located. I know this area well.

"Don't worry, she's with another woman. That's it. No one else is back there. Last one on the right. And it's good to see you again, Haley."

"Good to see you, Louis. I hope life is treating you well."

He laughs.

I enter the area, walk about fifty feet, and stand before you and a small, frightened Latino woman. You are both seated, facing each other. You're talking loud and slow while tapping your iPhone. The confused woman stares at you.

"Hey Mom. Déjà vu!" Years ago, the crow protests had resulted in arrests. Then the gas company fight landed you in jail. They weren't going to arrest you for pushing the truck driver because Dad had died a year earlier, but when you threw a large stone through his front window, they took you in. I was nineteen, home from college for the week.

"This time, we're dealing with a misunderstanding. Last time, there was a legitimate cause for my arrest. Haley, this is Maria. Maria, Haley, my daughter." You shout this then tap your Google translate. Maria smiles. "Maria's been with me most of the time, although she disappeared for a short while—bail stuff. One good thing about Connecticut, bail's done fast."

I speak a little bad Spanish but opt for the Google translation app. I type into my app. "Hey, Maria. I'm this woman's daughter. Are you and Mom having fun chatting?" I tap the Spanish speaker icon. It sounds OK to me, but she stares blankly. I type, "Isn't my mother fun?" I tap the Spanish speaker icon. She frowns.

"Nice." She points to you.

"Mom is nice. At the expense of the entire universe, she is nice." I type that in the app and Maria frowns again. Angst never translates.

"She doesn't speak very well," you say.

We stop by the desk because you want to inquire about this woman's bail, and you refuse to listen to every person's advice to please stay out of this. The dead fish are still there, but this concern has temporarily been put aside. You then call the bail bond company and offer to pay the fee, which comes to about $500. You give the bonding company your charge card. This takes a while, so I sit and tweet my friends. When you finally hang up, you talk with the secretary, sign papers, and we step into Louis's office. He walks in, tapping on his tablet. You start up again with a litany of complaints.

Bail money's too high.

Marijuana is actually good for you.

Who cares what happens at a four-way stop intersection since they should not exist anyway?

Is he going to do anything at all about dead fish?

"Let's see," Louis says. "Where to begin? We treat everyone with respect, Lorraine. You shouldn't get involved in bail for a stranger. No one calls police about fish murders. And can we discuss your situation?"

"Does she have a husband, children?" you say. "Do you know? I couldn't get her to respond using my Google translate."

He says nothing.

"You're not calling I.C.E. I don't care about the new laws. You will not do this because it's not who you are."

"Someone has already done that. It's the law now. She has no documentation."

"You can circumvent it. Distract, distract. Send them back. Tell them it was all a mistake." You stand to leave, even though Louis tells you he has a few more questions. You walk out his door, Louis follows.

As you trot away, Louis behind you, me following, you tap your cell phone furiously. You tell me to drop you off at the library. I tell you I'm not dropping you off anywhere. You know this, you know I will follow you, but I will never drop you. I figure Louis knows where to find you if he wants to arrest you again.

When I turn the corner, you wave back at Louis standing rigid at the door.

THE LITERACY VOLUNTEER at the cluttered desk is enthusiastic and eager. She shakes our hands, thanks us for stopping by, points at the empty seats in front of her desk. "Sit, sit." Obviously, she believes we are here to volunteer.

"I need an application form for ESL classes," you say. "English classes for a friend."

"Oh. I see." She opens her desk and slowly retrieves a few forms. "We have a long waiting list. Shortage of volunteers." She looks over the papers in her hand before placing them before us. We're still standing. You pick up the application and read it quickly. She offers me a quick, perfunctory smile before addressing you.

"We usually sit down with them and fill these applications out together. Can you tell your friend to make an appointment?"

"She's unable to come in today, but don't worry, I'll explain it to her." You pick up an application, look over the questions.

"Is she working? Because we're open till six thirty. She's welcome to come in at any time after work."

"I don't really know if she works."

"Mom just met the woman a short while ago. She's Latino, I believe. I'll just use my translation app to communicate with her."

"Sorry, we have rules. I'll call her, if you'd like. I speak a bit of Spanish. Where is she now?"

"She'll be leaving the courthouse soon. I just posted her bail," you say.

"She's in jail? Are you her lawyer?"

"No, I was in jail."

The conversation does not progress very well after this, so you steal an application and leave, and the librarian trots after you. I follow. This is always how things work when you escape—you leave, person you are escaping from runs after you, and I, the forgotten daughter, follow the procession.

You turn on the radio as I drive away. I know I should stop, explain my mom to the librarian, but I drive fast because I want to get you home, and what can a librarian do to us?

We are silent for a while.

"I told her not to say anything to the police," you say. "I used my translation app, which needs improvement, by the way. You have noticed how we have not progressed in ten years. I remember progression. We used to move ahead with technology. It used to be wonderful." You pause to consider what you have said to me—which happens to be about the thousandth time you've said it. "Anyway, I told her, I think, to remain quiet until the bonding company posts bail, then she can leave. If they let I.C.E. take her, I will camp out at the police station forever."

"That would do it for me if I were the police chief."

"Yes. I'm smart that way."

"Mom, why don't you call ACLU, or legal aid? And, you know, we maybe need to focus on your situation. They're letting you go with no bail, and we're to appear in court this Thursday, unless the owner drops charges. They're waiting for him to call back."

You quietly stare out the window.

"Mom, you OK?"

"Fish are dead. We have an ocean filled with dead fish and no one cares. And that girl has a right to smoke pot. And who in the hell can figure out four-way stops?"

I know why you're upset about fish. I'm disturbed, too. Don't you think it disturbs me, too? Sure, everyone should be disturbed, but you and I have other reasons. I don't believe in signs. I don't really care about symbolism. But truly all these dead fish are bringing back something we don't want to deal with. Something we have put to rest.

"Call the environmental department," I say as I take a sip of an old coke that's been in my car two days. It tastes too sweet and watery. "I've got to work late today, so can you promise to stay home till I get back?"

"Don't drink that sugar. It will destroy your beautiful teeth, and caffeine will make you crazy."

I take you home, return to work, but something tells me I should have stayed to make sure you remain home.

# Blue Jay Memo

*Keep up!*
*Where we going?*
*Keep up.*
*Follow!*

OK, so the protector takes female host to big white nest that protectors take humans sometimes. Female host has been there before. It's a large nest in the middle of small human tribal community. We perch on the roof. Perch, perch, perch, perch.

After time passes, female host and offspring exit and perambulate away from building to motorized mobile nest. We follow motorized mobile nest to another red nest, where female host and offspring enter, then leave. Fast.

We fly back to Children of Athena home nest. We force a few younger ones—the two-year-olds who have no nest—to remain at large white nest for extended reconnaissance. We have found extended reconnaissance is necessary at certain locations with human protectors. When two-year-olds return to home nest they sing to us, kind of.

*We're not doing that again.*
*Shut uuup and report*
*Where's food?*
*Stay on the limb*

*We want food.*
*Whaja see?*
*Big, brown motorized mobile nest.*
*Where?*
*It stopped on path to white nest where protectors are.*

*Squirrel! Burying acorn!*

*Come back.*
*On limb.*
*Perch!*
*Sing!!*

*Humans exited the large brown motorized mobile nest.*
*They had brown coverings over torso.*
*Symbols on back.*
*Symbols?*
*Yes, three symbols on back.*
*What did they do?*
*Why do we care?*
*Tell!*
*The usual protector came out, sang to them.*
*Which protector?*
*The one who always views whilst not wishing to be viewed.*
*He sings loud or soft?*
*He sings soft. Maybe medium. We were bored.*
*So, what happened?*
*Males with symbols on back perambulate back to brown motorized mobile nest.*
*They leave?*
*They leave.*

*HAWK, HAWK, HAWK*
*HAWK, HAWK, HAWK*
*HAWK, HAWK, HAWK*
*Hawk gone.*

*We perch, stop making two-year-olds sing. We look around. Perch, eat, sex, look around. Offspring leaves. We perch. Perch. Perch. Perch. Eat. Then, female host leaves.*

*Follow!*
*No we eat.*
*You guys follow.*
*No, you guys follow.*
*No, you guys.*
*Shut uuuup.*

*Two-year-olds follow.*
*No, all follow! Now!*

OK. So, we follow female host's yellow motorized mobile nest 11.4 miles southeast of Children of Athena home nest. She arrives at large brown nest-holding structure. Elders tell us there are fifteen nests per structure. They suggest perhaps these are for humans who prefer crowded conditions. Like us. Anyways, we note our female host exiting mobile nest, perambulating to nest-holding structure. We perch and wait.

*She's leaving.*
*Look who's with her.*
*Who?*
*Brown female human with her.*
*We saw her at large white nest earlier.*

*So, who cares?*
*Brown woman was at white nest.*
*Shut uuup!*
*It's important.*
*Why?*
*Now she's with female host.*
*Why do we care? Brown woman doesn't feed us.*

*Just note it, OK?*

*Insect!*
*Insect!*
*Insect!*

*No, dirt.*

*Follow!*

For crows' sake. So, where were we? Female host's motorized mobile nest travels down several paths until it arrives at exit/entry area for motorized mobile tube nest.[5]

---

5        train

This motorized mobile tube nest has several compartments and transports humans fast on tracks in northeastern direction or southwestern direction toward the Great Human Tribal Nesting Area. We never go to Great Human Tribal Nesting Area.[6] It's too big, nests too tall. No food except human leftovers. It's a pigeon kind of place.

Female host waits with brown woman. She sings, taps her communication enhancer, sings. Sometimes she sings loud. Motorized mobile tube nest arrives, brown woman enters. Mobile tube nest heads southwest, toward Great Human Tribal Nesting Area.

---

6    New York City

# Chapter 3

*A human nest which is a mess*

I TAKE A personal day today because you tell me, "there are a million things I need to accomplish today." I think it's best I'm there when you accomplish your "million things." I've accumulated ten personal days and while I have planned to use them for things that are actually personal, I don't mind a few used for you.

I take a quick trip to the deli for a bagel, return quickly, slowing down to regard our strangely configured house. Protest signs rise from the ground on either side of the gas company easement that cuts through the middle of the property. The signs are for the benefit of the crew who come for maintenance work. You want to make sure they all know they're still in your thoughts. Plus, occasionally, friends, or neighbors, drive by or visit, and it's important they know that your resistance continues. You don't want anyone thinking your attitude was simply a ploy in order to squeeze money from the government. Although you are happy to have the money.

After I park, I walk around the garage and notice a few protest signs resting against the wall. I take a moment to read them. My favorite sign has bold black letters lining the wings of a crow. "Say a Prayer for the Crows." I doubt gas killed the crows, but I'm sure you think there's a connection with fossil fuels and any death. We never really figured out why all the crows died. There were some dead fish problems back then, too, but that was related to the waste water treatment plant that's now been refurbished. I rarely swim, but when I do, I never swim in Long Island Sound.

I enter the house, which on this side of the gas line is a small study, a kitchenette, a large room divided into sections with furniture. The main kitchen is located in the second half of the house. Yes, the house is cut in two—the kitchen on one side of the pipeline, the kitchenette on the other, which makes eating interesting. Your design, your drama, your chaos. But of course, it became ours, too, including the stress. Dad didn't die of stress, although I'm sure if there is life after death, Dad's blood pressure is finally normal.

Life happened so fast back then, right, Mom? I was only eighteen years old when Dad died—a few years after the big crow die off and a year before the gas settlement and house reconstruction. Basically, my life trajectory after ten went like this: The Great Transition, which led to the beginning of your anxiety and activism; the big crow die off in New England; the gas pipeline proposal and government demand for our property; death of my father; pause for grief; a gas settlement; the construction nightmare; battles with gas company, battles with construction company, battles with town, battles with lawyers; end of house reconstruction; your depression that had been latent, then your withdrawal; your slow recovery and return of angst. Somewhere toward the end of this time line, I took a "conservative" job in order to be with you. And now, dead fish.

I peek into the study and notice the computer is off. Lolly, our rotund English bulldog, is snoring underneath the desk. I can't see the screen without waking her. I wonder if you're working on activist projects again or starting up another blog, or social media accounts. I pray you do not reactivate Facebook. After Dad died and our house construction ended, your social media activity went dark—which alleviated the intense anxiety my therapist said was related to having a mother screaming on social media accounts she didn't know how to use properly. You never managed your privacy settings; thus, your hysterical comments were always public. It's only a matter of time before your social media presence is fully restored and my therapist hours are increased.

The door at the end of the large room extending from the kitchenette opens to our "bridge," its transparent floor curving up dramatically. From the side it resembles a small hill. If one looks down, one sees the mass of dead weeds and black dirt covering the huge phallic monstrosity—the pipeline. The steel tube is supposedly several feet below ground level. This, we are told, secures and protects all of us—not just you and I, but the neighborhood, town, state, and nation, probably world—from the possibility of any leak due to what they refer to as human error and you refer to as "inevitable fuck-ups." You say "fuck-ups" relate to human stupidity, as evidenced by the "construction of a pipeline spewing more fossil fuel into the hands of our addicted and corrupted world." Technically, we are not supposed to walk on the easement because it belongs to the gas company under a lease. Thus, the bridge. You insisted the bridge curve up in the air dramatically. You said this was because no one owned the air. They didn't buy that argument, but you ignored them. For some reason, probably exhaustion, they gave up.

After we walk over the bridge to the other side of our house, I hurry to the kitchen and open the refrigerator, grab a hunk of cheddar cheese and some deli meat. I take a large bite of the cheese.

"And your job is still far from exhilarating, I'm assuming," you say as you sit at the kitchen table and watch me eat. You have always liked to watch me eat, particularly solid, protein rich food. I grew up underweight due to digestive problems that you obsessed over. I am over it and now quite fine. More than fine. You still watch me.

"Not the most exciting existence, but I'm basically OK with everything. Mom, here is the thing." I pause to swallow and study the cheese that has pretty blue dots that seem to rise from deep inside. Has blue cheese merged with the cheddar? Oh my God, mold! I drop the cheese on the counter, run to the sink and spit. The masticated blob falls from my mouth into the sink. I fill a glass of water, take a large sip, swish the water around my mouth and spit again.

"Is your stomach upset?" You stand. "It's back! You're sick. Let's go." You pick up the keys.

"I'm not going anywhere. How long has that cheese been in there?"

"I don't eat cheese. It's leftover from something. We'll take you to the emergency clinic. They can maybe do an x-ray."

I turn the water on and rinse out my mouth again. You pick up the cheese and turn it over, break it open. "Or maybe we call your doctor first? I think mold can cause cancer. Let me find vinegar. It'll make your throw up."

"I don't want to throw up now, maybe later." I fill another glass with water and carry it and the deli meat to the table. You follow, still studying the cheese. Beyond the bay window two bright red cardinals peck at seeds in the feeder. One blue jay perched on our old white pine stares at something in the distance then flies away. You put the cheese on the table and open your mouth to say something, probably about my stomach and the mold I just ate, or about some article you read on dairy products and mold, or maybe about my risk of cancer. I hold up my hand.

"Mom, yesterday you paid a fee to a bonding company for a woman you don't know who's probably an illegal immigrant. She will have a date to appear before a judge, probably soon, like today. She can't speak English and it looks like you're going to teach her or force the library to teach her."

You watch me now as I pause to sip my water. I put a slither of deli meat in my mouth. It's sour and oily. I eat it anyway.

"You want crackers, fruit. I have the fruit cut in there. It's organic, but that's meaningless nowadays because no one regulates that anymore."

"Can we try to stay on one cause at a time?"

"There's a legal procedure for all of this, and I can handle it. This will not absorb my days. It'll be like quick errands. We're not certain she's illegal, by the way. You probably said that because they told us she has no driver's license, but plenty of people don't have licenses because they can't drive."

"Of course, she was driving, or attempting to drive, through a four-way stop sign intersection."

"And that's why we shouldn't have four-way stop sign intersections."

"I give up."

"Why don't you get a bit of fruit? You need fruit."

"No, just the cheese and meat. Fish is healthy. Maybe some fish. You got any smoked fish?"

"And that segues nicely into my discovery and the need to retrieve the bike, which, mind you, has been sitting unlocked by the water overnight. Someone could have stolen it."

"Or borrowed it." You don't laugh. "Just trying to laugh, Mom. So I won't cry."

"Yes, laughing relieves tension as we all die. But you don't have to worry. Remember Darwin? The best of the world will always survive. Despite your conservative lifestyle, you're the best, my dear, by far."

The blue jay is back and flitters from limb to limb, then lands on the feeder and pecks at seeds before flying back into the tree canopy. I stare at the empty tree, the platter filled with bird seed but no birds, and think about that word, conservative. What does that mean nowadays? And what is my lifestyle?

"Hello?" you say, waving your hands in front of my eyes. "Do you now want to visit the fish and pick up my bike? You also need to see the fish. Most have probably drifted away by now, but you need to see the dead fish."

Just hearing the word fish and dead together sends a shock down my spine. I keep seeing my dad with his fishing pole, his lures, his fishing hat.

# Chapter 4

*Persistence can risk one's subsistence.*

WHEN DAD WAS alive, the only hobby he enjoyed was fishing. He was catch and release because he thought fish were the most important creatures on our planet. They were meals for other fish, birds, bears, and smart foxes. Dad would take me out to lakes in northern Connecticut where the water was less exposed to humans and all their pollution. We'd rent a boat and try to hook at least one fish. I was not thrilled with actually catching a fish because that meant I had to take the hook out of its mouth. But I did like sitting with my dad. Sitting and floating. I was a bad caster and we often sat near trees, which meant I spent a lot of time sitting and untangling. Dad made me untangle all my lines by myself. "You learn a lot by figuring out how to untangle line. Untangling knots helped me finally get your mother. Follow the chaos of string and you will enter your mother's mind."

WHEN WE ARRIVE at the Sound's edge, your bike is still there. No one has touched it. You stretch and look across the horizon. You tell me the population of carrion has shrunk only slightly overnight. I stand by your side and take in the scenery.

The sky is clear today, a crisp spring breeze tosses leaves and wrinkles the water. The tide is now retreating, the water hurrying away from us, carrying several dead fish to wherever water goes. There are still thousands of dead fish littering the muddy banks. White bellies refract the sun rays.

I like the feel of dry air tossing my hair and ruffling my shirt as I walk through the underbrush and slide down toward the mud. I look down at my white tennis shoes. You don't slide but jump down the embankment then trot through the mud. You grab a stick and methodically poke at floating dead fish near the edge. You roll one gently toward the bank, pick it up by its tail, raise the stiff corpse before your eyes, as you twirl it then hand it to me.

"Is it bunker?" I say as I gently take the fish. It has a pearly white, silvery iridescence with hints of green and purple. "No, not bunker. Herring. Alewife." I try to hand the fish back, but you've already stepped away. You've done this all my life. Before the transition, back when you were just my mom and your world was me, you would take me into the garden to show me a garter snake or spadefoot. You'd hold up that life, ask me to take it, then walk away. It was your sink or swim lesson. There I was, your five-year-old girl with a snake in her hand. Deal with it. (But you always looked back. You always looked back. Where are you, Mom? Why aren't you looking back now?)

"It's dead," I say. "It could be a fish virus." I toss it into the pile of carrion, then spend another moment looking out at the dead fish floating in the water. I have a quick image of Dad's sorrowful face regarding the death of creatures he used for bait on days we'd fish in the Sound instead of lakes.

"I bet they get viruses all the time," I say. I see your head filling with thoughts again. You lean over, pick up several fish, and lay them side by side on the mud.

"They tried to tell me this was a bunker die off," you say, studying the carcasses. You kick the fish with the tip of your now brown tennis shoe. "You're right. Alewife. They're here to spawn. Now those eggs won't be laid."

"There're millions of fish in the sea, Mom. It'll be OK."

"There're always a million more of everything, but we don't have relative figures as to what a million means in the fish world, now do we? What does this mean? We need to know why this has happened."

"And have you called the environmental department, or whatever they call it now?"

"Polluters Protection Agency. That's what I call it. I left a long message. What's new?"

"OK, it does look bad. So, just call other groups. Aren't there non-profits that'll look into this? You can go back to those activist groups. You're still welcome, right? Or are they retired? Or maybe dead. Weren't there a lot of octogenarians?"

You walk through the underbrush back to the car. We manage to squeeze the bike into your Prius. The wheel sits between us, and I talk through the spokes. You have to shove it aside to shift gears. We jerk forward. You drive faster than usual—your way of signaling to me your rage over everything, including my lack of passion. Ambivalence annoys you, and I expect another lecture on my conservative personality. You will lament your parenting, ask what you have done to cause this. I will assure you it was the fault of my college education. I took too many finance courses. That will lead to a discussion of how poetry is underappreciated by Wall Street. I will inform you that neighborhood retail banking is not Wall Street.

We pass our street, and you still haven't lectured me.

"That was Leroy. We passed Leroy. Why aren't we going home?" I say.

You don't respond. No lecture about my passivity. We are not homeward bound. There's a large wheel between us. I'm worried. I turn on the radio. NPR is walking everyone slowly through a homemade sourdough bread recipe. The woman sounds stoned.

"Yes, many of the best activists were old. But not dead," you say as you make a sharp turn. I have to rewind my brain to recall what I said that you are now, several minutes later, responding to. "The true Americans are the old ones who remember what it was like before the transition. They still fight the good fight. I knew this when I joined them. Some are octogenarians, a wonderful age, mind you, just an old age."

"So, what are you saying? That the dying or dead are better than the young because they have memories? You know, lots of youth are active and political but we also are broke and recognize how intractable our government is. Does this have something to do with where we're going?"

You turn down a few streets until we're in front of a red brick office building. A twelve-inch plaque with a name written in small gold letters hangs from a nail by the door. There's a deli across the street and I'm starving, so I ask if you're hungry.

"They're not all dead," you say. "And I have great respect for you, as you know. You are perfect. Your age group is not perfect, it's distracted. You have no peer support because no one your age has experienced the power of protest. I'll have to delay food."

"We've already had this discussion. Remember? Are we going inside?"

"Oh sure, everyone got upset when all the crows died, but then, nothing. Nothing. Crows are gone! Now fish are dead." You lean over your steering wheel and close your eyes. "Fish, Haley." I place my hand on your back because I know what this all means. You have this poetic soul, Mom. Everything is metaphorical. Everything is symbolic. I get you.

"The crows never returned here, but many live elsewhere, right?" I try to bring Dad back into my mind. What would he say? "There are so many birds, Mom. So, so many. And fish. Truly, we have lots of fish. There are fish swimming away from us and into the ocean as we speak." No, he would not say that.

"I don't care if a few crows still live somewhere out west, they don't live here." You finally turn off the car, the stoned sounding women leave us. I look through the wheel spokes at your profile—the slight upturned nose, ruddy cheeks, and teary eyes. "I plan on talking to these lawyers about Maria. I can save her. And I can save the fucking fish."

You open the door, tell me you'll be back, then clip off toward what I now understand is the legal aid building. The car grows hot, I grow hot, then I realize

I don't have to stay there, I'm not a dog. I can open a door. Which I do. I stare at the old building, hoping you'll return soon. I do not want to go inside and become entangled with you and lawyers and paperwork and discussions about the incarceration of the poor for minor infractions. I do not want to sit in the waiting room for an hour, then with a public defender type who checks his long waiting list of defendants and short list of volunteers. But there is so much in life I do not want to do.

SINCE I SPENT three years in high school studying Spanish, I can understand parts of the conversations in the waiting room. You sit between two men now talking to each other over your lap. The man is telling his friend that his wife is hiding out in New York. The other man's lips tremble. The man says, "They can't find you in New York." You pat the tearful man's hand and ask him if he needs help with anything. He has no idea what you're talking about, so you say it again in a very loud voice. He stares, but before you say it again in a louder voice, Brit Jacobs walks out and stands in front of us, which appears to startle you because you were not expecting Brit Jacobs. He's Nancy Jacob's dad, and I've always thought he was kind of cute. His hair is white, which looks cool, not old. He also has a permanent sunburned nose from playing tennis and walking his dog, which makes him look colorful. He lives alone and is probably still grieving. His ex-spouse didn't die, but she left so quickly it was like death. I've always hoped you'd notice him, or he'd notice you, but nothing ever happens when I hope for it.

"Hey, Lorraine, why don't you come with me?"

"These men were here first," you say. "And what're you doing with legal aid?"

Brit shakes the tearful man's hand and says, in very bad Spanish, the other volunteer will be with him soon. He turns to you, "I don't speak Spanish well." You don't stand, only wait for more answers. "I volunteer, Lorraine, a few hours every other week. Hey, Haley, nice to see you here helping your mom. We've got limited time, so why don't you both follow me." He walks briskly away. You stand slowly.

His borrowed office is a room slightly bigger than our walk-in pantry. His desk is piled with papers and brown accordion files are scattered on the floor. He rummages through a few papers until he finds some relevant to us.

"I saw your appointment and read up on the case. Thanks for calling ahead of time, Lorraine. Most just walk in."

He takes a moment to read one page of something that must be important. We sit. Your eyes skirt about the office. You have your usual censorious expression, which bothers me because Brit is one of the good guys. But you look like it all bothers you, or maybe you suspect Brit is about to divulge bad news.

"Let's see. You secured a bond for a Maria Lopez. You have her phone number, I assume, although you will find, like the police, that she is not answering it. I called the police before you arrived."

Your face turns blank, your eyebrows slowly point inward. You pull out your phone and tap contacts, then put it to your ear. You tap the phone off then tap the number again. Nothing.

"So, what're you telling us, Mr. Jacobs?" I say.

"I'm telling your mother that I called the police and they said the number and address Ms. Lopez gave them were invalid. Well, at one time the phone was valid, but now it no longer works."

"So, I lose $5000? Is that what this meeting has become? I have lost money. That is what you are saying?" You sit up, lean forward, back straight and stiff. I start to speak, but you put your hand on my thigh and squeeze.

Mr. Jacobs maintains equanimity. "Well, there's always a chance she'll call you on another phone. Did you give her a phone number?"

"Well, I kept her out of jail, out of a deportation plane. She is free. Brit, I know you're thinking I did something stupid."

"No."

Obviously, you forgot to give the woman your phone number.

"But there are worse things in life. For example, did you know our fish are dead?"


AFTER WE GET home, you look up all your past and present activist friends, then research previous volunteer environmental groups.

Cara O'Connor is your first call. Cara is the president of the Save the Water Environmental Association. They have the largest budget in Connecticut and most work is investigative—contamination of waterways, the impact of pollution on water fowl and wildlife. You used to go to all the meetings and attended every protest. You wrote letters to incompetent legislators who did nothing, posted to a blog read by no one, authored long articles for our paper, which resulted in very little commentary. That was when the crows all died, and everyone tested the carcasses, then the water. They studied oil spills, temperature, nitrate content, and issues with the wastewater plant in another town. I remembered when you helped collect water samples that were tested and sent to the EPA, who said thank you. The activists all filed complaints with the EPA, which are probably still being processed. The activists also sent obligatory letters and petitions to the state House of Representatives. One legislator submitted a bill that died in committee. This has become a way of life. Appeals. Appeals ignored. Complaints. Complaints ignored. Protests. Protests ignored, a few protestors arrested. You were the first person arrested from our town. You were so impressed with the publicity. Remember? So, you got arrested again. And again.

You finally reach Cara.

"Hey, Lorraine," Cara says. "I saw your name on caller I.D. and figured it had to be important. We haven't heard from you in a while. I tried to return your call but got nothing."

"They don't allow cell phones in jail, so I couldn't answer. They probably turned it off."

"I want to ask about the jail cell but I'm a bit busy. I figure it's the fish. You saw the fish and that led to activity that led to jail. Am I correct?"

"We've got a big problem with dead fish over here."

"I know. We've had phone calls from someone who worked at Westbrook Town Hall, some receptionist who said, and I quote, 'Lorraine is starting to heat up again. Could you come test these dead fish so she'll start cooling off.'"

"I think we're looking at another submission to the environmental department for their storage files," you say. "Then another legislative bill that'll die in committee. And more articles that will be ignored. And then . . ."

"Actually, New York is having a big protest the end of the summer," Cara interrupts. "Let me check." The phone clicks off and there's silence for a brief moment. She comes back. "Lorraine, you still there?"

"Do you think I'm going to hang up? What the hell else would I do? Help my daughter mow the lawn?"

Yes, I'm out mowing the lawn. See how well I know you? I can imagine your every move and conversation. I will find you, Mom.

"Like I said, Lorraine, there's a huge protest in New York at the end of the summer. The EPA is a voicemail, yes, and legislative bills go nowhere, yes, but protests get attention. We need you there. Meanwhile, we're testing fish. Most of them were alewife. Some bunker, which is surprising but not too surprising given the heat. We suspect low oxygen. Again. Bacteria count's very high. But as the fish die or leave and whatever is causing the oxygen depletion disappears, we will return to normal. I think. Although this die-off is unusually large."

"In other words, we do nothing, and the pollution will resolve itself. Cara, you know what I think. I think . . ."

"No, I'm filing a complaint and we're doing tests. We hope the EPA does not delete voicemail. And we protest."

"Well, I will do my local protest. Then, I'll do this march, I guess. Do I go with you? I've got a potential undocumented immigrant . . ."

"I'm not attending but you can certainly call around, see who is. But look, Lorraine, many just want to go stand a while, hold signs. You tend to complicate protests. So, don't be surprised if they kind of shrug you off."

You hang up and fume.

When I come back in from yard work, I hear your breathing, slow and steady, like you do in yoga class. I stand by you, say nothing as you breathe. You close your eyes.

"Fuck this. I will not let this go," you say.

But you did, didn't you, Mom? See, when you leave, you let things go. You let *me* go.

# Blue Jays Memo

*Follow.*
*Stop eating.*
*Follow. Now.*
*Squirrel!*
*Dive bomb!*
*Dive bomb squirrel!*
*Back on limb!*
*Follow!*

*OK, so, we follow. Female host and offspring travel in motorized mobile nest.*

*Dead fish observation. Big deal.*
*Come back!*
*We go back to nest. Eat.*

*We think female host, offspring, and other humans, mostly females, are exceedingly interested in dead fish. Go figure.*

*HAWK, HAWK. HAWK*
*HAWK, HAWK. HAWK*
*HAWK, HAWK. HAWK*
*Hawk gone.*

*Female host and offspring leave. We follow.*

*Female host and offspring arrive at red human nest. Both enter nest. We perch, perch, perch, perch. They leave.*

*We note male with white head fur and red beak observing departure through glass covered aperture.*

*We follow female host and offspring back to Children of Athena home.*

Time passes. We perch, perch, perch. We eat. We have sex. We look for insects. We look for acorns. We steal squirrel acorns. All of them. Dumbasses.

We have sex. We perch.

Look!
Where?
It's male with white head fur and red beak.
Where?
Way down path.
He's perambulating with dog.
Toward home nest?
He's now behind tree. Again.
He's viewing whilst not wishing to be viewed!
Predatory behavior.
No, male human stuff.

Offspring exits nest now!

Oh, not again!
Collateral annoyance!
Collateral annoyance!
We're out of here.
Come back!
Stay. On. The. Limb. Now.
Nope. Out. Of. Here.

Offspring is pushing a motorized mobile object that emits collateral annoyance and has no purpose except to reduce size of ground vegetation.

Now the beak! She has the beak!
Stop it! Stop it!
Stop it! Stop it!
Stop! Stop it! Stop it!

Offspring now has faux beak with two protruding sticks that move beak. She brings these sticks together with force, snapping beak shut and severing twigs of low-lying vegetation surrounding her nest. This vegetation provides nests for our friends, the cardinals, sparrows, wrens, and various other races. We always scream stop. Humans never care. It does no good.

We try to imitate Carolina wren to calm down. Too difficult.
We imitate hawk to tease squirrels.

# Chapter 5

*When you can't fight, you write*

Dear Editor,

Once again, we have death in our town, and this time it is not the death of our land, our air, our character. It is not the death caused by the fossil fuel companies drilling holes deep in our earth and vomiting liquid dinosaur remains through leak-able pipes, causing carbon to accumulate faster than dark money. It is not the death of plastic suffocating our sea life, littering our coast, filling the stomach cavities of fish, mammals, birds. (Well, who knows if it isn't this? Maybe the plastics have indeed contributed to this new problem I'm going to talk about). Oh, and it's not a mass Corvid death similar to the big crow massacre. No, no, at least so far, we do not once again have birds falling from the sky for an entire month.

This time we have dead fish. A few, you ask? No. We have hundreds of thousands of dead fish, a patina of fish bellies covering our Sound. Did you think it was foam? I know all of you saw it, and even if you did not have the curiosity to look out your window at the coastline—thinking,"Why do I care about the water, it's not hot enough to swim?"—you probably at least heard someone say something about it.

It's not irrelevant.

I called our town government's so-called Environmental Commission, who referred me to the Connecticut Environmental Department, where I left the usual two dozen messages for the robot that works there. We all know where that voicemail goes, or should I tell you where it should go . . .

Editor note: Lorraine Mulderon exceeded our 250 word limit and refused to edit her letter, so editors were forced to end her letter here.

YOU SAY, "FUCK this" under your breath before taking another sip of coffee. Lolly looks at me briefly, drops her head back on her paws. "Who has a two-hundred-and-fifty word limit? Who on earth can say anything in two-hundred-and-fifty words? No one. And I'm not going to limit my words. I read, I collect words, I share them."

I push the paper away, lean over to pet Lolly, and notice our soiled floor. For a while now it has needed the kind of cleaning that requires vinegar and sore knees.

"Well, I'll just make a statement at the Board of Selectman meeting this Tuesday," you say. "I've emailed a petition demanding we attend to the dead fish."

There are still dead fish in the Sound. In fact, dead fish have been seen at other locations. Ponds, rivers, even small creeks that flow toward the Sound from ponds northwest of us. I'm actually very concerned about it. I was young, but still vaguely remember when all the crows fell from the sky. The smell of death. The black carcasses. Feathers everywhere. The ambivalence. More ambivalence. Mom's hysteria.

I stand, stretch, grab a mop and bucket and look for vinegar as you continue your rant.

"I take a while to get to the point but when I do, my point is usually magnificent," you say to the air in front of you. I find the vinegar and pour it into the bucket then start filling it with warm water. "Richard cut my discussion before I was able to inform the readers of the consequences of dead fish. All the idiots eat farmed fish now and figure ocean fish are replaceable. They all think, 'Oh, fish are born to be eaten anyway, so why do we care?' I should have mentioned the dead sparrows I found. They would care about that. We live in a time of supreme ignorance and gluttony."

I finish the floor and straighten up, then start on the bay window, which opens the kitchen to a view of an acre of green grass—well, dull green, even a bit brown, grass and various species of weeds you do not want to kill. Our yard slopes slightly, eventually meeting a quarter acre of undeveloped property owned by the neighborhood land trust. Next to this wooded land trust is a large estate and next to that estate is more woods filled with underbrush and native trees—maple, black birch, red oak, and a few white pines. There used to an abundance of life up in that tree canopy, but now all that life seems to have migrated to our property. I've not discussed my observations with you. I've learned how to contain my concern in order to mitigate your anxiety.

"Do you think the sparrow deaths are related?" I say as I put the cleaning spray down and finally sit. I drag the newspaper toward me, flip the pages in search of any article about dead fish or dead blue jays. I do finally find a small write-up on dead fish. It looks obligatory, as if they decided to write something quickly to please you.

"Here's an article." I push it toward you. The article quotes another resident who has noticed the fish. Charlotte Culter.

"Well, of course they would interview Charlotte. She's soft spoken and thinks a lot before she talks, which comes across as wise." You curl your fingers in the air as you say wise. "And she lives in that gated community on Independence Island. I've wondered about them, what they're all dumping into the water."

You read. *"I saw all the fish, too, and was quite alarmed. I did call the Save the Water environmental group. They jumped right on it. I think it will probably clear up by summer."*

I look through the rest of paper and find something else. They interviewed a commercial fisherman. *"It happens more often than you think. We just don't really pay as much attention to dead fish. Actually, they provide good feed for the larger fish. It's a natural occurrence in our ecosystem."*

"Oh, yes, lots of dead things on the ground and water, all enhancing life," you say. "That's bullshit. Dead carcasses are not good food. Other fish do not feed on carrion. Christ, what idiots. I may as well move back to the woods in Alabama and live with the good ole boys again."

Maybe that's where you are now—Alabama. Are you there, hiding from your sisters? Somehow, I doubt you'd move back to the place you bragged about "escaping" from. You said back in your day, southern women had to go underground in order to have a different thought. Of course, you always exaggerated. And you're not that old. Back in your "day," is back in the 1990s. We used to visit your older sisters every summer and holiday. Mary Louise and Honee. They drank cocktails every night on their patio and told stories about each other and eccentric people who lived in the neighborhood, which was a large cluster of wooden A-frame houses about five blocks from main street. They had four dogs, but only knew where two were. They were sassy and suspicious of everyone else from any place but there, although they embraced me and tolerated you. I loved them. But after the entire South banned abortion, you only let me visit on Christmas. "They enslave women and I don't want you to witness it." I am sure you found out that I skyped my aunts and still do. Honee told me you skyped their daughters, too, which is why they both moved to Chicago. You told them to go anywhere "your uterus isn't shackled."

Blue jays gather in our white pine, ready for your routine morning feeding. When they gather, it's time for me to leave for work. They're my alarm clock.

As I back out the driveway, I see you placing your coffee and feeding items on the cast iron patio table. You begin filling the small plastic box with meal worms. You will hang that up then sit and toss one peanut at a time to the blue jays. You want them to learn patience. I imagine that after a moment or two, you'll push your paper away and simply look out at the blue sky and yard. Only a few tendrils of clouds interrupt the sun rays today; light freely falls through the branches, covering the ground with geometrical designs of light and shade.

You toss a few more peanuts and after several tosses, the jays disappear into the canopy, leaving you alone with yourself. You stare through the cast iron table at your huge, gnarled feet, then look down at your hands spread out on the table. You hate your hands. You told me you never put enough lotion on them, so now they look like the hands of a seventy-year-old woman. Your feet have been ugly all your life, you added. You said you avoided sex when young because of those feet. "Sometimes a large naked piece of you is just too much for a man to handle," you said once. You remember how your Lawrence, my dad, made you laugh at your insecurities.

You place one foot on the other, then cross them, then place your ankle upon your thigh and massage your foot the way Dad used to do on lazy summer days while both of you had cocktails and I sipped tea. The blue jays are back in your trees, no longer interested in peanuts, only each other and, oddly, you. One lands on the table, a meal worm hanging out of his mouth. There is a small noise that comes from his throat, so quiet, one would not notice it unless one listened the way you listen. The bird is probably trying to tell you it's a nice day and you should step away, do something, be alive.

"I can't fly," you whisper to the blue jay. "I want to fly. I want to fly away. But I can't, so the nice day is just me fighting gravity under the hot sun." He cocks his head. "I hate nice days," you say. "They shout my loneliness out to the world."

You stand, pull out a small pad from the back of your sweat pants. Another blue jay lands on a branch and watches you write in your to-do list. The grief counselor told you to carry a pad and write things to do. You were supposed to then do them. The process of doing helps one avoid the process of thinking. Apparently, the therapist thought you were one of those people who should never think, only do. She didn't realize that your doing always followed thinking. And that was not a good thing. The therapy experience was something everyone encouraged us to do. It's been seven years, and we're both still in therapy.

Dad died right when Connecticut Energy had discovered our land was the shortest route for the gas pipeline to a very large industrial complex near the highway. You actually blamed Dad's death on that gas company, although gas didn't kill dad. He fell off a ladder after apparently fainting from the heat. You also blamed his death on global warming, which you thought also contributed to the crow death, although who knows what killed those crows. Some people in town blamed the die-offs on the outdated waste water treatment facility.

The state built a new waste water plant with secondary treatment facilities to eliminate the nitrate and phosphorus that contributed to high bacteria counts. The new pipeline running through our property provided gas to power this new waste water facility. Thus, fossil fuels resolved the same issues that you believed they also caused.

After writing down your to-do list, you stand and do a yoga move. You know exactly three moves. One with the arms stretched up, one with them down, and one where arms are doing nothing—usually because the entire body is on the floor doing nothing. You do the one with the arms stretching down. And that is when you see it—the blue jay that had been staring at you earlier. It's now dead. At first you think it's sleeping, but birds don't sleep on their backs with talons up.

You pick it up, study its eyes, its body—bony and brittle—its legs—crisp like twigs. The bird has already lost the lightness of life. You recall Dad's body when he died. The breath gone, the frame sunk into the earth, as if wanting to disappear into the soil where it could revitalize and return as a tree. You look around our yard, up at the presence of life in the branches, down at the underbrush. The twigs shimmer. You regard your dead bird again. It suddenly occurs to you that the yard has fallen completely quiet. No chirps, no squawks, nothing beyond the rustle of leaves. There's barely a sound louder than your breath. Then, all at once, the jays start screaming.

"I didn't do this. I didn't kill it," you say, holding up the dead bird to the blue jays in the trees. "Don't think I'm killing things. I am not. I didn't kill the crows either. And how could I have killed the fish? I'm not doing this. I'm just a part of the human race that's doing this. Don't go profiling me."

The phone rings but you don't move. It keeps ringing. You do not answer phones when holding death. You watched your husband die, you are watching fish and birds die. You no longer have to be nice or polite. You are however curious, so you put the dead bird on the patio table and tap your voice mail. Cara's strident voice rises from the small speakers. You don't listen, just quickly tap return.

Cara answers in a huff, as if she's busy doing something very important but is so responsible she picks up the phone anyway. She probably knows you were not doing anything important and didn't pick up the phone because you don't pick up phones.

"Cara, it's Lorraine. Hi and all that."

"Hello, Lorraine, and all that back to you. I assume you either got my message or given the short time between my call and return, you simply listened to my voicemail and called before I finished. Whatever, and I do not care. Here is the big problem. As you know, we came out there a few days ago to collect a sample of the fish for testing."

"Yes, I know. Which was probably at least three days too late. You should have come right away, the day I called."

"As you know, we had to get a special permit to park at the designated beach to do our research. You know—all those rules they put in for environmentalists back when they eliminated all the rules for the polluters? Anyhoo, we got the sample and Mitt wrecked the van. Not bad. He's OK. I'm not sure you know Mitt? He's been with us for five years now. Teaches biology at Stoneybrook High. Got elected best teacher last year. It's the only award voted on by students. We're all very proud of him. So, anyway, he wrecked the van and the fish weren't frozen yet, so his side door flew open and let's just say, dead fish on I-84. He was shaken up. Then the police take their time getting there, then everyone takes their time exchanging insurance cards and such. Mitt's van had to be towed. The wreck involved at least six other cars. It was a biggy. All over News 12. So, we have to come out there again and get more fish. And more water. Too bad because, if the problem was low oxygen, we'd like to test for nitrogen and phosphorus in the water. But no can do."

"Didn't someone else come for a sample? Did you call someone else to come out? Are you going to come out today? You want me to do this?" Mom speaks fast because Cara the kind of person who interrupts, and if you talk fast, it's hard for her to interrupt.

"We have other non-profits trying to save our earth, Lorraine. I'd say, well, we have two dozen on the coast at least. I have a list."

"Cara, about the other group . . ."

"I'm not privy to anyone else you or the town called. Did you call anyone else? Did the town call someone else? I left a message on the state voice mail but that means nothing as I'm sure you know."

"Well, Cara, then fuck it. It's like the crow death. And here we are again, and I'm not going to simply sit on this because . . ."

"Lorraine, the mass crow death was complex. We've told you this how many times? It was a convergence of factors. We've spotted a few crows, by the way. They've come back, a few have, just so you know. Anyway, it's why we're marching. Global warming is probably indirectly related to this fish death. But, you know, when nitrogen goes up, dissolved oxygen goes down. But there are no real rules anymore. And fossil fuels are popular again. What can we do? I know voting doesn't matter but we got to still do it defiantly as if it does. Then march."

"OK, OK. I'll wait for all the phone calls, Cara, but I'm thinking no one is desperate to sit by me on the train to New York, and by the way . . ."

"Well, that may be true, but you can go with Haley."

"Look, I don't need a permit, as I'm a denizen of this town and can do whatever I please, so I'll collect samples."

"Nope. Can't let you do that. Since you just told me, if I let you bring me the samples that would be a violation of state and town ordinances."

"Oh, for crying out loud. Well, forget it then. And, Cara, I'm now dealing with a new environmental emergency in our yard. blue jays are also dying. I have a dead one in my hand, so I got to go."

"Oh my God, Lorraine. It's probably another bird virus. Go wash your hands right now. Run! Run wash your hands!"

You hang up the phone pour Clorox on your hands, then decide that's worse than a virus so wash your hands for ten minutes.

Your cell phone rings. You ignore it. It rings again. You ignore it. It rings again.

"Hello," You say, out of breath, annoyed at yourself for answering.

"Is this Lorraine Mulderon?"

"Yes, but I'm busy."

"This is Hackney Bonding Company. We have a problem with the bond you posted."

# Blue Jay Memo

*Female host holds our dead relative!*
*Female host holds our dead relative!*
*Female host holds our dead relative!*
*Female host holds dead relative!*
*Female host holds dead relative!*

We do not like humans holding onto our dead relatives. We recall humans holding dead crows.

We have yet to mourn this relative! We have noticed his slow deterioration over the past few days. This is the fifth death of our race in a few weeks. A high death rate for this time of year.

We're nervous due to elder's story of the great death wave of our crow cousins. Elders told us it was a dark time. They said, "Our honorable crows fell from the sky, covering the ground in great numbers. It was a time of terror. Female host filled the air with agitated songs. She perambulated down paths with other angry female humans, carrying large white boards that held black symbols. Female host spit mouth orifice fluid upon protector humans. She was then taken forcibly to the large white protector nest. She had been there before. Other humans collected the corpses of our crow cousins, placed them into bags, which were placed into large motorized mobile nests that traveled to a larger human nest where, apparently, crow corpses were deposited."

That is all we know. Many elders had mental trauma scars that lasted years. Eventually, all crows disappeared. Elders say some joined great western migration path travelers and never returned. Humans residing on western edge of our great land mass are rumored to be friendlier.

*Female host sings too loud.*
*Stay on limb. Observe.*
*She's singing in communication enhancer. Too loud.*
*Agitated songs!*

*Be quiet. Stay on limb.*

*We demand she leave dead cousin corpse!*

*We will scream until she drops corpse!*

*This is all too much. Dead fish. Dead cousin. Female host holding cousin's corpse. Augurs of doom. We scream. We scream. We scream.*

# Chapter 6

*Death inspires obsession*

WHEN DAD AND I fished on lakes in northern Connecticut, I did a lot of sitting. With Dad. If I chose to say anything, Dad would listen a few moments then remind me that silence was the most important fishing skill. "The best fishermen are quiet people," Dad always emphasized. He said fish could hear us. "They know what we're up to. They're curious, but also suspicious." I imagined those fish, desperate to rise to the surface and check us out, but so self-controlled they suppressed curiosity. I sat quietly practicing my self-control.

I actually felt I knew Dad more intimately because of that shared silence.


IT'S BEEN OVER a week since the discovery of dead fish, and you're adamant about conducting your own fish investigation. You barely understand science, although you've certainly read a lot of global warming documents and biologist studies. But you have the desire, you say to yourself and me and anyone who will listen, and desire is most of science, according to you.

You ride your bike to the same embankment where you discovered the die-off and stand by the water. The tide has ebbed and flowed so many times most of the dead fish are gone. Fish are still dying but there are no longer thousands of dead fish, only a few hundred, mostly scattered upon the bank.

When you jump down the bank, mud splats over the front of your t-shirt, the one that says, in bold letters, "If you say shut up, I'll yell." A few cars pass, one honks, a hand rises from the open window and waves quickly. You ignore the wave and take in the scene. It's a warm, cloudless day, and from where you stand, there's a clear view of the distant, arboreal Long Island. The water laps softly at the bank's edge. No scavenger is nibbling at the rotting fish carcasses, not even the turkey vultures or ravens.

You're looking for a freshly dead fish, or one that is in the process of dying. You think watching the fish die may inform you. A tail limply flips on a fish lying near the water. You lift your foot and place it lightly ahead of the other while balancing yourself with a stick. A squawk sounds from a nearby oak. Another squawk from a birch behind it, then suddenly many more squawks.

You wonder if Westbrook has more jays than any town you've lived in, certainly more than in Alabama. Of course, back in Alabama, the neighborhood kids had BB guns and shot squirrels and birds every chance they got, so maybe they were all there, too, but stayed quiet to avoid human pellets. You ponder all those kids shooting birds, as you reach out with your stick to roll one of the dying fishes toward you.

"Lorraine, what the hell?"

You drop the fish and let out a startled yelp.


BRIT JACOBS SITS in his orange Subaru now pulled over to the side of the road. His window is down, the engine barely grumbles.

"I'm fishing," you say, picking the fish up again. "It's the new twenty-first century fishing technique. You walk out to dead fish, lean over real quiet like, pick up the dead fish. It's not quite like fishing of the past with all the lines and lures. But we now live in a different country."

"I saw your letter last week. Don't we have environmental groups testing all this? And didn't all the dead ones go away?" He turns off his car and steps out like he's going to stay a while. "Let me help you with that." He regards the steep sloped bank as if reconsidering his offer, then kneels slowly, stretching his left leg out, then gripping the grass blades with his right hand.

"Just jump, Brit. Detergent gets dirt out usually, and, if not, you can always buy another pair of khakis." He ignores you and slides sideways down the bank to an area near the mud. You watch, holding your fish, now barely moving. You lose your grip; the fish hits the mud with a splat. You reach for it, trip, fall, both hands out. You are now on all fours in the mud. Brit, still on the grass, stands behind you. You suspect he's contemplating a big decision. Should he step into the mud to help you up or let you simply be? He seems to have the self-control to refrain from laughter. He knows that's very important.

"This does look bad, but I'm not hurt, and I have my fish," you say, not bothering to look back at him. "Don't worry, I'm a feminist so helping me would fill me with anger at the patronizing gesture. I'm fine just like this."

Brit tries to keep his eyes only on the fish.

"You're still alive, a good thing," you say to the fish. "I want you to be alive so I can observe how you die." The fish flaps lethargically as you grab its tail.

Brit shoves his hands into his pockets and cocks his head, like a hawk.

"You're thinking I may have a difficult time lifting my body from this mud, but you're wrong." With one quick push, you're back on your haunches, the fish still in your grip. You stare at the fish, ignoring Brit, although you hear his slow breathing, interrupted by a few blue jays' dulcet chirps. The fish tail moves only slightly, then the fish is still. It died right in front of the blue jays, Brit, and you. You wonder if watching the death educated you in any way. You stare at its now stiffening body.

"We're starting to dry out pretty bad this go around," Brit says. "Maybe that has something to do with these deaths."

You struggle to move from your haunches to your feet.

"Why don't you toss the fish to me? Standing in mud is hard enough with empty hands." You ignore him.

"I've got two years on you, Brit, but I'm in better shape."

You stand slowly while holding the fish. Mud covers your jeans, hands, and half your t-shirt. Even your face has splattered brown dots. But you have your fish. You raise one foot slowly, place it in front of you, and watch it sink in the mud. You do this over and over until you are at the edge with Brit.

"And what brings you home early today?" you say. Your hair hangs in your eyes because you had to cancel your hair appointment.

Brit wants to laugh at you in a bad way and you know this. You're right up next to his face so can see the jaw muscles restraining his emotion. You also notice the small moles and freckles on his face—which is very pale except for the permanently sunburned nose, as if he cares enough about skin cancer to protect his cheeks and forehead but gave up on the nose. You're not sure about his pale skin or fastidious behavior, but you like the burnt nose and the slight creases around his eyes. You always tell me eye wrinkles are one's medals of honor; they say this person has laughed through their hell.

Maybe Brit has laughed, but I've always wondered if his white hair implies something else. Brit's been mourning his divorce for about four years now. His daughter, Nancy, told me he woke one morning, and her mom confessed her sins and left him, Nancy, her sister, and the family's two Labs. Her mom took some money, but she didn't need much; her new husband owns The Travel Inns franchise.

"Our office is under construction, so I closed up, told everyone to go home. Hard to write legal briefs when it feels like the entire building will crumble at your feet." He looks back at the now dead fish. "So, Lorraine, where is this all going?"

Mom puts her fish in a paper bag.

"Cara lost their fish to an I-84 wreck. So, I thought I'd do an investigation myself. I wanted to get a dying fish, watch it die. I'm not sure what I saw. But there may be significance in his movements."

"And you're now going to do what with that fish?"

"They suspect suffocation caused by low dissolved oxygen. Who knows? So many things are dying and there is so little we can do but leave a message on the state EPA voicemail. So, I'm going to look at things myself." You reach for your backpack. "I've found a dead blue jay, too. They told me it was probably a bird virus. It died right there in my yard within minutes of perching on my patio table."

"Interesting. You know, I found a dead bird in my yard. Robin, I think."

You stare at your fish and ignore his comment.

"It's upsetting," Brit continues. "Finding dead things, I mean."

"He died right there," you say softly. "One minute he was there, the next he was gone."

"Are you still talking about the blue jay?"

You look away quickly.

"Of course, I am." You shove the paper bag holding the fish into your backpack.

"By the way, has the bonding company called you?" Brit says. "I think we have problems with your other advocacy project."

"I'll handle that issue. I'll call when your legal services are needed."

"I volunteer one day a month. But just call me, not legal aid, if you need questions answered."

You put your backpack on. "Thanks for stopping, Brit. I always appreciate your help."

"When you dissect it, why don't you give me a call. Nancy's a biochemistry major. I can get some tips on what we'd be looking for."

"You just wanted to take that opportunity to brag about your daughter, but that's OK. I have a perfect daughter, too. No, I need no help. I'm capable of doing this all by myself." You grab your bike, kick the stand, and get ready for the ride home.

"Let's say you find out that the cause of death is some strange chemical. Tell me the steps you will then take."

You put one hand on the handle bar, one foot on the peddle, and look back at him.

You hold up one finger. "I call my friends at nonprofit groups." You put up two fingers. "I write my letters to all the appropriate parties—blogs, legislators." Three fingers. "I leave another message on the voicemail at our state EPA." Four fingers. "I write letters to the editor." Five fingers. "I stand before our Board of Selectman and make a speech."

"Everything you listed is meaningless nowadays. Of course, I'd say skip all that and just march, but now that's dangerous. All that tear gas and police looking for trouble."

You don't argue, because you're in a hurry and challenging apathy takes so much energy. You're disappointed in Brit, because you remember when he used to fight like you. He was involved in civil liberty lawsuits and advocacy, even considered politics until it was obvious the elections weren't real. He eventually gave up. Why fight when no one accepts the case? Why file lawsuits that will never be ruled upon? Why call legislators who have no accountability? He joined everyone who went into survivor mode, concentrating on family, friends, and local community issues. That strategy has always made sense to me. It never made sense to you.

You take off slowly, yell over your shoulder. "Someday, Brit we'll get it all back. In the meantime, I collect dead fish."

# Chapter 7

*Obsession pushes dogs away*

WHEN YOU ARRIVE home, you let Lolly out and watch her squat to pee and lie flat on the slate patio, absorbing the heat into her fat belly. It's over eighty degrees, too hot for an old bulldog. You remind yourself to look outside in ten minutes.

Back in the kitchen, you set up at the table by the bay window. Lolly's back thigh is visible, splayed behind her like a sea lion's rear flippers. You place newspaper over the table but then reconsider because fish blood on a table where we eat may not be wise. You decide to remove the newspaper and cover the table with a plastic canvas you use for trash dump days. You cannot find the canvas at first, so that takes a while. You finally find the canvas beneath several platters in a cabinet you rarely open. You place the canvas over the table, then cover that with newspaper. This takes more time than anticipated, and by the time you finish, the blue jays are squawking at you as if you were a witch. You figure they want their special peanuts because the feeder is almost empty.

You crack the window and yell, "Go eat a seed. Or better, find a bug. No peanuts today." A few robins arrive and call to one another noisily. Soon, Chickadees, jays, nuthatches, cardinals, robins, grackles, all chirp, squawk, call, scream. The jays continue looking at you, which disturbs you but not too much.

You return to the alewife now lying belly up on the newspaper. You open your laptop and tap on a saved fish site. Up comes a picture of the alewife anatomy. You know from talking with Cara that low oxygen will swell the operculum, or gill cover. You don't know how to determine if this particular dead fish's gill cover is swollen, so you Google "alewife operculum size." Pictures of alewife gills but no details on size. You find a few alewife illustrations with identified parts and measure the length of the pictured fish with your ruler, then the length of the pictured operculum. The pictured operculum is about one seventh the size of the entire pictured fish. There's your ratio. Your real fish is twelve inches, and one seventh of this would be 1.72 inches, but the operculum is actually 2.6 inches. You therefore conclude the operculum is swollen. And that is your scientific method.

The birds are now so loud, their squawking so pervasive, you can barely hear yourself talk to yourself. (Yes, I know you talk to yourself.) There are almost two dozen blue jays now and at least four chickadees and what seems like a million sparrows but is probably twenty. They are not only on the ground, but also, trees, yard, and patio furniture. You stare out at the birds near your patio and wonder if there is perhaps something related to the patio you have forgotten.

# Blue Jay Memo

*The dog is dead!*
*The dog is dead!*
*The dog is dead!*
*The dog is dead!*
*The dog is dead!*
*The dog is dead!*
*The dog is dead!*
*The dog is dead!*

# Chapter 8

*Dog pushes obsession aside*

"OH MY GOD, Lolly!" You run to the patio door, shove it open.

Lolly's gums are blue. Her eyes are wide, her body is hot, as if the insides are cooking. The bulldog is not breathing. You hit Lolly's back hard. Again. And Again.

You pick up Lolly and carry her to the den, lay her on her side. Lolly starts gasping. It's not really a gasp, more like a desperate struggle for air. You stick your fingers inside the bulldog's mouth and clear the mucous. Lolly sucks at the air and mucous. It sounds like drowning. You run to the kitchen and return with ice and lemons. The ice you put on Lolly's chest and belly, the lemon you squeeze into her mouth. Lolly does not like the lemons but she doesn't fight it. The mucous build up is huge and the lemon juice begins to clear it.

"I kill everything," you say, now crying so hard mucous builds in your mouth, too. You squirt lemons into the bulldog's mouth again.

"I probably did something to kill those fish, too," you say. You keep rubbing the chest with ice. You imagine our vet, Nan, her wrinkled brows, her round, soft face looking at you with her disappointed eyes. She will also comment on Lolly's weight and how it contributed to the overheating. Nan always comments on Lolly's weight. You hate going to the vet for the same reason I hate going to my doctor. They always talk about weight.

You lay your head on Lolly's soft belly and listen to a faint thump and the swish of air in and out of her lungs. You other ear takes in the noisy birds.

When you walk through the kitchen toward the bridge that will lead you to the other side of the house, you grab the fish. You stop briefly in the kitchenette to catch your breath and put the fish back into the paper bag for transport.

Outside, the jays scream and flutter overhead as you shut the car door. You sit a moment in the barely muted car with your dead fish and dying bulldog. You start the engine, jerk the car into gear, jam on the gas, and screech out the driveway.

# Blue Jay Memo

*The dog is alive!*
*The dog is alive!*
*The dog is alive!*

# Chapter 9

*Passive aggressive vet pushes you aside*

NAN LISTENS TO Lolly's heart and lungs. She has placed a cool wet towel on the bulldog's chest and a small oxygen mask over the nose and jowls, which has stopped the heavy panting. Lolly seems happy, she is with Nan.

"Poor baby. You just got too hot." She reaches behind both of Lolly's ears and massages her neck. Lolly stretches her legs, so Nan rubs her belly—back and forth, back and forth. She lifts the mask and plants her lips on Lolly's large, pink and gray jowls and loudly kisses her.

Nan has streaks of red henna highlighting the edges of her hair today, giving her a younger appearance than her probable age, which we have guessed to be late thirties. There's a small tattoo on her left forearm, which looks like a cat, but you never study it. While the tattoo and henna streaks are hip and trendy, what comes out of Nan's mouth sounds like a 1950s mother from Iowa. You trust her, though. It's the tattoo and henna hair that say trust her, not the 1950s housewife-y personality.

"You are such a luuuv. Just a luuv," Nan says. "You tell your mommy to be careful in the future. Mommy needs to know English bulldogs cannot be left on a hot patio for God knows how long. Poor baby." She stops rubbing the belly, but Lolly kicks out her legs and paws Nan's hand for more. "And what is Mommy doing to exercise you, love bug. Is mommy not exercising you? Because it's even more dangerous to stay in the sun when you're a tubby wubby. Yes it is. Yes it is, luuuv."

"Nan, I'm standing right here. And I do walk her. Lolly likes to eat and I think dog diets are mean."

"Mommy is mad at Nan for talking to you, sugar cake. That's because mommy's feeling very guilty right now. Mommy needs to understand it's OK and learn from her mistakes so this doesn't happen in the future. We don't obsess over dead fish at the expense of our live pets. No, we don't my luuuv. No, we don't." She kisses Lolly on the jowls again and rubs behind Lolly's ear.

"And I'm not obsessing over fish," you say to Lolly's upside down face. Her pink tongue squeezes out of each incisor. "It was an accident. Thank God for my noisy birds. They may be dying, too, you know." Lolly yawns. "I've found three dead birds so far, one's a blue jay. It's probably related to the dead fish. Anyway, Lolly, please tell Nan, I'd appreciate just a bit of advice about the dead fish. After you finish receiving her kisses, of course."

Nan straightens up and looks at Lorraine then back at Lolly.

"Once an animal is dead, our job is over." She looks at the dog then Mom. "I doubt you will find anything in that dead fish now anyway. Maybe the liver could tell you something. It's probably low oxygen. There's always a reason and there's always a correction."

"Correction? You mean like when all the crows died? The correction was no crows."

She stops rubbing the dog's belly because Lolly's now asleep and oblivious. Even if Nan chose to finish the conversation through the bulldog, the words would simply enter Lolly's dream, so she turns and faces you.

"Lorraine, do you know how much it would cost to test that fish liver for toxins? And then what? What do you do with the report? We're not set up for that. Contact the state environmental department. Leave a voicemail like we all do, then walk Lolly or take her to the park, or buy another puppy. Life is short, Lorraine."

"Nan, I do believe I know all about the length of life. We don't have to accept the earth's life being shortened, do we? Can you look at the gill cover at least and tell me if you think it looks swollen? I read somewhere, the gill cover will swell with lack of oxygen."

Nan opens the paper bag, places the fish on a piece of wax paper. She points her flashlight at its pupils, runs her finger over the fish belly, pushes at the gills a few times.

"I'd guess these gills are larger than usual. The eyes have some parasites which may be expected if they were low oxygen and higher ventilation with the expanded operculum. Sometimes, predator fish can run these schools up the tributaries into brackish water where oxygen is naturally low. That can cause the entire school to die." She puts the fish back into the paper bag and washes her hands.

"But there were thousands. Thousands. And they were in the Sound, not up some tributary. Nan, the entire area was covered in fish bellies. Is that a school of fish? Has anyone else reported dead fish? And what about the dead birds."

"Are you still feeding those birds, Lorraine? It's late spring, plenty of food for them to eat. It's dry, but there's still bugs and insects." She looks around the room, as if trying to find a bird to deliver her lecture to. There are no birds, but Lolly is now awake and rolling over, so she talks to her. "Tell your mommy birds are fine in the summer. Please feed them only in winter. They will become too dependent. Do they mess all over your yard? Is she washing her feeders?"

"Lolly knows I wash my feeders. And I love feeding birds now when they're having sex and building nests. They're happy. Why engage only during cold misery?" Nan cleans the counter with intensity before grabbing Lolly's file and scribbling a long note.

"OK," You say, waiting for her to look up. She does not. "Forget this death. There's nothing to do anyway but march and write letters. Save the Water lost their fish and water samples on the highway. Car accident. No one was hurt, and the fish that scattered across I-84 were already dead. But even Cara says it doesn't matter. Whatever they find will be simply food for thought."

"So, OK," Nan starts up after a pause and long exhale, not wanting to talk politics. "Keep Lolly inside. She should stay outside no longer than ten minutes on days when the heat index rises above 80. "She holds out her hand for Mom to shake. You do. "Lorraine, enjoy life, OK?"

You put Lolly on the ground, leash her, and walk into the waiting room, now filled with five dogs and seven humans. Lolly freezes, lowers her body to the ground, as if ashamed, which provokes two large Labs to begin barking. Lolly lowers her body closer to the ground. You know Lolly is very insecure around other dogs. You've analyzed it in your anthropomorphic way. You tell everyone in the lobby that Lolly has a dog anxiety disorder related to her body image, "which of course is exacerbated by everyone emphasizing dog diets." Everyone is silent. The dogs continue to bark.

You grab Lolly around the chest, drag her through the waiting room as other owners put their weight into restraining their big barking dogs. Once outside, Lolly stands, shakes herself, and prances to the car. You shove her inside. When put your car into gear, you notice activity in the tree canopy. At least a half a dozen jays scattered among the branches. Maybe Nan's right, you think to yourself. You shouldn't worry so much about a few deaths when there are so many of these creatures. You should concentrate on the thousands alive, ignore the few dead.

That will be one thought, however, that you will not act upon.

# Blue Jay Memo

*The dog is still alive!*
*The dog is still alive!*
*The dog is still alive!*
*The dog is still alive!*
*The dog is still alive!*

*The dog moves appendages!*
*The dog moves appendages!*

*She's taking dog to motorized mobile nest.*
*Follow.*
*Come back. No not there.*
*Over here.*
*Follow!*

Female host takes dog to red nest located two miles northwest of our Children of Athena home nest. We believe this is a combined human and animal nest. Dogs enter this nest with humans, sometimes dogs stay, sometimes dogs leave. A few times, like today, humans carry dog inside. Same routine with cats and other species. We have also observed dead dogs transported to this location.

We increase reconnaissance. We fly high in order to better observe activity at many locations around female host's motorized mobile nest. This is what we see:

Black and white mobile nest that contains friendly human protector travels 1.5 miles southwest of our current transient location. He is traveling down same path female host is traveling down. He appears to be following female host. Protector takes a right turn at a path then left turn and another left turn on a path that will cross female host's current path. It appears intentional. Predatory behavior.

*Conflict!*
*Conflict!*

*Conflict!*
*Conflict!*

*Another motorized mobile nest is approaching path crossing.*

*Stay. On. Limb.*
*Watch out!*
*Watch out!*
*Conflict!*
*Conflict!*
*Conflict!*
*Shut uuuup. Listen.*

*Protector's motorized mobile nest has ceased motion on side of path and appears to be observing upcoming potential conflict.*

*Watch Out!*
*Watch Out!*
*Watch out!*
*Stay on limb.*
*Come back.*
*Watch out!*
*Watch out!*
*She's doomed.*
*Who will feed us?*

# Chapter 10

*Four way stops signs and conflict*

YOU DRIVE FAST, eager to get home and let Lolly rest in the cool air-conditioned kitchen while you do something with your dead fish. The smell of the carrion competes with the smell of Lolly's panting breath. You turn up the fan and point the vents at Lolly's face. Since Nan refused to conduct a fish autopsy, you have limited choices. You can simply throw the fish away and hope Cara will come back again in a few days to test a fish and the water. Of course, by then the dead fish will have been dead days in the hot sun, decomposing. The carcasses will have been pecked by turkey vultures, although to date no scavengers have appeared on the scene. You could also drive to New Harbor, march into Ivy University with your fish and your story, but Ivy tends to look down on people who barge into the school without an I.D. or nice resume or money.

Lolly pushes her head through the front two seats, sniffing vigorously. You lean over and kiss her cheek and tap on the radio. NPR drones on and on—updates on our terrifying world, sanitized for our consumption. Our forever war with Iran; drone bombings and civilian casualties; North Korea's ongoing nuclear testing and the lukewarm response by our country and our new alliance partners—Russia, Hungary, Poland, Indonesia; the usual "violent and possibly terrorist" protests by women in various southern states that abolished abortion after the overturning of Roe v Wade. Same ole, same ole. You tap the radio off.

You regard the distant clouds ominously rising. They do not appear to be moving eastward, however, only north, which means the clouds will miss the town, hit Connecticut residents located in central regions away from the coast. You wonder if those northwestern neighborhoods removed from the water care about dead fish.

These thoughts swell in your mind as you approach the notorious four-way stop intersection at Lawry and Slate. You at one time organized a petition and group advocating for the elimination of all four-way stop intersections because no one paid attention to the first stop/first go rule. Well, you never did. Your group consisted of a few members from your environmental activities and several octogenarians from the senior center, many of whom had ceased driving but still thought the four-way stop intersections were confusing

You see few cars today, not really, although a Toyota coasts toward the intersection. You slow your pace to one noticeably slower than the Toyota, but since the Toyota driver apparently does not believe in stopping either, both of your cars head for each other. The Toyota veers off the road almost hitting a police car before rolling into the ditch, then out of the ditch and back on the street barely missing another car that drives over a yard, back on the street.

You are out of the car and at the Toyota's door. A large man with jet black hair and a red beard opens his door, puts his meaty hands on his thighs, and pushes himself to a standing position, breathing heavily. While he is large, his voice is soft and effeminate. Louis is already there with his police computer tablet.

And we're off:

"You were coasting, not stopping," you start.

"You didn't stop, either, dear." The man puts his hands on his belly, like Santa Claus.

"I was coasting slower than you."

"I'm looking for a gas station."

"I'm not seeing how that relates to our rule about coasting speeds?"

"Rule about coasting speeds?"

"The question is who was going slower or who slowed first." You lean over to pet Lolly who has managed to escape the car and is now sitting between the large man and you.

The man stares at you, then at Louis, tapping his tablet.

"Can I ask you why you have a red beard and black hair?" you say, because why not?

"My red beard is relevant to this conversation in what way?"

"I've never seen a red beard with black hair. I'm just being nice. Noticing you, you know."

"Can I say something here?" Louis says.

"Where the hell am I anyway?" the man says, looking around for a sign. "Sorry, officer. Just wondering. What town is this? I took the first exit for gas."

"He doesn't know where he is. See, this, Louis?" You turn to Louis. "This is why we need stop lights, Louis." He says nothing, so you turn back to the man.

"We all know the town rules about this particular intersection, but you're from out of town, so there you go. Welcome to Westbrook by the way. We have a lot of dead fish. My dog is sick, and I have to go." You turn back to your car.

"I'm on my way to Vermont. And you didn't stop," the man shouts at your back. "Not really, you slowed way down."

"You didn't stop either," you shout over your shoulder. Lolly trots to the car door." You close your door, roll down the window half-way, and look at Louis, now at your car. "But Vermont has a ban on plastics, so okay. We all need these people from Vermont. I'll pay his fine."

The man looks confused and a little scared. You want to be home so Lolly can flop over the cool air conditioning vent and lick a bowl of ice cream.

"Lorraine," Louis says softly after you sit in your car with the engine running and air conditioner blasting for twenty seconds. He turns back to the man. "Excuse me, you're free to go." He does. "Look, I was here the entire time and no car stopped and we do not have a rule about relative speed of the cars."

"I've been thinking, Louis. It seems you're always where I am. Why is that?" You notice how the large man lumbers away, his legs rolling around each other. You imagine him making his own maple syrup, chopping wood before the snow, never using plastic. "Really, it's something I've noticed. Trouble, then Louis. Or at least trouble with me, then there you are."

Louis looks away a moment then down at his tablet then back at his car. "I just happen to be in the general location of disturbance, I guess."

"Are you saying you tend to always be near disturbances and, low and behold, I am there, too?"

"I guess that's what I'm saying." He looks at the intersection a moment. "You know, Lorraine, it's not that hard. You take turns at these four-ways. You just have to pay attention is all."

"I'm very good when there are a lot of cars, Louis. I have patience, I take turns. I'm not good on low car days. Give me a ticket if you want. I agreed to take it on the chin because the man is a Vermont man. I like Vermont."

You lean over and kiss Lolly, now by your side, panting again. Louis stands there for a moment as if he wants to say something but has forgotten what he wants to say.

"You aren't going to search my car?" You say over the half open window. "I do recall, now that I think of it, another civilian, Maria Lopez? I helped her with bond. She ran a four-way, too. They searched her car."

"We're allowed to do that now. New cases, new precedents. She was an illegal immigrant. We have . . ."

"Oh, please don't tell me what you can do now, versus what you could not do a thousand years ago. Marijuana should not be crime." You roll the window down the rest of the way and place your bent elbow out the opening. "We almost legalized it before the transition. And calling I.C.E. on that woman was wrong according to human laws. Human laws, Louis. I still operate under those and you should, too."

"Has that bonding company contacted you?" Louis says. You remain quiet. "Just a question, it's not part of your current violation, Lorraine."

"Yes, they have called. I told them she was coming back, just had to take care of some family issues. I enrolled her in a literacy class, but the library said she could not attend unless she was interviewed. Well, so much for that. Libraries now have to ask if the students are citizens according to the new laws. I guess I'll teach her English."

"When's the last time you talked with her?"

"You know, Louis, I've got to get Lolly home." You start to roll up the window, but Louis places his hand on the edge of the glass.

"You tried to enroll her so everyone would think she was around. Right, Lorraine? I guess you'll be out a few thousand bucks and then you go on with life. Just a miscalculation on your part. Unless you knew she had no intention of showing up. Unless, you paid the bond and told her to get the hell out of town. Right, Lorraine?"

"Oh, please. You have no proof of that. We never have that proof we all need, now do we?"

You put your car into gear, wait for him to step back, and drive away.

Were you nervous, Mom? He was right, wasn't he? Just where is Maria and why did you do that?

# Chapter 11

*When the gone return*

WHEN WE CAUGHT a fish, after sitting for hours, my dad would always do the same thing. He'd place his thumb in the mouth of the fish and slowly work on the hook. Occasionally the hook would be lodged deep in its mouth, but Dad was always determined to remove it without injuring the fish. I couldn't do it. Removing a hook from a fish felt like the beginning of a horror movie—the eyes of the fish looking at you, the tail flipping hysterically. And it probably was being tortured, although Dad insisted fish feel little or no pain, although they did experience anxiety of sorts. If removal of the hook was impossible, Dad clipped the line and let the fish go. He said this was no big deal because the hook would eventually come out, then he'd quickly change the subject. I never thought the fish would survive with a hook stuck in its throat or on the side of its stomach, rusting. I suspected the fish would die, and I wondered if it would be best to kill the fish and eat it, put it out of misery. Just once, I begged Dad, just once, can we take the fish home and fry it. But not once did he kill it for food.

YOU DON'T THROW the fish away. You lay it carefully upon the unfolded newspaper on your table and continue to poke at it as you rub Lolly's side with your bare foot. Lolly's front legs stretch out before her, her back legs stretch out behind her, like a baby seal. You have already given her a few scoops of ice cream, which you believe enhances endorphins and eliminates bad memories. You pick up a knife again and turn the fish over, noting its slimy, scaly feel. Its eyes are clouded over with death and yet it still has a presence. You consider this, imagine its previous life with no real thoughts, only one concern—finding food. It would move in order to breath in dissolved oxygen which would allow it the energy to keep going in order to find food so it can live another day to breath and find food, until someone or something eats it. A fish exists to provide nourishment for another fish, which will provide nourishment for another fish, which will provide nourishment for a bird or mammal. When poisoned, the life is valueless. This is what bothers you. All this death humans cause renders life and its ultimate demise worthless.

You cut a straight line down its belly and study the gunk that is its insides. The gunk does not resemble the insides of a fish now on your laptop's screen. You lean closer and pick out the tiny red blob that apparently is a heart. You gather the big blobby gray thing, that is probably a stomach, then peek at the stuff beneath that, which according to the picture are intestines. The liver evades you. Everything looks pink and filled with something. You don't know what a liver filled with toxins would look like or what you would do with it, if you did know what it looked like. Is there a point to this? You decide, no, there is no point, you are simply passing time with a dead fish.

You roll up the fish into newspaper and shove it in a large paper bag. You then stuff that into a large plastic bag, because that is what you use for the large garbage bin rolled to the street every Thursday. You pause to consider this plastic garbage bag you stuffed everything in, now deep in your bin. It will be barged to the incinerator. En route the wind will toss the plastic bag around until it's torn, pieces will escape into the Sound, and vulnerable fish will eat it. The fish will have a weakened immune system or develop weak livers, which will make it susceptible to viruses. Of course, maybe the fish will not eat plastic, but try to escape the plastic by swimming up tributaries that used to have enough dissolved oxygen, but now due to warm waters have limited oxygen. So they die. You stare at the garbage bin containing your cruel plastic garbage bag. You have killed fish. You take it out and sit it in a corner. You think about the dead fish in this plastic bag for a while until you develop a solution. Cardboard boxes? No. Several paper bags? No.

There are no solutions. You have almost killed your dog. You are probably contributing to dead fish due to your occasional plastic bag use. You feel depression creeping up. You tell yourself at least you care. That staves off the depression for now.

The trill of your iPhone startles you. The caller ID says Dr. Sarah Ableman, an old friend who's gone AWOL for a while now. Dr. Ableman was a quiet, unemotional participant in past environmental activist causes. Actually, Dr. Ableman is the most self-controlled, methodical, steely woman I've ever known. She's almost six feet tall, wears thick round glasses and rarely smiles or exudes passion. You usually let voicemail pick up all phone calls, but this is Dr. Ableman.

"Sarah!"

"Lorraine, hi." Silence.

"So. Wow. Long time, no hear."

Silence.

"I'm so glad you called. Where the hell are you?"

Silence.

"Lorraine. I heard about the dead fish."

"Yes, they're dying. And how are you?"

"I still live here."

"But you've been gone."

"Why did the fish die?"

"No one knows why. No one cares."

"The waste treatment plant down the way has secondary treatment now, so that's not the issue."

"Yes, Sarah, I know. The gas pipeline running through my property reminds me every day I am contributing to the secondary treatment for our sewage."

"Well, I don't know if that's exactly accurate, Lorraine. Anyway, how are you otherwise?" She says it softly, slowly. It's been seven years and there are still sorrowful comments like this. Even Nan occasionally treats you sorrowfully. I get them too. But with Sarah, it's as if she also feels the pain. Completely.

You take a while to think, then think some more. Most people would interject a comment, change the subject. But not Sarah. She simply breathes. You feel like talking to her, saying something profound. She has this effect upon you.

"I'm moving on. Actually, I'm glad I stumbled upon dead fish. It's time to get involved again, change the object of my life. I've been involved intermittently, you know, ever since . . . But not this kind of involved. I was going to send out invites to my home for a meeting of sorts to discuss the dead fish."

"That would be nice. I've been on the outside of the community, too. Work has taken me out of town."

You put your foot back on Lolly's belly and slowly move it back and forth, thinking about this comment. Sarah's marriage disintegrated six years ago, because the One Party outlawed it again. She had been married to Malinda five years. Then, the courts ruled it was OK to fire gays, not hire gays, refuse to do business with gays. Malinda eventually chose freedom and left the country to live with Canadian relatives. And just like that, the relationship was over. We assumed Sarah stepped away from life because that's what you do when you grieve. That's what we did for a while, or what you did, right Mom? But you came back. And so has Sarah.

"Sarah can you help us out? Get involved again. I'm going to petition the city to investigate. I've found a few dead birds, too. We can't have another bird die off. There're so many dead things nowadays."

"Yes, there are."

Again, the silence.

"I noticed they found dead fish down in Maryland," Sarah finally says carefully.

"Really. Where did you read that and why haven't I read it?"

"It's spreading, I think. I've been reading, researching. I called our U.S. senator. He said, 'We all eat farm fish now. So, until they die, we're not going to go nuts over fish deaths in the wild.' Then he hung up."

You consider this for a moment. Sarah, who's been gone for a while, is more informed than you about your dead fish issue. Also, something about her seems changed.

"So, I guess the solution will be legislation mandating more fish farms," Sarah says.

"Maybe we toss our plastic in the fish farms," you say. "Starve the legislators in Washington."

# Blue Jay Memo

We must follow.
Off the Limb
Come back
We stay.
No, follow!

We have nesting responsibilities, but we still follow.

Bored. Bored.
Stay behind her.
Bored.
We go back, sit on eggs.
No. Follow.
She's at water's edge again.
Same thing.
Bored, bored.

Female host is overly concerned with dead fish.

OK, so we're also concerned with dead fish. We're not that oblivious. We notice. There's lots of death waves. They come and go. We don't like it. Not. At. All. It's just that female host's obsessions tend to result in conflicts and no resolutions. A human trait. Humans lack natural perspective.

See, here's the deal. When you're above it all, like us? We have whatcha call a natural perspective.

She's sitting.
Bored. Bored.
We need to sit on eggs.
Shut uuup. Pay attention.
Back on Limb.

*OK, see our perspective allows us to understand origination of events. For example, we know the fish death wave started at the large land cut off from coast. It's 1 mile south, approximately 2 miles west of Children of Athena home nest. During a great storm, this small, cut off land mass was covered in water. Afterwards, we noticed arrival of many large motorized mobile carrying dirt. These nests dumped large quantities of this dirt near water. We suspect the soil was meant to dry wet ground. We laugh. Haha (Yes, we laugh. How do you think we live around squirrels?) Soil is futile. Green vegetation now covers water where it meets land. First great death wave was here.*

*We suspect female host does not understand the origin of this fish death wave but there is no way to tell female human about death wave origin since she does not sing our song. Even our basic, easy songs, songs of warning, she ignores.*

*Bored.Bored.*
*She's sitting.*
*We go now.*
*On limbs! Now!*
*Stay. Come back*

*We follow female host back. We are sick of observing her worthless endeavors when we know more than she does.*

*We meet with elders. Elders decide we need to intervene so female host will cease worthless activity. They suspect she needs a hint, a bit of guidance.*

*We send a two-year-old to reconnoiter the land cut off from mainland, where original death wave occurred. We tell him to gather object that may serve as a marker for the area.*

*He travels there in ten minutes, takes another minute to find object clearly attached to resident humans. He brings it back. Object is oblong, fits neatly into our talons and refracts light. We've not observed it at other human locations, therefore conclude it's a good marker. We decide to share object with the female host.*

*We know we're only supposed to dictate memos, but we feel we must do this. We have perspective, OK?*

# Chapter 12

*Let go of the stick to catch the gift*

DAD HAD ABOUT twenty fishing rods. Some could be taken apart for travel, others were long and sleek and could only be transported by SUV. If he wasn't fishing, he often cleaned and worked on his rods, sometimes replacing all the lines. On lazy summer Sundays, he'd sit out in the yard, while you weeded or fed the birds or drank wine, and methodically take apart and clean his reels or fix his lures. I'd come home to a yard filled with parts. Lures, lines, reels, spools, small screws. The entire process was way too mindful for you to witness, and you would usually start complaining around the third reel dissection. But I loved seeing everything splayed upon the grass, alone, separated from its purpose. One time a jay swooped down and snatched a shiny, stainless-steel fish lure for no reason. It simply picked it up and flew off, which made Dad frustrated but not really angry. Lures, which were part of a collection that numbered in the hundreds, were expendable. If it had been a screw or part of a reel, or handle, the theft would impact the entire get up. But they never took pieces integral to the whole.

"They know," Dad said once. "They know what is critical, what is not."

Mom had lifted her glass of wine. "Well, once they took the cork for my wine. One must have a cork to keep the wine fresh. I think that disproves your theory."

"Unless they wanted you to stop drinking," Dad said.


TODAY IS AGAIN cloudless and hot. Our yard is brown and dusty. You now ponder whether the drought may have something to do with the dead birds. I disagree because we've had droughts before with no dead fish or dead birds. Of course, this drought is a record breaker. Everything is always worse than before. The storms, the rain, the wind, the droughts, the heat waves.

You have all Dad's rods on the patio. You have placed them side by side the way he used to. You've never really known what to do with them. You gave away all his clothes and didn't keep much memorabilia except letters and photos. But you couldn't quite give up the fishing rods. You placed them in the attic, away from me, thinking the sight of them may upset me because I was Dad's fishing companion. But they don't upset me, only frustrate me. I suspect Dad would want them with another fisherman, not in an attic.

You stare at the rods. You've called Wills McNeil, an old fisherman who operated a fishing boat Dad and I fished on a few times with our deep-sea rods. You asked him to please come pick up the rods; they were too much work. He said nothing to that. He knew you were not working on rods, you barely knew how to cast them. "They need homes. Some father and daughter or father and son who fish, you know. Someone who will take care of them the way Larry did. Take them apart, put them together. That kind of thing." He told you not to worry, he'd come get them. "Then, you'll be free, Lorraine."

You look them over, recalling the care they once had. You regret never learning the art of fishing. Why hadn't you learned the skill? What skill did you have? You pick up one rod and gently run your fingers down the line to the reel. A small snap swivel is slipped into the hook keeper. You detach it and open the bait box, choose a random lure, a green plastic frog. You manage to attach the lure to snap swivel. You stand and cast your green frog out into the yard then quickly reel it back in.

"There're no live fish in dead grass, only dead fish in water."

You drop the rod. Brit Jacobs stands near your large hemlock, holding the leash to Fred, his labradoodle. Fred pulls at his leash and bounces around, his ears flopping around his jaws. When Lolly is around, Fred pounces on her until she stands up. But today Lolly is inside splayed over the air conditioning vent, so Fred just pounces on nothing.

"Can you possibly announce yourself first? Dear God, Brit. And why are you not lawyering today. Is it still the construction or have people stopped suing each other?"

Brit walks to the patio and tells Fred to sit. Fred sits the way dogs sit who expect to spring up at any moment. He looks over the rods. "Are you going to fish or is this Larry's collection?"

"I'm giving them a home today. I was thinking maybe I'd keep them and learn to fish, but all the fish are dead."

Brit picks up a rod and Fred leaps up and grabs it and takes off around the yard. You start after Fred, which leads him to assume, like all dogs do, that you two are playing a dog, human game. He now runs faster around the periphery then into the front yard, you behind him, screaming, Brit trotting behind you, laughing. Since Fred is probably trained to never pass a driveway, he stops suddenly at the end of our property.

"Drop. Sit," Brit commands.

The dog drops the rod and sits. You grab the rod as if it were a baby, holding it tight to your chest as you lean over.

"You're very bad," you say. "Very bad dog. This is my favorite one! You are a bad, bad dog!"

Fred lowers his body to the ground, cowering.

"It's OK. I'll discipline him, Lorraine." Brit leashes his dog quickly, annoyed with you for yelling at his dog, but when he turns, you're on the ground, hugging the rod.

"Oh, Lorraine." He drops the leash. Fred lies down, his head shamefully resting on both paws. "God, I'm so sorry."

"No, it's just me being stupid." You lie still now, the rod to your chest, eyes closed, tears squeezing out of corners, one small drop sliding down your nose. "I'm just tired, I think. I'll just lie here a short while."

"You need to walk. Get away from the house a while. Come with us."

"No."

He sits down by you.

And then it happens. It falls from the sky, like a rain drop, hitting your shoulder, bouncing lightly onto the grass before your eyes. An oblong crystal chime with several octagon indentations around its surface that refract the sun. You touch it, then hold it. It fell from the hemlocks and when you sit up and bend your head back, you see them squawking down at you.

# Blue Jay Memo

She's down.
Stay on the limb.
Quiet.
She's down with long stick.
Man with white head fur is above her.
Predatory behavior!
Conflict!
Conflict!

The dog sings too loud.
Dog sings too loud!
We do not like dog!

Loud dog tried to devour female host's stick. Female lies horizontal on ground. She still grips stick. We are concerned. We chirp, imitate sparrows, to calm ourselves down.

He touches her!
We attack!
No. Come back.
Stay on limb.
We dive bomb!
No!

What are Elders saying?
They say drop marker!
Why?
Distraction.
What marker?
Pay attention!
Back on limb. Now!
Who has marker?
Two-year-old.

We find two-year-old who finds marker.

Drop it now!
On him?
No, her!
Good shot.

She has it.
She has what?
Marker!
Why?
On limb now!
She holds it.
She stands!
She's OK!

We are proud! She has marker, she looks at us. She has recovered and understands our message.

What is he doing?
He holds her!
Danger!
Danger!

Come back.
On limb now.

He's touching her!
Beak touching?
He wishes to mate her?

This has been a mating ritual all along? And he wears no colors?
Humans never cease to amaze us.

# Chapter 13

*The chime connection*

Dear editor,

The dead fish have now moved out to sea. Maybe they have decayed. Maybe rotted pieces of them have sunk to the sea floor where crabs nibble on their remains. Out of our minds, out of our way, gone.

Another disaster we no longer have to witness.

I know that nowadays when we all wish to understand environmental issues, we must search the deep bowels of our media. Our environmental disasters are not entertaining enough for the front page. But maybe all of you should peruse the internet. If you do that, you'll find that dead fish are a problem in many coastal areas. No one offers an overarching reason for these deaths, but there are a few theories. There is plastic littering the waterways. Fish nibbling plastic which they cannot digest. There is global warming raising local water temperatures, bringing fish north, which confuses fisheries and renders regional regulations and quotas moot. That doesn't cause fish death, but it's a problem. There are waste treatment plants that are not required to have secondary treatment, raising nitrogen and phosphorous levels. And on and on.

Do you think everything is OK because you buy farmed fish? Have you ever visited a fish farm? Do you know what's in fish farm water?

And by the way, I've found a dead blue jay.

So, let's talk about how fish can impact the bird . . .

Editor note: Lorraine Mulderon exceeded our 250 word limit and after numerous requests for editing were ignored, editors were forced, as usual, to end the letter here.

To: <advocategroups, family, old school lists, church lists, anyone who ever emailed you >
From: Lorrainismad@gmail.com

Dear concerned citizens of Westbrook and everyone else who cares,

I am requesting signatures for a petition demanding that our legislators form an investigative committee to study the dead fish issue, which may be related to dead blue jays. Not too many of you have noticed, or cared about fish, but I am assuming a few of you do care about dead birds. I have found three dead blue jays so far. I know others who have found dead birds.

My letter to the editor was cut off at 250 words. But there were theories out there relating the dead fish to the dead birds. Some scientists believe water polluted the birds' food supply. Or the water could have impacted the garbage landfills where crows picked at discarded food. We don't know now do we? (Don't worry, I'm not going to pontificate. I will make this short and sweet. Well, not sweet. Or short.)

OK. If you think it wise to explore how and why our nature's most important creatures are dying en masse, then sign this. Yes, your name will appear somewhere. Yes, maybe this will impact a One Party government official's opinion of you. But during these trying times, bravery is critical. And bravery is signing petitions, bravery is establishing where you stand, bravery is marching, bravery is having a purpose.

The great transition took our vote but not our letters and our ability to march. We can do that. And can't we at least control our lives at the local level? I thought that was the idea back when we lost everything. Oh, we'll just huddle here at the local level?

Anyway . . .

Please tap this link which will take you to the gopeition.com site. Type in Dead Fish Petition, then the password, CAREABOUTFISH52. Type your name on the designated line, then date it, type your email address.

As always, united in love for our planet,
Lorraine

THAT LETTER IS sent to at least three hundred people. You succeed in obtaining twenty signatures. Thirty people return your email, suggesting they don't have the patience to finish reading it. Another twenty write back with ideas, a few suggesting dead fish are common nowadays, so they don't care.

I sign the petition because I'm your daughter.

Your email and snail mail drive for a petition to investigate dead fish doesn't achieve the fifty needed to qualify for an invitation to speak at the town hall. But I'm concerned you may speak at the town hall with or without the signatures.

It's too bad no one pays attention to you, because you've looked into Sarah's comment about incidences of dead fish up and down the coast. She is right. While most of the carrion in Connecticut litter affluent neighborhoods that line the coast, other states don't have concentrated areas of dead fish, but scattered intermittent pockets of death. However, only a few states raise alarms, primarily because the one Senator who talked with Dr. Ableman appeared on the news network and informed viewers that the fish issue is not a big deal because "we have good quality farmed fish in our country." Everyone simply stops eating wild Atlantic fish. Sales of farmed fish skyrocket.

Dr. Ableman has done quite a bit of research into this area and finds that the large fish farming lobbyists have succeeded in convincing FDA to loosen farmed fish regulations. "No one knows what's in those ponds," she tells us. "For all we know that's where our garbage is going nowadays."

We stop buying fish.

Somehow, Sarah also manages to dig up a list of forty Senators who've invested in fish farms stock. Did I mention Sarah Ableman has a Ph.D. in computer science? You suspect there are lots of politicians with significant investment profits.

You continue your obsession with the petition and drag me along with you around the neighborhoods, begging for more signatures. We start with our neighborhood because most people who live near us like me. I used to babysit for many of them. A few neighbors listen and take your email address and link to gopetition.com, but, for the most part, no one signs your petition. You suspect they don't want a government official seeing their name on anything negative about anything. Nowadays many citizens don't sign petitions because they don't want to be categorized as trouble makers. Once in that category, life could become complex. Like yours.

We still walk all the neighborhoods.

We now walk toward the homes in the Harbor Association neighborhood with our petitions. The area is closer to the coast, so the air smells of decay, and the heat index is over 100. It's early summer but a very hot early summer. The heat wave that came in spring has lasted longer than usual. My t-shirt clings to me and tendrils of hair stick to my forehead. For some reason, you're not wearing shorts but, instead, long khakis, and damp material clings to your legs, slowing your pace. Your tired look is freshened a bit by your fish earrings dangling happily from both ear lobes. Gifts from Dad that you've started wearing after giving away the fishing poles, as if signaling to Dad's ghost that you are still loyal.

Your face is red after knocking on a dozen doors. We forge on past large houses, mostly colonials, sitting behind one-acre lawns dotted with a few sick looking maple trees. A few women are outside gardening, which, to you, means wasting water. One woman shifts her eyes over our way before she turns the hose on her long line of impatiens. You open your mouth, I squeeze your forearm, we keep walking. Thank God we pass a bald yard owned by a more responsible citizen. This calms you.

We finally arrive at a long driveway leading to Margaret Hathaway's door. You've actually chosen this neighborhood because of Margaret. You always think if you can convince one important person, just one, you will get your way. I don't care anymore. I simply want a drink of water. When Margaret Hathaway opens the door, we are so hot and red, she insists we come in and drink tea. Which we do.

The kitchen looks fresher, more open, airier since I was last here. I was one of Margaret's regular babysitters. There's obviously been a major expansion. A granite island establishes the center. Viking stoves, large and shiny, make a big statement about the priority of cooking. A stone floor with such interesting mosaic designs one feels guilty walking on them. We sit at an oak kitchen table and wait for our tea.

"I suppose you know why I'm here, Margaret," you start. "You've read my letters to the editor and my petition mails."

Margaret finishes pouring tea into the glasses and brings them to us. "I've got some crackers and cheese. You want a bite to eat?"

"No thank you, Margaret. We're not here to eat," you say.

"Sure," I say. I'm starved. "But I'll get it. Let me fix a plate for us while you talk with Mom."

"You're so sweet, Haley," she says, sliding her eyes toward you.

"She takes after her father."

"I'm not anything," I say, opening Margaret's refrigerator door to peek inside at all of her food. Her cheese is expensive and plentiful. You would approve of its unprocessed quality. I select a round hunk of something that is orange and looks hard. I cut several pieces, then search the cabinet for crackers. I hear talk behind me—something about the danger of walking in the heat. Margaret has ignored the introductory statement on politics. You always bring politics up, everyone always ignores it.

"So," Margaret says in a sigh when I put down the cheese plate. "Thank you, sweetie. Now, Haley, are you as passionate as your mother about all of this death? Or are you walking with her to make sure she survives the heat?"

"I don't think we should all ignore fish dying," I say. "And I want to make sure Mom doesn't die, too, of course."

"Florida ignored it and then it was too late," you say to the cracker. "Florida's coast is disappearing due to erosion and no one would be caught dead eating their fish. But the phosphate and sugar cane industries are going strong. And the average age has dropped significantly."

"Yes, but we have no fishing industry," Margaret says. "Fish farms are slowly taking over. Clamming is coming back, but I don't really eat clams anymore."

"I bet you don't. And clams are impacted by the rise of acidity. Toxins, bacteria, all absorbed by Mollusca. I wouldn't touch an oyster from this area if you paid me. And I'm sure people are paying people to eat them nowadays. So, look, Margaret," you say as you take a long sip of tea. "You're on the Finance Board, right?"

"Lorraine, this fish thing is not even something we have local control over. It's probably caused by national and global issues. Warming waters. Plastics. Toxins. You know. I don't know what we can do but inform the environmental authorities. We've restricted some forms of plastic, but we can't control other communities. We just have to live with this dying wild life."

"What about septic tanks?" I say, suddenly. I have no idea where that thought comes from or why I blurt it out. I'm usually quiet around you and your friends. "We have septic tanks." You slap the table with both hands and sit up as if I've said something profound. "You know, I'd love grapes with this cheese. Do you mind?" I look at Ms. Hathaway who ignores me because she is focused only on you. I wonder if it would be rude to stand and retrieve grapes. I can ask again, of course, but something stops me.

"Septic tanks!" you say. "And there we have it! Proof that some of my genes were actually delivered to my daughter." You look off into space, as if searching for my genes. "Why have I never thought of this? Why hasn't anyone thought about this? My daughter is a hero."

"Actually, Dr. Ableman is the hero," I say as I stuff a cracker into my mouth. I chew for a moment. "She said something to me when she stopped by a few days back. She was dropping something off for you."

Margaret taps her iPhone.

"Septic tanks near the coast," you say, now walking around the table to face me. "The rise in water levels would impact leaching fields and contaminate the water. I bet we could walk around the coast and locate areas that are at risk."

"We check all septic tanks and are on top of that," Margaret says, in clipped voice. "I doubt this relates to septic tanks."

I recall when Dad explained our septic system to me one night. He stood before me with his large erasable marker board and drew the tank, the underground piping, the leaching field. I was ten years old and working on potential science project ideas, and Dad wanted me to research septic system efficiency. The entire explanation terrified me. My poop was outside in the yard? I was constipated for a week after his lecture. My eventual science project had nothing to do with septic tanks.

"Haley, how's your job over at Carver National Bank?" Margaret now uses me to change the subject. "I bet you're doing great. Before you know it, you'll be promoted to a position at their headquarters in New York." I get a feeling there's message in the question.

"I'm doing OK. I'll stick around at least until the dead fish mystery is solved."

"Then you have to stay to resolve the dead blue jays, too. It could be a long time before Haley is allowed to leave," you say.

Margaret's smile is there, then gone. "You think bird deaths are related? How could birds possibly be related to dead fish?" She continues before you say anything. "I've had a few sparrows die. Two were missing heads, Lorraine, so I suspect hawks ate them. I've heard other reports of dead birds. A few just plopped down in Sallie Redgrave's lawn. I don't know what kind. A bird is a bird to me. A few dead birds every season would be expected, don't you think? All the bird viruses and raptors."

"It's all related," you say. "Water impacts all of us in some way. And I don't want birds dying unnecessarily. Death is death."

"Mom loves her birds," I say.

"Birds will communicate with you if you give them a chance," you continue. "They give you things sometimes. For example, yesterday, this blue jay dropped a crystal tear drop at my feet. I was lying in the driveway and felt something hit my shoulder." Margaret looks at me then you. I suspect she is trying to visualize Mom prostrate on the driveway. "It bounced and landed by my chin. A chime, I think. It was very charming, almost like it wanted me to have it."

"How cute," Margaret busies herself with cheese. "What did it look like? What do you mean chime?"

"It looked like a chime. Shaped like a tear drop. It was crystal. Lovely. I have no idea where they found it."

"Susan Pasternick had gorgeous chimes," Margaret says. "Crystal tear drops. Made the loveliest, dulcet noise. They were blown down a while ago. The one rain storm we've had. They were hung in her yard, over near the water. Isn't that interesting? I wonder if the birds found one of them. Maybe they were attracted to them for some reason. Crows used to love glitter in our yard when we decorated for Christmas." She stops, realizing she has said "crow" in front of you and not wanting to start another rant.

"Where does Susan live?" you say.

"Independence Island."

I see the light in your eyes. Thought generation is occurring. I prepare myself for words or action. Either one can be traumatic. Your eyes, however, have that dull look that indicates latent thoughts, the kind that tend to be more innocuous. Still, I'm cautious, so I stand and say we must be going, it's late.

"I bet it matches those chimes," you blurt. "The birds picked it up and brought it to me, because they know. They know it's Independence island." You stand. "Two winters ago, Independence Island went under water after a big northeaster. I'd say that water line has moved up, what, six feet? How many houses on that island? They all have septic tanks. That's where we begin."

"Begin what, Lorraine? This is simply not going to happen. A million things are killing fish. Mostly hot water. This is ridiculous."

"But we can't do anything about a million things because we don't have anything protecting us anymore. No EPA. No people there. We can do something about local ordinances. We can control this locally. We don't have to call our corrupt politicians at the state or, God forbid, national level."

"So, you're convinced of septic tanks erosion now because blue jays sent you a message? Why, how scientific." She looks at me and smiles.

I do not smile back. I agree with you. I'm beginning to get what you get, feel how you feel. Is this my aging process? Am I becoming you?

"How about this." Margaret brushes her table, clasps her hands and rests them comfortably before her, like a judge. "How about you put the petition away. I'll talk to Sally and the selectmen about all of this. But you put the petition away and don't bring up Independence Island. We have families out there who enjoy their privacy. Let's leave them alone.

# Chapter 14

*Impact of wine upon the environment*

THE LEFT SIDE of the house, which holds the biggest room in our house, our living room, has been dusted and smells of lemon. The fake Persian rug is clean, and bright red and white roses rise from a thick oriental vase that sits upon our small glass coffee table. A few white lilies bend over jars on the mantle and book shelf. The fragrance of roasted garlic vegetables in the kitchen make my mouth water. I want to pick at the cauliflower, slice a big piece of cheese, but all the activists, or friends who call themselves activists, will soon be here, ready to talk. It's been years since you've called one of these meetings and you want everything perfect, which means no missing cauliflower or sliced cheese.

You're anxious and overdressed. Elegant black linen pants, sleeveless cotton blouse, fish earrings. You're nervous because your invitation—which ignored Margaret Hathaway's advice and pontificated endlessly about the impact of rising waters on septic system leaks and resulting algae blooms—did not receive the expected responses. While a few said they would attend, most wrote back vague statements of intent. Like, "So good to hear from you. Hope my life will allow me to attend. I'll let you know."

You drive your car down the street to make room in our driveway for those who are coming and those who vaguely intend to think of coming. After you turn the corner, you're distracted by an image reflected in your rear-view mirror. Lolly running after the car. You lean out your car window and scream at Lolly to go home, but Lolly, who rarely walks, chooses this one time in her life to run. She doesn't run toward you, she instead runs away from you, toward something else, something she now understands—freedom. You jam on brakes, turn off the car, jump out, leaving your car in the middle of the road, merely twenty feet from an intersection. You catch up with Lolly, scold her, lift her up in your arms, and wobble back home.

I see all of this out the kitchen window. I feel guilty for not helping, but helping would take time that I don't have. I'm in a hurry. For once I'm attempting to have a social life, which means I'm going out to listen to one of my beautiful, connected friends talk about her social life. My joy is usually vicarious. I'm not really thrilled with the prospect of listening to my friend talk about herself, but the alternative—staying for an activist meeting with middle-aged or older women is worse. Women like this ask too many questions about my future, which leads to questions about why I'm here and when I plan to leave, all of which inspire your face to fall into various expressions of both guilt and terror. Guilt that I am here, terror that I will leave. No thank you.

I kiss Lolly when you bring her into the house and say goodbye, but you force me back to help you set out the tea, seltzer, and baked vegetables. There is never alcohol at any social meeting at our house because you stopped drinking alcohol after Dad died. If you don't drink, then you don't offer it either. "We have to stay sober when the world is on its edge. At least some of us have to remain alert or we'll all miss the end."

I finally escape before most of the activists arrive. Yes, I am gone, but don't worry, I know what they will do, I know how you will behave, I understand all the chain reactions that will lead to the tragedy of this night. Trust me.


IT TURNS OUT, the "vague intents" actually leaned more toward yes than no. Women arrive in carpools—groups of four or five—a few alone, some by Uber. They all wander around our strange house, joking about the easement that separates it into halves, all laughing at the half they are squeezed into. Several grab their seltzers, but their expressions imply they can't wait to get home and pour themselves a large glass of wine.

The meeting is supposed to begin at nine, but at nine-forty everyone still picks at the food and shows no desire to sit and listen or talk about whatever it is they are meeting to sit and listen and talk about. You clap your hand right when someone knocks on the front door. Dr. Sarah Ableman steps inside, nods, speaks quietly, and stands alone, smiles only when you welcome her. She fixes herself a plate of vegetables and walks into the living room, gravitating to the mantle, where your collection of mallard duck manikins are lined up, tail to beak, between lilies. She picks up a male mallard and stares at its head. You watch her a moment, then clap your hands again, calling the meeting to attention.

Everyone takes a seat, but before everyone settles down, the door blows open without the usual warning knock. Several more women enter, chattering, a few laughing. Bonnie Hamilton—eighty-five years old and never without words—is in the lead. She has an arm over Marcy Finnegan, the driver, who is mid-sentence—apparently regaling everyone about a small personal event in her life. She ceases her story-telling to say hello to you and everyone else, then walks with her group to the kitchen, trying to hide her bottles of wine clanging together.

"Lorraine, we're drinking," Marcy says, not bothering to turn and look at your expression. "Nice to see you upset about everything again," she shouts. "We thought we'd celebrate your renewed activity. Dead fish is not exactly something we can discuss without a drink. These meetings have always been boring as hell and we have a right to a glass of wine. I do respect your teetotaling self, though."

"I was not intending this to be a party, Marcy," you shout back. "Did you get my email? Or emails? Has anyone here gotten all my emails or have you put me on spam?"

No one in the kitchen is listening now. They are studying the insides of the refrigerator. Drawers open and shut, open and shut. The sound of faint barking drifts down from your bedroom where Lolly is locked away.

"Where are your wine openers, Lorraine?" someone shouts. They assume that even though you have stopped drinking, you still have a wine opener. You do not. I always buy cork-less bottles. Yes, I drink. Of course I drink!

You remain in the living room with a few women and Sarah—still holding one of your male mallards. You can still hear them talk. An older, husky voice, probably Bonnie, says, "Oh I know how to open a bottle. Who has on tennis shoes?"

You trot to the kitchen. Bonnie has the end of the bottle in the heel of a tennis shoe. She winds up and rams the end against the wall. The cork pops across the room, hitting the door and bouncing around the floor.

"You do not have my permission to drink," you say.

"You want to talk about dead fish, Lorraine? Then we drink," Bonnie says. Bonnie always confronts people because she knows no one wants to have a conflict with an eighty-five year old and be responsible for a stroke or heart attack. So, most back off when Bonnie disagrees or stands her ground, which she likes to do. The kitchen now contains everyone, as all the women who were waiting for the meeting are now there waiting for wine. Except Sarah Ableman.

Sarah sits patiently on the couch in the living room, empty handed. The mallard manikin has been returned to the mantle. When you return, you say nothing because you have reached that rare point of fury that leaves you nonplussed. Sarah allows you to stew. You bond. Again.

"Sarah, you can have a glass of wine if you like," you finally say. "It's the way of the world now, even though we know for a fact now that alcohol kills us. We have to numb ourselves."

"I don't want wine. I'm fine." She picks up a carrot and stares at it, then puts it in her mouth and gently bites down. She chews slowly staring at Mom's mantle again.

"They can all get drunk, but the alcohol won't make the dead fish go away. Go ahead drink wine, just don't eat fish. Ever."

The women now wander back to the living room. Marcy holds onto a freshly opened bottle of wine. "Well, one of these days, Lorraine, I'm going to park on the other side of your house so I can walk over the gas bridge." She throws back her glass of wine and pours herself more, then pours a few other glasses for others. "Margaret called me about your petition. Why didn't you tell me you were going around with a petition? We could have gone with you. I do have my name on it."

"Yes, you do, Marcy. You have your name on my petition. Can we all get seated?"

A few women look around, as if trying to figure out if there has been any rearrangement or redecoration since their last visit. They both hold glasses of wine, one of them holds a tray of baked cauliflower. They decide to join Sarah on the couch, so that she will have company. Marcy doesn't sit, preferring to stand by you with her wine. She sips it as she smiles at you. Marcy is somewhere in her sixties and sturdy like a pile of bricks. She wears thick linen pants that hang slightly low on her hips, which would look silly at her age if she didn't have such a thick, strong build.

"Marcy, can you at least sit down? You can drink but please drink seated. I don't want you falling all over my floor. Thank you for signing my petition."

Marcy sits heavily in a club chair and breathes out loudly. "Dead fish!" she says, then chuckles.

"Do you think dead fish are funny or is that the wine talking?" you say. "This is what happens when we drink at these activist meetings. Dead fish becomes funny."

"Lorraine, we're concerned about the dead fish, we've always been concerned," Bonnie says, taking over. "We do have other issues, like the new proposal for development on Reynolds Lane. How many trees are they going to mow down for that?"

"And when was the last time we organized a cleanup?" Abby Schmidt says as she steals a cucumber from Sarah's plate. "I remember when the crows fell from the sky. Remember that? Just dropped plop on your head if you weren't watching it. That clean up took forever. We all threw a fit, but so much was going on at the time. We had five projects. What can you do? And a few eagles died too, right? Or was that another year? Then they shot all the gray wolves in Yellowstone Park. That didn't really impact us, but I was concerned. Hell, we were all concerned, but you have to choose your battles."

The meetings usually start like this, which is why I could never make it through one. You try to steer the discussions toward the more important topics, but most of the time they want to organize—a park cleanup, grants for another land trust addition, and so forth. Or they want to complain about commercial real estate development. Today, however, you notice they try to a bit too hard to distract, so that you will not discuss dead fish.

"I'd like to start," you say in your most stentorian voice. You stand in the middle of your living room, everyone around you—a lion in her den. "What're we going to do about the dead fish and dead birds? We've found some dead birds, or people around here have found some dead birds. Not as prevalent as the crows but dead just the same. The petition died out, but, well, I have an idea about that. I also plan a speech for the town hall meeting."

"We meet, we beg everyone to do something, we organize petitions, Yada, yada, yada," Marcy says.

"And your point?"

"There's just so much that can be done, Lorraine. We can march, though. There's another march coming up in August. Anyone have the date?"

"Are you suggesting it's futile?" you say.

"They've finally tested a few of the fish, I hear," someone says. "They made it back to the lab with all fish intact, right? Oxygen depletion, I heard. Nothing too surprising. Global warming. Pollution upstream."

"Yes," you say. "They made it back and found what I expected because did you know I analyzed the fish? There are signs of oxygen deprivation. But apparently the livers were swollen with toxins of some sort, too."

"Pharmaceutical plant," Abby says in a spit. Her face is shaped like a kumquat and she always talks while eating. You still look. The rest of the room cast their eyes elsewhere. "They dump crap upstream. But they don't make anti-depressants, so no hope of us benefiting." This sentence comes out in a slight slur.

You are disgusted with the direction of the meeting. These are the activists. These are the ones left to engage the public! This!

"I've contacted the company," you say to the cumquat, mainly to stop her from talking. "I also wrote a letter to the public relations office. We can't do anything about the low oxygen if it's due to global warming."

There's a collective sigh when you say global warming. This is because the battle has been lost so completely.

"Oh, we can always try to write another bill to protect local tributaries. Ha ha, right?" Marcy is now talking loudly. She stands and pours herself another glass of wine. "Of course, we did get the waste water plant expanded. We did that only by agreeing to the gas pipeline. The very one we all will stomp on when we leave. And I do want to stomp on that. Can we stomp on the easement tonight, Lorraine?"

The meeting is out of control and you realize your attempts at controlling anything lately are failing. You look around the room and catch Sarah Ableman's eye. She's the only woman who seems sober and interested in what you have to say. You sit on the coffee table opposite her.

"Septic tanks," you say to Sarah. "We are here tonight to discuss septic tanks." The meeting goes silent.

"Septic tanks," Sarah says, waiting perhaps for anyone to add something. No one does. "I agree, Lorraine. I think that's where we should start. Yes. The facts point there."

"Water levels are rising," you say to Sarah.

"Yes, I know. Leaching fields," Sarah says.

Everyone in the room looks at Sarah, then you—two people having a loud conversation, ignoring everyone else.

"It's a local issue, one we can handle locally," Sarah says.

"Hello? We're also here, Lorraine," Abby says. "And I don't know about this. We have no research and it's a bit too personal."

"Personal?" Sarah says.

"It comes directly out of us, onto our property then into the water. It's an intimate pollution," Abby says. "And I think it's all a rush to judgment. I don't think we need to go there. To septic tanks issues."

A collective moan of agreement rises from the other women.

"Who here lives by the water?" Sarah says looking around. Silence. "Show of hands, please."

Marcy, Bonnie, and about six other women look down at their hands but don't raise them. Many in this particular group are wealthy and thus live by the coast.

"A blue jay dropped what we think is a chime in our yard," you say, ignoring the obvious conclusion concerning why the women staring at their hands don't want to talk about septic tank systems. "We think it was from a landowner over at Independence Island. Dropped it right by my feet. Just plop, right there. I suspect it is a chime from Susan Pasternick's estate. Blown away by a storm a while ago, I hear. Independence Island was flooded a few years back, and of course the water levels are quite high. I think the jays are trying to tell us something about that island. Maybe about what's going on with those owner's septic tanks. Maybe we can start there and move up the coast."

Everyone has poker faces.

"Sure, there's so much going on right now we can't resolve because national politics won't allow us," Sarah says suddenly. She has come alive, as if woken from a deep sleep. "This is one thing we can do. We can finally resolve something."

"We can fix our sewage," you agree. "We can do this one thing. This one thing. We need a mandated sewage system. Septic tanks on coastal properties are no good anymore with the water levels as they are."

Marcy stops drinking.

Bonnie closes her eyes.

"This will kill our property values. And a sewage system? Can you imagine the taxes on that here in this small town?" Marcy stands. "I'm an activist, but this is . . ."

"A sacrifice?" you say.

"Let me get this straight." Bonnie says. "A bird brought you a chime and this has started a theory about our septic systems? Lorraine, you need to start drinking again. Just a little." She picks up the bottle and brings it to you.

The bottle gives you another thought, which is not good because it combines with existing bad thoughts, and you've been restraining yourself, which has built thought energy to combustible levels in your brain. You grab the bottle, walk to the fireplace, and pour the contents onto the old firewood. You step back and throw the now empty bottle against the brick chimney. A bit of glass hits Marcy—who has run to your side to stop you—causing blood to bloom on her chin. She wipes her chin and regards the blood on her fingers.

"I've had enough of this. I think this meeting is done." Marcy gathers several women, Bonnie included, and they hurry to the door. The door slams shut. You sit back down by Sarah Ableman now quiet and alone, again. Dr. Ableman moves not one facial muscle.

The other women stand and leave. You pick up a carrot from Sarah's plate and take a bite. Engines grumble and hum.

Then, you hear it—the crack of metal on metal. Then nothing. Then screams. And more screams. And more screams. And squawks.

# Blue Jay Memo

*Look, blueberry colored motorized mobile unit!*
*Go to sleep.*
*Traveling backward out of nest path!*
*One side, other side.*
*What?*
*No straight line.*

*conflict!*
*conflict!*
*conflict!*

*Collateral annoyance!*

*Is female host in motorized mobile nest?*
*Female host is at home nest entrance.*
*Conflict!*
*Conflict!*

*Female driver exits, perambulates to other side of motorized mobile nest, pulls elderly female out of mobile nest. The less elderly female driver beats chest of dead elderly female.*

*Female host sings discordant songs!*

*We are concerned!*

# Chapter 15

*Environmental clean-up requires lawyers*

IT'S DEBATABLE WHETHER the accident kills Bonnie Hamilton, who is an octogenarian with a heart condition, or the trauma kills her. You stay up all night at the hospital, even though Bonnie was pronounced dead on arrival. You sit with the family, who make it clear they do not want you there. They don't want to see anyone from what will forever be known as Lorraine Mulderon's wild party that killed Bonnie Hamilton.

Louis arrives at our house the next day, and when you open the door, he immediately assures you there will be no arrest. You always suspect an arrest after any incident, particularly when you open the door and see Louis.

"This is a horrible accident, and I emphasize accident. I suspect it's all the more upsetting for you since you threw the party."

You both sit in the kitchenette. You keep him on the right side of the house because you don't have the energy to cross the pipeline. You apologize to Louis for not offering food or tea.

"I didn't have a party. You know I had an activist meeting. We discussed the dead fish, of course."

"Drinking's not illegal."

"They smuggled the wine into my house against my wishes. I don't drink, as you know."

"I'm proud of you for that." He stares out the window.

"I wasn't an alcoholic, if that's why you say you're proud of me. I quit after Lawrence died because I would have simply drunk every afternoon to get over it. The loneliness of it. Death is lonely. You know."

"It would keep you thinking about his accident, too."

"I think it's time to change the subject. That's what Marcy wanted to do. That's why she drank then rushed off. Change the subject. I wonder if she wrecked the car to change the subject. Maybe you should investigate that. Oh, forget I said that. I hate myself sometimes."

"Bonnie wrecked the car, not Marcy. Look, I called Brit, just to make sure he comes by. He said Haley had already called him. You may need representation. Bonnie's family is litigious. Remember when her grandson was bit by the

Anderson's Labrador? Her daughter wanted us to charge them with negligence, which of course didn't fly at the department. Then they sued."

"The women are lying to protect Marcy," you say, suddenly realizing what he said. "She's the one who should be sued."

"I believe everyone interviewed indicated that Bonnie was driving. It was Marcy's car, but Marcy didn't want to drive due to her drinking."

You know Marcy was driving, but you say nothing. No one wants Marcy in prison for manslaughter.

"It's mostly my fault because I left my car poking out there in the middle of the road, so, whatever."

Louis sits a while longer, as if he wants to say something profound to you, but nothing comes. He tells you not to worry, to wait for the coroner's report, then simply attend the funeral and be discreet. You both look out the window at the now empty feeders, brown yard, and one male cardinal on a distant limb. A blue jay lands on the feeder.

"Blue jays are the bird police," you say without looking at Louis. "I can count on them to warn me about approaching hawks, foxes. They alert me to problems with Lolly's health, too. I just realized this a while ago—that they warn me. It takes a certain perspective to warn others." A finch lands and the blue jay pecks him away. You tap the window. "But they push the little birds away. They protect them when the hawks come, then bully them."

"Are you saying something to me?"

"No. I don't know what I'm saying. Just talking about blue jays."

"Don't over-think the world. Sometimes things are just what they are, nothing more. Fish die, bigger fish and birds have no food, so they fly away, move on. Birds protect each other, then eat the weak one's food. Then the weak fly away."

"Or get stronger, Louis."

"OK, enough of this." He stands. "I just wanted to assure you that we find no negligence on your part, no criminal negligence that is. But, like I said, talk to Brit. These people are like the hawks. OK? Squawk, squawk."


THE CORONER REPORT indicates that the cause of death is a massive coronary probably brought on by alcohol and trauma. Two weeks after the report and one week after the funeral, you're informed of the lawsuit by their attorney's intern. Apparently, you've been negligent for serving alcohol in excess at the meeting, then allowing Bonnie, a very old, inebriated person, to drive. They also find you negligent for leaving your car parked around the corner in the middle of the road, not on the side.

Brit meets with you even though you insist you will not participate in a frivolous lawsuit. You tell him this over coffee at a local deli. The meeting turns into a disaster because you cannot speak appropriately about private matters in public—your stentorian voice fills the room regardless of location. The meeting is interrupted several times by customers who ask you to speak quietly, then finally a waiter who asks you to leave.

You and Brit try to talk again, this time at home, on the patio. The day is warm, the air heavy even though there is no humidity. Maybe it's heavy with dust or allergens, or maybe just your thoughts. Brit sips lemonade and stares at a plate of sliced apple and cheese.

"All we do is present our case strongly, insist we're willing to go to trial. They'll bring down their price, then we settle." He crosses his legs, talks, moves his fingers delicately in the air. You notice his graceful movements, his khaki pants with thick creases down the front, adding weight to his thick waistline. Poor sartorial taste, you think to yourself. Pretentious, delicate behavior. But, then, the eternally burnt nose and laugh lines offset this so you decide he's OK and pay attention.

"It's like everyone's out there waiting for anything, anything to happen so they catch you, get a little money," you say. "Our energy is needed for the dying world, but, no, no, we have to store it to fight each other. We're a weak species. I'd rather be a bird."

Brit raises both hands and flaps, then stops when you don't smile. He carefully picks up a large apple slice and looks it over. The sun is particularly angry and small droplets of sweat form over his lips and forehead. You are dry. You take a few peanuts in their shells from a bowl and fling them upon the slate walkway for the birds.

"They have no case," Brit says after he bites into the apple and chews. "The car belongs to Marcy, who brought the wine. It was not your wine. But here's the thing. They know this. They're simply fishing, seeing if you bite. I tell you what. We do the deposition, with me there, of course, and tell them we want the case to go to trial."

Up until today, Brit had chosen to delay this deposition discussion. The funeral was quite the occasion. *The Westbrook Weekly* front page was a full picture of a more youthful and energetic looking Bonnie Hamilton, accompanied by a long article outlining all her contributions to the town—years on the Board of Education, fundraising for activism, marches she organized back during the Great Transition.

"I've agreed to the deposition," he says, not looking at you, only at his apple slice. "For this Thursday afternoon. I'll pick you up at around one. How's that?"

"I'm going to present my petition this Thursday night at the Board of Selectman meeting." You sip your tea, pick up an apple, turn it, put it back on the plate. "They tell me now I can't be on the schedule unless I agree not to discuss septic tanks. I agreed. What're they going to do if I talk about it, call the police?"

"Did you hear what I said about the deposition? This is real, Lorraine." Brit leans into you. Today your hair is pulled back into a tight, small ponytail. You wear shorts and a loose, cotton, sleeveless blouse, which, combined with your pinched lips, makes you resemble a frightened little girl, impervious to reason, ready to become apoplectic if pushed too far.

"I'll go to jail. They can send me to jail."

"Why do you do this? Why do you always say, 'I'll go to jail'? What is it about jail that you like? And by the way, if you're referring to the civil suit, no one sends defendants in civil suits to jail. I thought Louis explained this to you."

"It's a betrayal. We've worked on countless issues over twenty years, and all these women do this to me. They're lying, you know. Marcy was driving. It's because of the septic tanks. They want me to shut up about the septic tanks."

"How about we let the lawyers just do this. They can come out to interview you, and I'll sit in. You sit, say nothing, let me talk. Just do it, get it over with."

You stand, walk inside, and return with seeds. Brit's eyes follow you to the bird feeder. You methodically fill it as two goldfinch land on the overhead bar and two chickadees perch on the roof of the feeding house. You believe the birds know your world has turned upside down again. Perhaps, you reflect, they know you wish to fly away with them.

You think about this idea—flying away from life, from your divided house, your town that has rejected you, the world of humans that is intent on killing the world of animals—the death of which will kill humans, too. You want so desperately to be like the birds who teach their children survival, then leave. But, of course, in your nest, life is reversed. The child has taught the mother how to survive, and now the child must fly away.

"But she can't fly away," you whisper. "My daughter is too good a person to leave a mother not yet ready to survive." Your eyes burn.

"Lorraine? Are you talking to me?"

Brit stands, approaches you. You concentrate on pouring seeds. You hate the kind ones because they always make you cry. Maybe he'll just go away. But Brit remains there with you in that tragic space where you reside.

"Sarah Ableman has agreed to be a witness for you," Brit says quietly.

"She shouldn't risk her reputation on me. I don't know why she would." You put down your bird seed and grab your hands in front of you. "Of course, it's probably good for her, a way of establishing herself again in town, in opposition to something. She has finally engaged again, finally lifted herself out of her daze we've all watched her live in for so long. She's come out fierce. And why not? Why not come out fighting?" You turn to Brit. "I think I may have inspired her."

"That's what you do, Lorraine. Inspire those who need to fight to survive."

You step back. "So, I'll comply with the judge's order. We do this deposition, but on another day so I can present my case before the town. We'll threaten to go to trial—a ridiculous trial about a woman who drank even when I told her not to. And the person who does not drink but still fails to rip wine glasses from guests' hands must sit through this charade. But I did leave my car in the middle of the road. I did do that. So, OK, I'll follow your orders. There's too much else I need to do to waste time fighting them. I'll do this, because, Brit, fish are dying."

"Yes, dear, do this for the fish."

# Blue Jay Memo

Female host's mate with white head fur arrives, sings to female host. He wears no color but again succeeds in mating ritual. We see mate often now. Today he leaves after much singing and time in nest. We notice female host leaves with him. We send two-year-old for reconnaissance. We feed our offspring, imitate hawks to tease squirrels. Bored.

Male human!
No, mate left.
Mate left with female host!
Eat.

No. Another male!
Perambulating toward nest.
Predatory behavior!

Conflict!
Conflict!
Conflict!

Come back now!
Back on limb!
Female host is not in nest.
Female host gone. No conflict.
Stranger male!
Perch. Back on limb!

Although juveniles are always hysterical, we admit this is unusual. We usually ignore motorized mobile nest activity on paths near female host's nest, but this time a large, black motorized mobile nest ceases forward motion and a lithe, rather youthful male human with small beak and black head fur perambulates to female host nest. This is alarming.

*He touches nest!*
*Everyone shut uuup.*
*Come back. Perch! Now!*
*Shut uuup.*
*No, don't go there.*
*Danger!*
*Danger! Danger! Danger!*

*No. Stay on limb.*
*GO AWAY!*
*GO AWAY!*
*GO AWAY!*

*Shut uuuup!*
*Come back. No dive bombing!*

*GO AWAY!*
*GO AWAY!*

*Screaming does no good. We all still scream.*
*We chirp to calm ourselves.*

*He looks through glass covered apertures.*

*He touches our feeders!*
*He. Touches. Our. Feeders!*

*GO AWAY!*
*GO AWAY!*
*GO AWAY!*

# Chapter 16

*Dead fish meets leashed dogs*

IT'S NOT LIKE you never fished with us. We always asked. Remember? You didn't like the idea of luring a creature toward fake food only to torture its mouth with a hook. But occasionally you'd grab your binoculars and fishing rod and walk around a lake with us. We would inevitably lose you in the woods; you'd follow a hawk, stop to study a rare colorful bird, run after a fox. We'd find you, bring you to the lake, and force you upon a rock, where you'd reluctantly cast the lure. And sit. We would hope the fish would avoid your lure, because nothing on earth was worse than the trauma of a hook piercing the rubbery mouth of your captured fish. If the fish swallowed the hook, then we would have to listen to your pontifications about the impact of metal upon not only the fish but also the raptors and water fowl who ate the fish. Ospreys, fish hawks, egrets, herons, eagles. The hook's impact upon our universe would be discussed for weeks afterward. If Dad or I caught the fish, you would not complain. Only if your line captured the fish.

It was always the actual doing that sucked you into the drama of wrongness. If we kept you away from our fishing, we kept you outside of everything wrong with fishing.


THE LAWSUIT PERSISTS. I wonder if the family would have dropped the lawsuit if you had simply said, "I'm sorry for your loss," or "Bonnie was a fine woman," and then remained silent when you ran into Elaine, the oldest daughter, at the drug store. That is what a normal person would do, but you said, "I'm sorry your mother, who was eighty-five, mind you, died the way she did. Although, I do think right before she succumbed, she realized she had damaged my car bumper extensively and we can only hope that allowed her to rest in peace."

The deposition is moved up to Wednesday because you're speaking at Thursday's town meeting. The deposition does not go well because they ask open-ended questions and when anyone asks you open-ended questions, the conversation does not go well. The law firm for the Hamilton family is Sterns,

Howell, and Logan, a well-established Stratton firm that specializes in real estate development. But they also enjoy a reputation for civil suits and have quite the track record in that regard.

The lawyers ask several questions about alcohol—your reaction to Bonnie's drinking, your reaction to her driving, your attempt to stop both. The questions assume Bonnie was driving and that you were aware she was driving. There's been a court precedent concerning serving alcohol to the elderly. It was appealed up to district court, now stacked with post-transition judges, and the plaintiffs won a huge settlement.

Brit emphasizes there has been a difference of opinion as to who was driving since the car was owned by Marcy. One lawyer then shifts through his notes and reads aloud a few sworn statements insisting Bonnie had volunteered to drive since the owner of the car could not find her glasses.

"Are you contesting these statements, Ms. Mulderon? Are you contending that these statements are false?"

Brit looks at you. You say nothing for a long while. You know Marcy drove that car. You have heard no discussion about glasses. You remember seeing Marcy with the keys as they all hurried out the door. They wait for you to accuse the women of perjury and Marcy of manslaughter.

"I have no idea what the truth is. The car belongs to Marcy. I suppose she let Bonnie drive it."

"So, we're talking to the wrong person here," Brit says. "Apparently Marcy Finnegan should be questioned. She handed over the car to an inebriated driver."

"Yes, but your client allowed that driver to leave inebriated. She gave her the wine."

"I don't drink. I've not had a drop of alcohol in over seven years. Well . . ."

They shift the focus, because no one knows how to question a nondrinker about serving alcohol she didn't have. They show you several pictures of the accident that indicate where the car ended up after the accident, pointing out the obvious—that a car traveling around a corner fast will of course hit a car parked in the middle of the road.

"How did they arrive? They should have known about my car if they drove around it to get to my house. Yes?"

"There are two routes to your street," a lawyer says. "They arrived on one lane, departed on another."

"I see. Well, it was out of my control. My bulldog escaped the house and ran down the street. Bulldogs don't have great eyesight, it's easy for them to become confused and run after a car or into a car. So, I stopped, jumped out, and saved her. I know this probably means nothing to you because she's an animal. Dead animals seem to have no real impact upon all of you nowadays. We care about death only if it's a human death. We then freak out and sue each other. What if I hadn't jumped out of my car to save my dog? Let's say she ran into something, or a car hit her, and my sweet bulldog died. Who would represent her? Dogs have no lawyers. Birds have no lawyers. Fish have no lawyers. And right now? Fish need lawyers."

Like I said, the deposition does not go well. Brit files for a continuance to give him time with you.

It's not like you don't care about what happened. You didn't know Bonnie well, but you miss her. Well, mostly you miss her old age. Bonnie's liberalism didn't die with years, which has always given you hope that you will never succumb to conservatism, never give in to the One Party that rules us now. You also miss everyone associated with Bonnie, since either due to her death or the lawsuit, or your inappropriate post mortem remarks, the activists don't invite you to meetings anymore. This marginalization doesn't stop your mouth and activity, it only makes you a rather lonely activist. Of course, there's Sarah Ableman, who lives inland so has no reason to fear septic tank regulation. She has completely broken from her chrysalis. She researches septic tanks, leaching fields, and writes small reports she emails to you.

Sarah's papers do come in handy for the speech you've prepared for the town meeting. This particular town meeting's ostensible agenda has been listed online. You print it out to understand the other topics—the potential reorganization of the four main parks, various budgetary considerations, and dog leashing laws. To leash or not to leash has been a favorite town debate for years. It has led to nasty letters to the editors, speeches posted online, and lost friendships. Arnold's Bar and Grill was forced to close one night due to a bar fight over leashing dogs. That incident was followed by the obligatory lawsuits over bruises and ruined clothes.

You notice the agenda does not include your speech about dead fish.


THE TOWN HALL is a large red brick building which was originally a storage facility before being sold to a developer who transformed it into a large office building. He intended to rent out extra space to retailers and restaurants, maybe even affordable apartments on the third floor, but none of his intentions were taken seriously by anyone, and no one wanted affordable housing anywhere. He sued, then made speeches at town halls ridiculing town government and threatening to sue again and again. The town purchased the building with bond money, and now everyone who does anything for the town has an office here. The occupancy is about 40%, and its emptiness and old linoleum floors transform the slightest sound into loud, hollow echoes, inspiring most people to immediately whisper once they enter. Except you, who now stands before Ellen at the front desk.

"Why, Lorraine. How long has it been? How are you?" You detect a slight pity in her question and pause before slowly assuring her you are OK. She asks what she can do for you in a voice that doesn't have a tone of a secretary but of someone who owns the ground beneath her. And at one time she did. Her husband was the developer who sold the building to the town right before she was appointed secretary. "Can I help you find something?"

"I know where I'm going, and I know she's there. I called earlier."

"I wondered if that was you. The caller ID just gave your cell number. I almost called it back. Sally's busy." Ellen is standing now, her loud voice echoing off the floors and high ceilings. You ignore her, walk to the elevators, step inside, slap the third floor. The elevator doors close as Ellen approaches, like the end of a movie.

The First selectman's office is as large as two offices because it's actually two offices. Why not combine rooms when you have such a large building? You have always imagined how many trees could be planted if the building was obliterated and local leaders simply rented space elsewhere. You knock. You hear "come in," and you walk in.

Sally rarely shows emotion beyond a smile. You saw her laugh once several years ago after her first election. She's been head of the Board of Selectman since before the great transition.

"The agenda?" You put it on her desk. "Does not list the problem with our dead fish."

"The reason is because you aren't speaking. How are you, Lorraine?" She remains seated.

"I had to rearrange my legal life so I could write my very short speech and be here on time. I understand, Sally, due to your One Party, we no longer have a valid democracy, OK. But we still have a free press. Or on paper we have a free press. OK, maybe we don't have that either. But we have town meetings here in New England. New England still has that."

"I would never interfere with your freedom, Lorraine. And national politics has no place in our town politics. Big difference. How are you? I know these are trying times for you."

You pause to consider the pity, because while you believe Sally displays feelings of concern, you're not sure she actually has these feelings. Also, she's simply too calm.

"Lorraine, we actually do have rules and procedures." Sally remains seated and has not asked you to have a seat. You don't want to sit, so that's OK by you.

"All the rules are excuses for you not to do anything. You guys do nothing."

"We don't do things like snatch boats when we have the urge to see a dead fish up close."

"Borrow a boat. And the charges were dropped once everyone realized the gravity of the situation and things we do under pressure. I have a right to talk, and you know it. If you don't let me, I will protest."

"Lorraine, you cannot discuss septic tanks. And we all know you'll discuss them. Septic tanks are complicated, you have done no research, have absolutely no expertise. We'll have to discuss this another time, OK? Maybe after study."

She is of course technically correct, and her lack of emotion and correctness cause you to pace.

"I'll simply point out that we have a lot of dead fish and that some people have found dead birds. We don't want another crow thing. That's all I'll say."

Sally begins to look through papers, a hint that you should leave.

"Look, Sally." You put your hands on her polished mahogany desk, free of papers, detritus, clutter—making you wonder what she actually does. "You guys, or your Park and Recreation Department guys, have spent the bulk of their two years analyzing ways to gut all parks so that we can add one soccer field. We're putting parking lots in parks that don't need them, dog parks in parks where people are fine without them, all so we have one more soccer field that, mind you, eliminates five trees. Trees are homes for a multitude of birds, squirrels, and raccoons. Two years. Everyone's still yelling at each other over this. I could write some letters about that."

There is silence as Sally ponders the relative annoyance of a dead fish speech versus poor park management letters—something that most of the town would probably agree with.

"All I'm going to say is," you continue, " 'hey, can we look at these dead fish? Stop walking your damn dog for one minute and look at these dead fish. It's real. They are dead.' Sally, it's probably due to something we can't control, right? Global warming. Plastics. Lack of any viable water pollution regulation." You know everyone loves to talk about things they can't control locally.

"OK. You will talk about the dead fish, maybe the possibility of global warming impacting the quality of water. Something like that. That's your speech. You'll talk for precisely two minutes after the leashing regulation discussion."

"I hear you."

You leave, return home, work on your speech. About septic systems.

THE TOWN AUDITORIUM seats about two hundred people and has a stage with heavy, soiled, beige curtains—always closed—and a large American flag drooping from a pole in the far right corner. The five Board of Selectmen sit at a rectangular table in front of the stage—Sally Staysim is dead center, two Selectman on either side of her. All wear business suits, the two men in bright ties and dark suits, the two women in colorful jackets and white blouses. Sally's suit jacket is bright yellow with black trim, making her look like a bee among flowers and dull bark.

I'm in the middle section, Brit Jacobs, our lawyer, on my right, an empty seat on my left. I stare at your back, covered in a lavender button down. Your fish dangle playfully from both ear lobes as you talk to a woman next to you who appears to be the leader of the Unleash Our Dogs crowd. The dog women hold signs that say, "Free Our Dogs NOW." I am wondering if you want Lolly— who rarely moves from her bed—to go to the parks without a leash.

Sarah Ableman arrives, lugging a portable plastic file box, which she drops at her feet after sitting down by me. She proceeds to go through the box quickly as if researching something—only looking at me briefly to smile. I actually like this about her—how she doesn't engage me. Most women her age strain to make small talk, usually asking about my job at the bank, then moving on to friends I know, then—not knowing how to proceed given controversial you and noncontroversial me—they slowly fade away. But Dr. Ableman doesn't fake anything. She has nothing in common with me, so she doesn't talk. I feel strangely warmed by this.

The meeting begins and you stop talking with the Unleash Your Dog crowd. The First Selectman quickly goes over the state of the town, emphasizing its financial health. She mentions the drought and warns about potential forced water restrictions if we're not careful. She asks Margaret Hathaway, the Chairman of the Finance Board, to quickly go over the finances of the town, the projected growth in our mill rate, the overall health of our property values, business fees, etc, etc. It's quite boring, and I find my mind wandering until it's time for the citizens' speeches. The dog woman is first. She marches to the podium perched at the far left of the stage and taps the microphone.

Her name is Lydia Russo and she brings a poster and places it on a stand by the podium. The poster is an enlarged picture of a labradoodle. She announces the name of her dog, "Daffodil." She tells us she named her dog after the daffodils in her garden that her dog ate as a puppy and regurgitated, which was a good thing because daffodils, she informs us, are poisonous.

"I'm sorry, Lydia, but I just want to remind you everyone has only five minutes," Sally says into her mike.

Lydia ignores Sally and begins her speech about how critical training is for a happy dog. It was critical to teach Daffodil not to eat daffodils, for example, because they would kill her, or make her sick. It was also important to teach her how to behave herself at a park so she could run free and not have to be on a leash. Lydia becomes quite passionate about her dog's ability, due to intense training and work, to now walk anywhere without a leash.

There is a slight sound of movement in the audience. Coughing. Whispers. Sally hits a small bell. The ding reminds me of boutique bells attached to doors that alert salespeople of customer arrivals. It does not stop Lydia who has moved on from the training to the freedom of dogs and the enjoyment of parks. After a few more moments, she finally finishes her speech and her opponent rises and takes the stand.

This woman is older and does not bring a picture of her dog but instead a large bar chart, which she carefully places on the stand. Apparently, the horizontal line on the chart represents years and the vertical axis represents numbers of various dog incidents, which include dog fights and dog bites. The blue bars are towns with leash laws, the red bars are towns without leash laws, the purple bars are hybrid leashing regulations, which she doesn't really explain. It appears that the red bar has the most incidents, the blue bars have the least, but Lydia interrupts her and offers opinions about the inaccuracy of bar charts in general. Sally asks Lydia to please respect the speaker.

I am thinking you and Lydia will be best friends forever.

The other woman stands quietly while Lydia continues to yell. Finally, Lydia quiets down and the woman, named Brittany I believe, continues her speech, now emphasizing the invasive nature of dogs and how they disrupt the natural park ecosystem. Lydia interjects again, emphasizing that dogs are not an invasive species because they are attached to humans, who never invade.

Sally picks up her gavel and slams it down.

The audience sits stoically through this drama. It's a New England town meeting and it doesn't matter what happens on stage, you cannot ever display emotion. If one displays emotion, it proves one does not have true New England blood. You are of course originally from Alabama. I suspect Lydia is from outer boroughs-New York, given her accent. Therefore Lydia, like you, displays inappropriate emotion. After one more interruption and another bang of gavel, it's over.

There will probably be leash laws.

"Next is . . ." The First Selectman looks at her list. "Lorraine Mulderon."

My heart rate rises. Sarah Ableman sits straight and takes a big inhale as if starting meditation.

You grab each side of the podium and look at me. "There are dead fish everywhere." You stop for effect, looking around the room like a minister. "I know all of you know this. I've tried to call some of you. I've tried to get a petition going. A petition to investigate. I called an activist meeting specifically to address this serious issue. I am very sorry for the loss of our beloved Bonnie Hamilton. I'd also like to ask everyone to please be careful when you drink and drive." There is not one sound in the entire auditorium. Brit closes his eyes and breaths in and out slowly. I can barely hear his breath. I don't close my eyes, but I hear this voice inside me begging the gods above to shut you up. "Oh please," the voice says. "Please have her say a few more words then sit down."

You pause. There is not one sound in the auditorium. "Septic tanks!"

The gavel goes down hard. Sally leans forward. "Thank you, Lorraine, for talking about the dead fish. We have a history of algae blooms here and I believe this's not the first wave of dead fish we've seen."

"We all need to talk about septic systems," you say again, ignoring the gravel. "The dead fish are predominately around the coastal areas that have a history of flooding. Like, for example, Independence Island. I want these areas tested. I want the septic systems investigated."

"Unless you have engineering reports or a background in plumbing," Sally says into her mike, "we are not prepared to discuss theories about causes of dead fish. We're very aware of this problem and we thank you for taking the time to share your thoughts. I think we now can move on to the park reorganizations."

"Either," Mom says into the mike, "we test our septic systems, or I will take this national."

"National?" Sally says then laughs. We all know what happens when anything goes national. There is no national media anymore. Not really.

"Yes," you continue. "I will contact the national dark web. We do have that."

"They're illegal. Please sit down," Sally says.

"I will ask bloggers to come visit our coastal septic tanks. We cannot destroy our fish. What will happen to our Osprey? We've found a few dead birds. We need animals. For crying out loud, our damn animals are dying!"

The gavel again. Brit puts both hands over his face. Sarah Ableman looks straight ahead, no emotion, no expression. She's a perfect New England resident.

"And I think dogs should run free, too," you say suddenly into your mike. "Sure, they're invasive but they'll be supervised. I used to feel differently about this, but my mind has been changed. See? It can happen. This nice lady over here, Lydia, has convinced me dogs should be unleashed. I get it now. My dog is also well-trained." You look at Lydia, who vigorously shakes her head. I ponder

Lolly's stubborn refusal to walk or do anything beyond eat. "I support the Unleash Our Dogs movement," you say again, this time very loud. "Clean our water and free our dogs!" You lift your fist into the air and start chanting, "Clean our water and free our dogs! Clean our water and free our dogs!"

The Unleash Our Dog crowd chants with you, their fists are in the air. The gavel bangs. The Unleash Our Dog movement stands.

"Clean our water and free our dogs!"

"Clean our water and free our dogs!"

"Clean our water and free our dogs!"

"Clean our water and free our dogs!"

# Blue Jays Memo

She's off routine today. No morning travel to tablets. We're concerned so we scream.

Off routine!
Off routine!
Off routine!

We get nervous when female host engages in nonroutine activity, OK? Nervous. We're not anxious by nature. She's not exactly a predictable human, we know this. But female host rarely skips land of tablet visitation. Sometimes she adds other trips after visitations. For example, she has visited path leading to land cut off from coast, where one of us discovered shiny marker that was later dropped on her. But today no land of tablet visitation.

She's driving too far away.
Shut uuup.
Keep following.
Too many paths
Shut uuup. Follow
Where are we?
Elders?
We are 10.5 miles southwest of Children of Athena home nest.

Female host finally ceases forward motion. We perch and observe. Female host leaves mobile nest, perambulates then perches at what appears to be one of those human outdoor feeding nests. Another female human brings a cup of fluid for female host.

After a few moments we see another female perch with female host.

We know her!
Who?
Two-year-olds know her.

*Know who?*
*The brown human female.*

*Come back.*
*Perch.*
*Shut uuuup.*
*Two-year-olds!*
*Sing to us!*

Two-year-olds sing. Song suggests this is the brown woman who was at big, white protector building. The one the female host took to motorized mobile tube nest.

*Female host sings loud.*
*Brown woman sings soft.*
*Different songs!*
*What does this mean?*
*That's not our job!*
*Come back. No back.*
*Perch.*
*Shut uuuup.*
*Quiet. Observe.*

Let's see. She's off routine. She's meeting with familiar brown woman. They sing different songs but eat the same food, drink the same fluid. This could be an important observation. We don't know.

They leave. We leave. We return to home nest and those who remained have songs to sing to us.

*We saw something!*
*What?*
*While you flew away, we saw something?*
*Who?*
*Us?*
*So, sing!*

*HAWK! HAWK! HAWK!*
*HAWK! HAWK! HAWK!*
*Hawk gone.*

*Oh for crows' sake, it was a seagull*

*We're teasing squirrels.*
*No. Come back!*
*On limb!*
*Are you going to listen?*
*Sing. We're ready.*

*We saw young male human with small beak and dark head fur*
*When?*
*While you guys were gone!*

*Hush. Eat that worm.*
*Now, eat it now!*
*Don't just leave it there!*
*On limb now!*

*Go on.*

*So, he perched in black motorized mobile nest again.*
*Where?*
*Hush and listen.*
*They never listen.*
*We listen!*
*No they don't.*

*The male was viewing.*
*He was viewing what?*
*Female host's nest!*
*Viewing whilst not wishing to be viewed?*
*Yes.*

*Predatory behavior!*
*Predatory behavior!*
*Predatory behavior!*

# Chapter 17

*Complications of Unleash Our Dogs membership*

THIS MORNING YOU ride your bike the usual route, ending up at Shoreline Road where you still monitor fish mortality. There is always an ebb and flow of odor—death overlaying the fecund muddy banks. You bend over to check fish carrion, noting the date, time of day, tide, number of dead fishes—inaccurate, of course, because who can count them?—in your log. There's no place to send these statistics so you keep them in a computer folder.

People notice you walking up and down the coast bending over, lifting a fish into the air, dropping it. Some probably consider joining you—expressing concern, asking questions—but no one ever does. Why complicate life by dealing with you? You feel their eyes, hear their cars behind you as you log data, but you never turn, never wave. You simply stand among the life and death as your shoes imprint themselves into the transient mud.

After you leave the coast, you return home to work on more letters to editors of daily papers in contiguous towns. Our town's paper, *The Westbrook Weekly*, now refuses your letters. Jim Hardison, the editor, told you the fish problem has been overdone. "Lorraine, we're all looking into the dead fish, we get it. You've stated your concerns and expressed your misguided theories. No more dead fish letters." That's OK by you because you now avoid our local paper because of all the articles on themes surrounding the Bonnie Hamilton tragedy. Two articles about alcohol—one on driving under the influence of alcohol, another about a party host's responsibility when alcohol is served in abundance. Then there was a long essay by a lawyer about legal liabilities associated with double parking. And the best—a rather long, self-righteous pontification by a local psychologist about how guilt can make grieving an angry process. A few journalists had called you, requesting comments about the alcohol articles. Brit had warned you to practice saying, "I have no comment" over and over so that it would come out on impulse. You for once followed his advice, except the wording was a bit off. "I have no fucking comment" didn't appear in the article. The paper simply included the statement, "Lorraine Mulderon refused to comment."

You focus on septic tanks to get your mind off the accident. You talk with plumbers and engineers about septic systems design. You go online for hours and research rising water level's impact upon septic leaching fields designed to clean water flowing away from the sludge and scum of the septic tank. The fields leach only when the soil is permeable. Rising waters can interrupt this natural filter. You still try to call activist friends to share this information, but most continue to distance themselves from you. Cara has completed testing of the water, tells you that, while septic tanks are a risk, she cannot say for certain they are the only risk. "Too many other factors," she says in a hesitant voice that sounds frightened. Frightened of what, you wonder? Her taxes? The cost of reconstruction? Or frightened of those who are in control of the town.

I notice a few cold shoulders at the bank after your attack on septic tanks. Septic tank owners are bank customers, and the wealthiest customers live on the coast. Your big confrontation years ago with the gas company was nothing compared to the growing anger over your septic tank theories.

Once again, the world battles you. Except for the Unleash Our Dog group. So far, Lydia has offered verbal support and help with email chains. Her dog friends tend to interrupt the email chatter with cute canine stories, which you tolerate because they are all you have now. You do want structure because it's important to always have structure. Meetings. Committees. You think someone needs to be called the President (you of course) and Vice President of whatever it is the group has now become since its purpose has broadened beyond dog freedom. Lydia agrees, kind of—mostly to meetings, not so much to the rest. She tells you to call yourself anything you want, and the group will contemplate their definition at some point. She then plans the first meeting.

YOU PUSH LOLLY'S butt into the car while I stand behind you. She immediately spreads out over the seat, her front paws stretched before her, her back legs disjointed behind her. This is her "I'm-not-going-anywhere" position. I imagine the difficulty of pulling her out of the car once we arrive at the park.

Unfortunately, the first Unleash Our Dogs meeting is at Golden Grove Park and everyone is supposed to bring their dogs. You have begged me to go with you. While Lolly rarely obeys anyone, she's more likely to obey me than you. "If you don't want to help out, Haley, then stop behaving so well. If you made a few mistakes, I'd let you off the hook." I agree to help you, not because of your compliments, but because I'm optimistic this group will remain loyal to your cause. You will belong to something again, and I can slowly fade away, observing your activism from afar.

Most of the Unleash Your Dogs' members live inland—something you discovered right away at the town meeting. It was one of the first questions you asked. Lydia told you the group was composed primarily of neighbors on streets that bordered the Golden Grove Park, which is about three miles from the coast. So, of course, the coastal septic tank problem would not really impact any of them, just like the leash laws would not impact anyone who owns a fat, lazy bulldog. You caught on to this mutual beneficial relationship. Furthermore, Lydia has told you she's not intimidated by large coastal homeowners. "I'm used to influential people opposed to free dogs. I also support affordable housing filings, so they hate me for that, too. The poor have no place to live anymore. You do know this, right? And I have discovered that many poor have wonderful dogs who like to roam around off leash."

Her activism for affordable housing worries you because your environmental advocacy groups have historically protested developers who cut down trees and overdevelop land. A few of your activists—unfortunately the ones in the car accident—are involved with the Land Trust, an organization that fights overdevelopment. You usually agree with their land protection efforts, even though their reasons differ from yours. The wealthy hate real estate developers because of their support of affordable housing. You hate developers because of their lack of support for trees. But after five minutes of thought, you decide to shift your opinion. Affordable housing and free dogs are squeezed into a space in your cerebral cortex right next to dead fish. And so that is your new belief system. Latent, ready to fly out at any moment.

The park is mostly a large soccer field surrounded by grass—which now resembles trodden hay and dirt. There're a few oaks and maple trees. The western edge is anchored by a pretentious gazebo fifty feet from a small dirty pond. Two dozen women linger about the periphery of the soccer field. All the dogs are on leash because Unleash Our Dogs obey laws. There are one Goldendoodle, two Wheatons, a Portuguese water dog, two Labradors, three Bernese mountain dogs, two golden retrievers, a few mixtures, probably rescues of some sort, and one very curious looking corgi. Lydia's Labradoodle sits quietly on the steps of the gazebo, but most of the other dogs sniff each other and pull at their leashes. A few of them bark as we drag Lolly toward the crowd. Lolly hates moving in the heat but she does like to sniff dog butts, so she waddles over to the panting huddle of fur. She stops at a Lab butt momentarily before collapsing in front of a large Bernese mountain dog.

"Is your dog tired from a long walk?" Lydia says. A large whistle hangs from her neck and a thick bulging belt circles her waist.

"She's fine," you say. "Heat's not particularly welcome with a bulldog but I have water."

The Portuguese water dog has pulled her owner over to Lolly. He sniffs her wrinkled face then growls. Lolly jumps up, as if preparing for something. She always jumps up and back as if preparing to defend herself, which we know would never happen. Our bulldog is a coward. When the Portuguese water dog growls, Lolly runs toward the pond. She's able to do this because you have let go of the leash—which now bounces on the grass by her. You tell Lydia it's OK, because your dog is trained. But she is not trained, you simply think she will soon collapse from exhaustion. Which happens. But the problem with letting one dog wonder away unleashed is the impact upon the other dogs. If the fat bulldog gets to walk to the pond by herself, then why can't they?

The Labrador, who has been sitting nicely, leaps up and runs before the owner can grab the leash. He then proceeds to pounce upon Lolly, which looks like it could be friendly or maybe unfriendly, depending upon one's mood. Lolly's mood is one that allows an unfriendly translation, so she goes full coward mode. She lowers her torso to the ground—an anxious gesture, which for some reason sets dogs off. You have always pointed this out to me. "Dogs annihilate others who don't stand tall and assured of themselves. If you get dogs, Haley, you get men." I will just say, I do not have a boyfriend.

You take off toward what now appears to be a dog fight, but before you arrive, Lydia's "trained" labradoodle, Daffodil, leaps off the gazebo steps and runs to join the fun. The owner grabs the Lab but now Daffodil has the Lab's collar and won't let go. The corgi has also escaped its owner and leaps upon the large pile of dogs that have piled on top of Lolly. The Bernese mountain dogs could probably kill two dogs at a time if they desired, but they lie together in the sun and ignore the violence. I can only see Lolly's back legs, held by you as you try to pull her away. There seems to be a bit of blood on the ground, not too much, just enough to cause you to react the way you always react to injured animals. You scream.

"Mom, Lolly seems OK. Please let go of her," I say. You have your arms around Lolly's belly and are rocking her, which seems to make Lolly's breathing even more stressed. There is a small tooth mark under Lolly's left ear, but for the most part, her skin is barely broken.

"I've killed her. It's me. It's me. This is the second time, I've murdered."

"What was the first?"

"Third time. I killed a cat once."

"Lolly is OK, Mom." I'm trying to remember any previous murders.

"Call Nan."

"No, I'm not calling our vet, Mom. Everything is fine."

Lydia blows her whistle and the dogs pause a moment to reflect upon its noise. The pause gives the owners time to grab leashes and you time to not do anything. I like this whistle. I imagine blowing it when I see thoughts germinate in your head.

The world's order returns and everyone has their dogs by their sides, controlled and legal.

"You maybe shouldn't bring the bulldog, Lorraine." Lydia stands before us with her dog, Daffodil, who appears to be laughing, but is probably just hot and panting. "I think it provokes other more normal dogs."

"The dog bit her," you say.

"I'm not sure she should be allowed anywhere until she's been treated for her anxiety disorder," Lydia says to me.

"Well, I used to drink and that seemed to help it." You sit up now but don't stand. "But now I don't. So, I'm healthy and nervous. What can you do? You either live unhealthy with low anxiety or healthy and nervous."

"Mom," I say. "I think she's talking about Lolly's anxiety."

"Oh, then never mind."

"Are you sure you want to join this cause? I wonder if a leash is the best thing for your dog," Lydia says.

"She ran off and Bogey probably just wanted to run up to her and play," another woman, apparently Bogey's owner, says. "But maybe she misunderstood your bulldog's dog expressions." The short, frail woman has her leashed and panting Labrador close to her thigh. I move a few steps over because the Lab's stare makes me nervous. "Bogey is a sweet, well-trained dog. This has never happened. I'm so sorry, but really, I've never, ever seen Bogey growl at another dog. I think your dog's anxiety may trigger this in otherwise calm dogs."

We have reached the Lolly criticism saturation point. I see it in your eyes. You take a breath and your whole body seems to expand as the words fill your brain, then lungs. You let go of Lolly's belly, unleash her, and stand.

And then we hear it. It's not loud, just a pulse that tells us the police have arrived. The red and blue lights flash in the parking lot and we see two cops step out of their cars and slowly lope toward us.

Lydia whispers "shit" under her breath and you pat her shoulder. "Don't worry. I've been through this many times. Let me handle it."

"Hello, everyone. How're the dogs today?" the young officer says. He's tall, lanky, and looks my age. "We heard there was some sort of commotion. Got a call."

"Nothing us experienced dog owners can't handle," you say, walking away from Lolly.

"Ma'am?" the other older, rounder officer says. "The leash? Is your dog not leashed? It appears to be in your hand but not attached to the dog?"

"I don't believe in leash laws, so, no, my dog is not leashed. There was a bit of commotion due to a misunderstanding. It had nothing to do with the unleashed bulldog. I don't want her leashed. Leashing is bad for her anxiety."

"It's the law."

"And until we change the law," Lydia says, now by Mom's side, "we follow it. I'm sorry for the disturbance. Lorraine, let's leash our dogs."

You do nothing for a moment until I say, quietly, "Please, Mom, for me." You slowly unwrap your leash and approach Lolly. Lydia winks at me, leans into my ear. "I can't believe your mother's willing to go to jail for our cause. Stupid, but wonderful."

So, the group keeps you.

# Chapter 18

*Environmentalists must know how to climb*

FOR THE MOST part, Dad and I fished from the shores, only occasionally in small rented boats. We'd stand in the tangled underbrush—me terrified of whatever creatures lived in tall coastal weeds, Dad quiet by my side. In in our efforts to diversify our fishing experience—and due to occasional laziness— we explored fishing spots near us, like Independence Island. It was called an island because an asphalt drive crossed marsh grass and muddy water to connect two dozen enormous houses on fifty acres of land. The residents tended to be prominent members of our community—doctors, lawyers, investment bankers, all members of prestigious private clubs.

So, when Dad suggested we fish there, I was excited because I knew, given the large gate that separated the island from non-island people, we would have to sneak onto it. Unfortunately, we didn't sneak like I imagined spies sneaked. Dad simply parked his car outside the gate; we put on our fishing boots and walked over the rocks, into the water and around to the causeway. We then strolled through the neighborhood until he found an empty lot, which he told me was part of the Westbrook Land Trust and so belonged to the town. He said the island did not want any developer to buy the property and possibly build a tacky house, so they bought it and put it in the Land Trust. "Your mother of course supports that, because she wants to protect the birds nesting on the property." This made me think maybe the people were nice, because they agreed with my mom. I was young.

We fished a while, but we only caught a robin fish, a particularly strange fish that croaked like a frog when out of the water. I felt successful because I never tangled my line, was able to change lures with no help, and kept my mouth shut.

It wasn't long before we heard a siren on the causeway. The patrol car parked on the side of the road and two officers slowly made their way to the edge of the water where they stood staring at us fish.

"You guys catching much?"

Dad kept his line in the water and glanced back at the officers, as if they were friends asking him how his day was. He told them he'd caught one fish and that I had not tangled my line.

"Well, that's good, but we've gotten a call or two about you two. Seems the caller is concerned because you guys are not members of the Independence Island Association. Is that correct?"

"That is correct," Dad said, this time not looking at the officers, only his line.

"Sir, can I have your name?"

"Lawrence Mulderon. This is Haley, my daughter." Dad started reeling in his line, so I reeled in mine. "I thought this was a land trust, which as you know my property taxes fund indirectly. When you take property that was previously taxed and place it in the trust that is not taxed, the rest of us must make up the difference. So, I support this land with increased property taxes. I therefore get to fish on it."

"No, no, Mr. Mulderon, that's not how it works. These people funded the purchase with their money. They just used the land trust to facilitate the deal. It's part of the Westbrook Land Trust but it's also part of a private agreement."

"Which defeats the purpose of the trust and intent of the trust. It's just a park funded by the neighbors and should be treated as such. A land trust is for the community."

Dad was beginning to show the effects of living with my mother for sixteen years. I was always slightly nervous when Mom argued with police, but I was terrified when Dad did it. Because it was Dad!

"Mr. Mulderon, I'm not a lawyer, and if you want to handle this arrangement, you can address that through the courts. Even if you had a right to this particular land, you do not have a right to walk on the causeway, nor the property leading up to this coast."

Dad stood with his fishing rod for a minute or so, thinking. The officers stood. One looked over at me and winked. We waited for Dad to mentally sieve his options, then choose one. That is how Dad dealt with conflict. He went through all the possible choices and consequences of those choices, then chose a path. He chose leaving. So, we did not go to jail. That's how Dad got onto the island and off the island. You do things differently.


YOU DECIDE TO collect proof that coastal homes, particularly coastal homes on Independence Island, are polluting the water. You're not sure what you will do with it. Write an article for a blog? Spread information on the dark web?

You have called a few residents of Independence Island to request water samples to test for nitrogen and phosphate levels. They don't pick up the phone, nor return any messages. So, you decide to test the waters yourself. You discuss this with Sarah Ableman, your best friend forever, informing her that you will simply walk over there and collect the water yourself. Sarah tells you the gate has cameras and even if you waded around it, security would be contacted. The next day, Sarah calls to tell you that while there are cameras, she has detected a blind spot in their views. You tell me this over dinner.

"What do you mean she detected a blind spot?"

"When she hacked the system, she was able to look at the precise screen on their computer system"

"She hacked the system?"

"Why do you think she has a PhD in computer science?"


SO, HERE YOU are, with your best friend ready to sneak onto this island in a slightly different way than how Dad and I sneaked onto it many years ago. Lydia was going to join you two but backed out when you mentioned your climbing skills in an answer to questions concerning your experience with this kind of expedition. Sarah didn't ask the same questions as Lydia.

You park the car down the street from the island causeway. While both of you wear backpacks, yours is twice the size of Sarah's. When she asks what you're carrying, you ignore the question because you don't wish to spend time with all the questions about your ropes, climbing gear, and sheets. Her backpack contains Tupperware containers and small glass tubes.

You walk near the water and Sarah tells you precisely where to approach the corner of the gated entrance to insure invisibility. The cameras are located in two large bronze eagles perched on top of the gate's two spires. The eagle statues are famous antique relics imported from Mongolia by the original developer of the island. Sarah told you the eagle eyes—which were damaged years ago—are actually small cameras.

You point to the regal birds. "You sure we're not on a screen now?"

"It's not live, they record," Sarah says. "So, no one is watching now. And, no, blind spots are in this area right up against the gate."

"Great. I'll make my climb here," you say.

"Climb?"

This is what Sarah, with her controlled personality and analytical mind, misses about you—those subtle clues that suggest you're about to make an amazing bad decision.

"What we have to do is toss sheets over the eagles," you say, ignoring her squinting eyes. "I brought sheets, and if I climb the gate, keeping my body very close to it, they won't catch me on the screen. Sarah, I see your concern. We need water from one of the lots. Not here. Listen, there're no security guards sitting at a screen with coffee and newspapers now. Later, much later, they may look. Actually, they may never look at this particular recording unless someone tries to burglarize their homes. Then, they will look at it." You pause a moment, as if reconsidering. "And when they look, they will see—"

"A sheet thrown over the eagle at precisely," Sarah interrupts, looking at her phone, "9:42 am."

That should have provoked more reconsidering, but you retrieve the rope in your backpack and toss it before Sarah can talk. It sails over the gate—which may or may not be in the blind spot—and drops to the ground on the other side. You reach through the spires, grab its end, hand it to Sarah. She looks down at the rope as you harness yourself.

"Why am I holding this?"

"When I begin the climb, hold it tight and lean way out. Don't worry, I used to be a climber in college. I joined a climbing club, actually won a few competitions."

Sarah's not used to this. She generally takes notes, records them in computer files, and, well, OK, hacks computers for you on occasion. But she has never held a rope for a climber. You think this will help her move out of that quiet, methodical state where her mind has been eternally parked since she lost her wife.

"Lorraine, this isn't wise." Sarah glances down the street. "I'm not sure how we look here, climbing over a fence."

You stand with your rope and sheet, annoyed and ready to climb.

"Who looks out their window around here? We've got to do this. Blue jays brought me evidence for a reason."

"Lorraine, about those blue jays . . ."

"Yes, blue jays," you say. Sarah becomes quiet. "You were doing so well, Sarah. I'm a little disappointed. You and my daughter are alike in so many ways. I am thinking you may have leanings toward the One Party, which, by the way, is the source of your civil rights crisis. But OK. How about this? How about you tie that rope to something, maybe the horizontal bar down at the bottom? Just tie it then step down the road a way so no one will see you."

Sarah finds this more acceptable, so ties several knots, steps away and watches you grab the rope, lean back and walk up the fence. From a distance, one would see a middle-aged woman horizontal to the ground, holding a rope, and another middle-aged woman in neat linen pants and a black sports shirt standing near the water. And that is precisely what Brit, your lawyer, sees as he drives down Leroy Street and approaches the entrance to Independence Island.

# Chapter 19

*Environmental vandalism*

BRIT PARKS HIS car on the side of the road and slowly walks up to the gate. Sarah says hello and nothing else.

"Brit, they can see you. Walk closer to the gate," you say, turning your head slightly.

"And I would be concerned about the camera catching me because?"

"If, say, something was to happen. Like someone collected samples of water on one of these lots, and the owner's association checked the tape, they would suspect you were also involved."

"I'm not here for water samples. I'm here to pick up Jack Westerly for tennis. His car won't start. If they see me in the camera, they'll suspect me of tennis. Is this what you're doing, dear, climbing the fence for a water sample? Because this looks a little dangerous."

You walk up to the fence, then pull your body up with the rope. Walk up, pull your body up. Walk, pull, walk, pull. It's a slow, careful process.

"I find her strength surprising," Sarah says. "She's so thin. One would never know she could do this."

You are now near the eagle and you toss a torn sheet over one. It moves slightly, and a small piece of something falls and hits the asphalt with a ping. You ignore the piece of eagle and swing the second sheet over the other eagle, about twenty feet away.

"Can we possibly rethink this, Lorraine?" Brit says, looking down at the ground searching for whatever fell.

"That was exceptionally well done, Lorraine," Sarah says. "I think something from that eagle broke off, though."

"It was already broken," you say as you back down the gate. "What a metaphor right? Is this not perfect for our situation—blind eagles?" You jump out, then hang backward from your rope to talk to Brit. He looks at your mouth, then nose then eyes. "I used to climb solid rock. I won a contest in Alabama." Your eyes look strange upside down. He looks back up at the covered eagles. "There were rocks in Alabama. Most people don't know this about Alabama. I've won contests, Brit." You pull yourself up, drop your feet to the ground, untie your rope, and step out of your rappelling harness.

"What's the next step here," Brit says.

"We can walk around, wade through the water, or climb over. Sarah here can't climb so we'll wade. The Eagles' cameras are blinded, so we're clear to go now."

Sarah begins to coil the rope.

"I've got an idea. How about I buzz Jack so he can open the gate for us, then we walk through."

Sarah shoves the now tightly wound rope into the backpack.

"You'll be involved," you say. "It's best you just go on your way and do your tennis thing."

"I'm feeling nervous about all of this, actually, "Sarah says. "Brit's strategy is best. If we knew Brit had a friend who lived here, we could have avoided all of this." She doesn't look at you while she talks but at your backpack. She's probably frightened that any eye contact could trigger another impulse. At this point in the renewed friendship, I suspect she's beginning to recall other moments in the past when you jumped into an action without thinking. Vague, fuzzy memories of anecdotes emerge from the depths of her brain. She realizes you're the same person she knew four years ago, and the only difference is the desperate actions have become more ridiculous. She looks at Brit, her eyes pleading.

"Lorraine, I really don't want to have to represent you again. The sheets over the eagles are going to lead to calls to the police."

You think about this. "But the sheets are over the cameras and we're ready to do this."

"I'll collect the damn water, and Jack will never know. As your lawyer, I can't let you do this, Lorraine."

"I think we stop now before everything gets out of hand. We need to focus on more important things," Sarah says.

"Yes, like your lawsuit, dear. As your lawyer, I'm going to have to order you to stop this kind of thing. You can't do this anymore, Lorraine."

You hand Brit some Tupperware. "There're empty lots here. Find one. Fill our Tupperware, drop it off after your tennis game. And this officially makes you one of us now. You're on the Dead Fish team. It includes Sarah, me, and everyone in the Unleash Our Dog group. Well, actually, the dog people are temporarily on hold due to prejudicial behavior toward bulldogs."

AFTER YOU DROP Sarah off, you drive back toward Independence Island and turn into a side road to hide your car. You want to try to uncover the eagles before they cause trouble, but when you walk toward the entrance, you see Brit at the gate with a short man who gestures as he talks. The man taps his phone, talks into it, and marches to Brit's orange Subaru parked on the side of the causeway. Brit opens the door on the passenger side, but the man does not enter. He instead shouts back at Brit. A patrol car arrives. Louis steps out, rubs his eyes, and shakes his head. He taps on his iPad and looks around. Soon, another patrol car parks behind his. Then another black Ford van with WBCT TV in bold white letters painted on both sides. A man gets out with a camera and takes pictures of the covered eagles. One of the reporters leans over, picks up something from the ground. It's bronze and appears to be part of a wing.

# Blue Jay Memo

*Female host is trying to fly*
*Shut uuup. Perch on tree.*
*She's trying to fly over barricade!*
*She walks over it, not fly. Pay attention!*
*She will die!*
*She will die!*
*Shut uuup. Perch!*

*Ok, female host tries to walk over barricade at land cut off from coast. We're happy she understood our marker, but we're concerned about her reaction to it. Barricade has vertical sticks and fake model of another nemesi—the dreaded eagle—perched on top.*

*She's climbing to eagle!*
*Eagle's fake!*
*What's fake?*
*Eagle's fake.*

*She'll fall and die! Humans cannot fly!*
*Shut uuup*
*Come back.*
*Perch!*
*Watch out!*
*Watch out!*
*Watch out!*

*Man with white head fur and red beak arrives. Female host and large female with glass covered eyes leave together.*

*We decide female host's behavior around this large female with glass covered eyes is too dangerous. So, we send some reconnaissance teams to follow this large female with glass covered eyes. We send only females, as hawks are in the area and males stay behind to aggravate hawks. Females are actually better fighters than males but they're eager to escape nests.*

Females fly away. Much later, they fly back. They sing observations.

OK, first, large female human drives blue motorized mobile nest
Who cares?
Hush, we're singing!
What did the female do?
We think it's important.
What?
Blue. Motorized mobile unit is blue.

Oh, for crows' sake!

OK, she travels 12.6 miles southwest of Children of Athena home.
Then what'd she do?
She perches. Outside on wood by water.
OK?
Oh, and with folding metal slab with buttons. Tap tap tap
Bored. Bored. Bored.
She perches alone?
No. Male human.
Familiar male human?
No. Unfamiliar male human.
What'd he look like?
Brown head fur. No color over upper or lower appendages.
Obviously not interested in mating.
Yes, but mate with white head fur has no color?
Female host easy to please.
Shut uup! Continue!
That's it.
That's it?
Oh, also, he wears tight lower appendage cloth coverings.
And he also taps on metal slab with buttons.
They sing, they tap, they sing, they tap.

We perch, sing, eat. After meal of seeds we meet and decide to keep following large female with glass covered eyes.

# Chapter 20

*I'm OK, are you OK?*

FOR TWO DAYS you anxiously wait for the *Westbrook Weekly*. You retrieve the paper as soon as it hits our driveway. The front page is a close-up picture of the Independence Island eagles covered with torn sheets. The caption reads, "VANDALISM AT INDEPENDENCE ISLAND."

Over tea, you read the article and all the letters to the editors. An expert suggests the damage to the eagle wing is irreparable. The letters to the editor discuss the historical significance of the eagles, the symbolism of the eagles, the symbolism of blinding the eagles. Everyone is outraged. "These bronze eagles meant something to our community, our town, our country! It's anti-American," Sally Stayism, our First Selectwoman, says in an interview about the incident. "There's a warrant for the arrest of the intruders who vandalized the community relic." Louis is quoted in the same article. "We'll find the perpetrators and bring them to justice."

You put away the paper and sit for a moment contemplating yourself. You don't know why you act on bad ideas, nor why this behavior has not changed with age. Dad used to talk you down from chaos. When the crows started dying, and no one paid attention to your letters, you decided to dump dead crows at the Westbrook Town Hall. You rented a large dump truck and found crazy volunteers willing to pick up crow carrion. Dad cancelled the rental contract. He invited a corvid specialist to dinner to discuss other ways to research the deaths, which led to activist groups who did normal activist things like meet, organize petitions, raise money for foundations that investigated crow virus epidemics. Dad focused your energy, redirected your actions. After your hysteria, you calmed down, and eventually we were all grateful because Dad made sure the world around me was safe.

You take your tea outside and sit in the silence that blankets the neighborhood when leaf blowers are absent, the dogs aren't barking, the construction has ceased. But it's never completely silent for you, only for other denizens who pay no attention to passerines.

Two cardinals talk across the expanse of properties—repetitive, mellifluous songs—one melody rises from the immediate area, then comes the response from a distance, the same melody with one slightly changed note. Back and forth, back and forth. You think the repetition is conversation, each assuring the other that they are still alive and well. It's important to know a partner is safe because at any moment a creature can die. Eaten by a raptor or a cat. Infected by a virus. Knocked out by an unmarked window. Shot down by a boy's BB gun. Killed by human poison. The back and forth says, it's bad out here, but at least you are there, and I am here.

You tap my number into your cell phone. I pick up and quickly say I'm too busy to talk. You quietly tap off. You hold you mug firmly in both hands and decide to walk. Down the driveway then down Turner Avenue. You don't know where you're going, you're just going. You need to walk in order to fully ponder your anger over the covered fake eagles. Meanwhile, the real birds, the ones not duplicated in bronze, fill the air with their language. Their words are calm and hopeful, rarely impulsive and bitter.

You've dragged Sarah and Brit into your insanity. You wonder how Brit has managed to evade police questioning. Will he eventually have to report you to avoid problems with the bar association? You suddenly realize as you walk that he is on that camera tape. The video will reveal him talking with people in the blind spot right before the camera is covered. You suppose you have to save Brit, you have to turn yourself in. This time you will not spend just one day in jail for activism. This time you may be in real trouble. And it will definitely impact the lawsuit.

The street you stroll down is lined with maples, hemlocks, white pines, and old oaks with thick gnarls and cavernous holes. The trees anchor themselves, roots reaching out like arms of greedy gangsters stealing water from smaller plants. Despite water restrictions, everyone tries to save their favorite plants. Some neighbors ignore the drought restrictions and sneak out at night to turn on sprinkler systems briefly to prevent shrubbery from browning and shriveling. It's not enough water for color or luster, just enough for survival. It's frustrating to witness; the water shortage is real and dangerous. But you know people break rules because they love the life they're intimate with—the plants near the home, the annuals brightening the driveway. And this life needs so little from us. Water and no poison, that's it.

You pause a moment to listen. The cardinal song rises from a limb right above your head. You look up as it finishes, see the flash of red. The distant return song is louder, more strident, like you. I'm OK, it says. Are you OK? I'm OK, says the cardinal above your head. Are you OK? Yes, they both sing, we're OK. You reach out and touch the oak tree bark. You used to send WhatsApp messages to Dad daily.

You regard the acorns at your feet. You pick one up, noting its brittle, empty feel. You crush it against the tree bark and a small white worm crawls out. You take a few more acorns and shove them in your pocket for later study. But when you turn to walk, you almost step upon a dead baby bird. And then another. You kneel down, take one up in your palm. It's fairly large, yet frail. All white and brown fluff. Large eyes. Owlets. Dead owlets.

You feel your rage rekindle then flow through your body, like water through roots.

# Chapter 21

*Analyzing death*

THERE ARE FOUR dogs in the veterinary hospital waiting room, and the dead owlets in your box are getting their attention. A Portuguese water dog barks, and two Labs desperately pull at the leash to get at your shoebox. You have both arms around the box, protecting it from a small beagle who has managed to escape its owner to sniff the death you are holding.

"No," you say to the beagle. "They're no longer alive and do you no good. You have other more pressing concerns." The dog puts its paws on your legs and howls. You lightly bop the beagle's nose, which causes a melodramatic yelp. The owner quickly runs to her dog.

"What happened?" The beagle wags its tail and looks back at you. "Did you hit my dog?"

"This is not a bird hunt. I was protecting your dog. Dead birds are bad for him."

The woman stands before you. You do not move, only stare, as if contemplating her reaction. You imagine yet another lawsuit, this time over a bruised dog nose. Can one sue on behalf of a dog? You see yourself bringing birds into the deposition—at the table with all the lawyers and Brit, shaking his head every time you open your mouth. The dead owlets would probably be decomposed by then. You could of course place them in the freezer in case of a lawsuit.

All these thoughts race through your brain within seconds, but stop when the receptionist says, "Lorraine Mulderon" in an annoyed voice. The woman and beagle return to their seats. You step up to the reception desk.

"Nan says she does not handle dead birds. We do have wildlife experts who rotate around the various vet clinics, but they handle live birds."

"Haven't we had this conversation? I told you to simply squeeze me in, that I have something important to say to Nan."

"Yes, and I told you I would ask her, and I did, and that was her answer. She is very busy today."

"It took you an hour to ask her?"

"We're busy. Like I said before, live animals take priority."

"I'm live. Where is Nan now? Is she back in the examining room?"

"Nan's in her office returning a phone call. Lorraine? Lorraine, you can't . . ."

You are already through the swing doors and down the hall. The receptionist clips after you. You open the door as Nan places her phone down.

"I have an emergency," you say.

Nan stares at the box in your arms. The office is more like a closet—papers scattered around a phone, pictures of client dogs posted on a bulletin board hanging at an odd angle on the wall. A large filing cabinet covers the back wall. Nan closes her eyes and says nothing. You ignore the closed eyes and open the box, revealing dead owlets.

"Two dead owlets," you say. "Two together, as if they died in the nest and the parents pushed them out to show me. You need to perform an autopsy. Just test their livers."

Nan takes the box and stands. "Nestlings die all the time. Come with me." She leaves the office without looking at you. "This woman thinks your mom pushed you out of the nest," Nan says to the dead birds as she walks into a small room. "She doesn't realize they don't do this." She places the shoe box on the examining table and yanks two latex gloves out of a plastic container, then freezes to study your appearance. Baggy cargo pants and a T-shirt that says in black letters, "Someone's Gotta Care!"

"That's a good one. I like that one." Nan returns to the shoebox and gently removes the dead baby birds and places them on the table. "I'd say this is a barred owl." She flips them over, searches inside their beaks, feels their chest with her index fingers. "Nothing seems broken, but it's hard to tell. I'm not thinking predator because the heads are intact. But these cuties show no indication of a predator attack. This makes me think they fell out of the hole in the tree. Of course, you two are quite emaciated, which tells me Mommy has not been diligent with food, or Mommy has died."

"I'm sure their spirits appreciate your thoughts. If a mother jay dies, the father takes over. And even if the father dies, other blue jays feed them. Aunts, cousins, even uncles. Blue jays are very community oriented. Protective of themselves, protective of others. I know nothing about owls, though."

Nan looks into your eyes a moment.

"I've found a total of eight dead birds, some blue jays, around my area," you say. "And I've found these acorns." You take a handful of acorns from your purse. "I crushed one and a worm crawled out."

Nan takes the acorn rolls it in her hand, taps it against the side of the table, looks inside.

"Weevils," she says. "Strange ones. I've never seen these before."

"Is this related to the fish?"

"Lorraine, I just don't know. Everything is related to everything. We have species of insects here we've never seen before because of global warming, our development, our disregard for native vegetation. We probably have a very low crop of acorns. I'll report it to the EPA. Maybe they can spray the trees, but that will cause all kinds of complicated side effects."

"Our fish are dying, and I've been right—whatever is happening to the fish is an indication of what is to come for the birds, then mammals."

Nan puts the birds back into the box and speaks down to the box. "Blue jays are quite different from owls. They don't eat fish or anything in that water. But, yes, fewer acorns could impact the ecosystem dramatically. Squirrels, birds, deer."

"I don't know about squirrels. I have squirrel guards and yell at them when they steal seeds."

"Also, depleted fish would have some impact on raptors, and that would impact the ecosystem. We all evolve to survive, Ms. Smarty-pants, except humans. Or *modern* humans. Anyway, I do suspect you're right about the damaged septic systems. Leaching fields. I grew up in Waterport. We had a town waste treatment plant with no secondary treatment facilities, and well, my dear, let's say we had no fish because the fish avoided our wonderful coast like the plague." She touched the baby owl body with her index finger, as if about to pet it. "I'm not sure nitrogen and phosphorous are going to impact the owls, because they don't eat fish." She turns and looks at you, her tone changed, more intense, less chirpy and shallow. "I've read your letters. I saw you on that local TV station that covers town meetings. I watch the local network. Most people don't watch town meetings because they're so boring. Our version of CSPAN. But if you look at it with an eye for irony, you can see it as our own reality TV channel."

"I'm glad you're finding it all entertaining. I know I'm entertaining everyone. I'm not very popular. Even my activist group kicked me out. Most live on the coast so my complaints hit home, I guess." You open your mouth to say something about your water sampling at Independence Island, but for once you show self-control.

"It's their personal waste you're talking about. Lord, you're saying their poop's in our Sound. These are old Connecticut families. Well, some are." She chuckles and looks over Lorraine's head, as if thinking about all of the wealthy citizens in their bathrooms embarrassed by their pollution. "I live right on the water, by the way." She removes her gloves. "Right there on the Sound. We replaced our septic tank and moved the leaching field far back when we bought the house. That was about ten years back. I suspected sea levels would be rising. I read, you know."

"It's all we can do. Read. And march. I also write letters and yell."

"I know."

"So, do you want to join my Dead Fish activist group? It's two people, plus the Unleash Our dogs' group. We merged."

"I know the Unleash Our Dogs people, I'm the vet for Lydia's Daffodil. I actually don't like the idea of unleashed dogs. They disrupt the parks natural vegetation and wildlife. They're invasive. But, look." Nan turns back to the box and picks it up. "I've sent off the fish livers. We'll see what the test results say. I doubt we'll find anything. Maybe these owls have damaged immune systems related to the water. Maybe toxins dumped into unregulated upstream waters. You can pretty much dump anything in that river now. And we have that drug plant up there. I have no earthly idea what they're making."

"I'd appreciate a look, even if it's useless. Just send me the bill." You open the door.

"And, Lorraine, just so you know, and you probably do know this, dear, but my neighborhood hates you."

You shrug. "What's new?"

"It's just that, well, there's big money living on the Sound. Some of those houses are eight thousand square feet. My goodness, one house went on the market for $7.5 million. Can you imagine owning a $7.5 million house and worrying about fifty thousand dollar septic system replacement? But my daddy used to say, "Baby doll, how'd you think those rich people got so rich?""

"Whatever. Let them cry. I'm still going to yell and write my letters."

Nan catches your arm as you turn to leave. "No, I mean it, Lorraine. You, Haley, and sweet Lolly have been through too much these last six years after losing your husband. It's rough. I remember when we lost my dad. You need to listen to me. I saw your letters in Norwik's *Daily News* and the *New Harbor Advocate*. And on the internet, some of those sites hidden from the monitors. You just keep writing about this and posting your name all over the place. In one letter, you threatened to go national, whatever that means nowadays. National truth has been blocked, as you know. Still, that kind of talk ruffles these people. Seriously, don't roll your eyes. You don't want to keep messing with this crowd. They can be scary. Be careful."

# Blue Jay Memo

We send two-year-olds every day to follow large female human with glass covered eyes.

This female has several excursions to same location. She sings and taps buttons on folding metal slab alongside male human with brown head fur and tight lower appendage covering.

Meanwhile, female host has taken interest in owl progeny. Owl offspring are dead, something we have gleefully noticed. Unlike us, however, female host reacts with sorrowful song and collects the corpses. As with other collections, she takes them to red human nest—same red nest that cured dog.

We ponder these observations as we eat.

Strange male human is back!
Go away! Go Away!
Go away!
Go away!

Large black motorized mobile nest is back. Male human with black head fur perches quietly in his motorized mobile nest on path that leads to female home nest.

He follows female host who has left.
Predatory behavior!
Predatory behavior!
Predatory behavior!
Predatory behavior!

Male in black motorized mobile nest suddenly takes detour. We send two-year-olds to follow.

They return and sing.

*He's a predator!*
*He's a predator!*
*Shut uuup. Tell your observations.*
*Predator!*
*Where does he travel?*
*He travels to land cut off from coast.*
*Where?*
*Where fake eagles perch on barriers?*
*Yes.*
*He travels there often.*
*He also travels to exit area for motorized mobile tube nest.*
*So, what happens there?*
*He enters motorized mobile tube nest.*
*Which direction?*
*Southwest toward Great Human Tribal Nesting area.*

*We're concerned.*

# Chapter 22

*Lunch, an anxious dog, guilty ex-friends*

I SIT FACING the lobby full of bank customers, my back to the floor-length window that faces the parking lot behind our building. I don't know why they have windows but force all of us to face the lobby. I suppose they want the customers to look outside. And they do, they all stare outside as I talk, because our discussions are mind numbing. I ask questions. They answer them. The questions are all the same. What is your name, what is your address, where do you work, how much do you make, how long have you worked there? That is my day.

I see your car first. When I'm free of customers, I always turn my chair so I can stare at cars, pedestrians, and across the street the park where you and I will eat lunch today. Your bright yellow Prius enters our parking lot and pauses. I can barely make out your face. Your car turns into an open parking space near the street, then quickly back up. The car idles. It turns back toward my bank building and idles again. You sit straight and confident in your idling Prius. I wonder what's bothering you. Did you forget to fill your car with gas, or are you contemplating the handicapped parking space because our lot is full today? My bet is on the handicapped parking lot. You are tempted because of Lolly. Your car now moves forward, turns sharply, slips into a space in the left corner, far removed from the handicapped space and our front door. Your expansive, generous view of humanity beats out your desire to shorten the walk for your dog. You step out of the car, open the back door, and retrieve Lolly. I turn back to face the lobby.

Lolly is leashed, and loudly panting. She quickly pulls you over to Nic Rodriquez, our assistant manager, so she can sniff his legs and obtain a back rub. Nic greets you, quickly pats Lolly's head, then talks to you, probably about rules precluding dogs into the lobby. You're of course arguing, which is leading to a discussion about the purpose of the bank rules and importance of following rules. Lolly flops down, front legs stretched before her, disjointed back legs stretched out behind her. A woman stops to pet Lolly. I walk out right as you begin to explain to the woman what Nic has told you and why you disagree. The woman rubs Lolly's belly and listens.

"There's no food in a bank, so I don't understand the safety and health factor either," the woman says. She's now apparently an accomplice in your new activism against bank rules banning dogs. You look at Nic, raise your eyebrows. The woman continues to rub Lolly's belly.

"In fact," you say, "I bet she'd bring in business. She's been trained for therapy, only needs to retake the test. She's technically a therapy dog."

"Hey, Mom." I'm eager to move the conversation away from Lolly, who is clearly not a therapy dog. You did bring Lolly to a dog therapy training seminar and the teacher gave her an initial test, which she failed. She couldn't even come on command. You told the instructor that Lolly required a certain inflection, a "sing-song voice of sorts," and if he could use this calling technique, Lolly would come. He didn't. You left.

"Can I just bring Lolly to my daughter's office for a quick second while she gathers her things? We're eating in the park today."

Nic stands quietly and considers all the wrong choices one can make with a woman like you. One can argue—the worst choice. One can reason—a slightly better alternative, but, of course, you sometimes take reasoning as permission for pontification. Or, one can simply be a wimp and give in without comment, which I call the best option. Nic puffs his cheeks on exhale, winks at me, indicating he is tempted to go with the best option. His wink sends a quick flush down my neck because I have a crush on Nic. I work very hard at ignoring it since office crushes can become sexual harassment, in a reversed kind of way. I am not someone he would like even if I weren't working with him. I doubt he would ever learn to appreciate a plain woman who still lives with her overbearing mother. I also don't have that sexual come-hither way about me, something I actually like about myself because it eliminates annoying problems most of my friends always have to deal with in their careers.

"Look," Nic says, "Ms. Mulderon, why don't you stand here with me while your daughter goes to the office to retrieve her belongings. Then I can walk all three of you to the door. That way we're not breaking rules, I'm just helping you follow them." This is why I have a crush on him.

IT'S A CLOUDY day and a small zephyr tosses my hair, but not yours because your hair is pinned tightly to the top of your head. You always look sophisticated when your hair is up and away from your face like this. Your cheekbones are high and colored by the true ruddy tone of healthy skin. You wear little makeup because you don't need much. You're a green woman and most of it shows in your figure and skin.

We have to cross the street to sit in the park, and on the way, we see Abby Lawson, one of the activists who attended the tragic party that resulted in the death of Bonnie Hamilton. She's walking with a group of women, all laughing and talking, but when she sees you, she raises her hand and waves, as if the tragedy of the party that resulted in death and a lawsuit has been forgotten and we're all simply passing each other on a normal day in town. You've been trying to forget about the accident, which Brit calls about daily, usually with bad news concerning the obstinate plaintiffs. Now, suddenly, you're reminded of that nightmare and your tragic life because Abby and her friends stand before us. You stop, back straight, hands clasped in front, waiting for verbal punishment. Lolly wags her butt and Abby pats it, inspiring a roll-over for a belly rub. Abby obliges. Lolly is happy. You are not.

"We've missed you at all the meetings," Abby says, as if you were supposed to attend. Lolly kicks her feet as Abby rubs her belly harder. "We're gathering support to stop the Lowland Avenue development. The town land trust is on our side on this one. You're welcome to join us, Lorraine." She doesn't introduce the two women who stare down at Lolly's belly.

You regard the other women briefly. "Well, Abby," you say. "I didn't really think I was welcome. The group doesn't seem particularly concerned about water quality. The fish, Abby, are still dying. Actually, since they do have brains, wee brains, but brains, they're swimming away from us, so we no longer have dying fish, we simply have no fish. A fishless coast."

"Lorraine, Haley, do you know my friends?" Abby introduces us. She stops rubbing Lolly's belly and stands while we all shake hands. I lean over and rub Lolly's belly. "I'm not going there with you, Lorraine. If you want to work with us against this development, then I will be glad to have you. Otherwise . . ."

"We need affordable housing. I've learned all about the housing crisis through my Unleash Our Dogs group. I think Lowland development plans to have fifteen percent affordable units, yes? Where will the poor live, Abby? Or will they just go somewhere else, like our fish? The poor are the most impacted by our ruined environment. We just dump crap in their neighborhoods and forget about it. Well, we can't forget about it. And the poor will die along with the fish."

Abby smiles quickly, says something trivial that I miss, then leaves with her friends. You watch them march away before we begin the ritual of dragging Lolly across the street. For some reason, Lolly refuses to cross streets. This forces us to drag her as the traffic wait. While we drag, you ponder your various losses to date. These friends are a chosen loss. Dad was a non-chosen loss. Brit could very well be another loss, although, so far, he's been a good lawyer. I suppose when you age, these losses represent a peeling away of priorities. The lifetime partner goes, and so friends are more important. Now, the friends disappear, so new friends are important. After every peeling, Lolly and I become more important.

When we sit, you open your canvas bag and pull out Lolly's treats. Chicken, rice, and organic dog biscuits. You take out our salads, yogurts, containers of cut fruit, and V-8 juice bottles. We eat in silence a while. I ask you about plans after lunch. You say you will be returning home and "just doing things at home." You eat quietly, and I see it in your eyes. I always see it when you say "home," particularly when you say you're going home, or staying home. It's been seven years, and despite your efforts that changes its appearance, our home is still the place where Dad died. I wonder sometimes if we will ever talk about our loss, our pain, our new home without Dad. There is so much we have pushed away in order to survive. Since you've been strangely incapable of facing the accident, I don't touch it either.

"Are you still asking dull questions?" You smile, as if you know my thoughts and are changing the subject on purpose.

In the distance, a chipmunk races across the grass and disappears into its hole. Since the town is allowed to ignore conservation guidelines, the small one-acre park looks vibrant, its grounds green and healthy. The four large oak tree branches cast flickering images of themselves upon the ground.

"Same things. Occasionally I ask about length of time on their job."

"I've been thinking about how you deal with this. This is what I have concluded." You finish chewing your salad, swallow. A small breeze pulls a few tendrils of hair from one of your bobby pins. The hair tosses around your face as you talk. "Ask your customers if they think man is inherently good and molded by life's hardships, or if they believe man is inherently bad and molded by rules, moral codes, religion, and mothers."

I open my mouth to respond with some witty, ironic comment, but you do not let me talk.

"Ask them if they think reality is solipsistic. That is, is their world view simply their life experience transposed onto others? Or, alternatively, do they believe reality is ethereal, impossible to determine, an amalgamation of global world views? Ask them, if man were left alone in an unregulated world, would he ever consider societal costs when making profound life decisions? The answers to these questions will tell you a lot about whom you're dealing with."

I let that sit for a while and stare at the strands of hair, now limp and still because the zephyr has passed. One strand lightly lines the right side of your face.

"Does anyone really know the answers to those questions? Do you?"

"Yes, I do." You take a long sip of your V-8 juice. "You will know better how to manage a customer if you know his world view."

There is a quiet screech overhead. The hawk flies high over a distant cluster of trees and disappears. Lolly starts to snore. A few house sparrows hop about begging for bread, which we do not have. You reach into your purse and retrieve a bag of peanuts you always have on hand and toss a few into the grass.

"Or," you say, slowly. "You can quit and create problems for your bank's management because, of course, they will lose a tremendous talent. They didn't challenge you enough, and thus lost an opportunity. Then, you go back to school, become a scientist. Invent something enormously helpful. This will be wonderful for your resume when you eventually run for Senator. State elections are sometimes honest. And who knows, one day we may be back to normal. There is always hope that a real democracy will return. Vote this year, by the way." You look up and stare in a strange way. "This year, it's important."

"Why?"

You ignore me, toss a peanut into your mouth.

"We're going through a dark time, and since you're young, you don't really know any other time. I do. I do know another time. I know enough to not give up. You don't have to act like me, but you should operate like there is hope."

"I have hope, Mom. You always think about big hope. I see things on a smaller scale, I guess. You know, getting along, creating a safe little world."

You look into the space above my shoulder, then stare at the corner where we stood with Abby and friends, as if studying ghosts of the past conversation. I recall you wandering in the yard a year after Dad died, staring at the area where he fell. I suspected you were trying to recreate the tragedy in order to change it. Maybe you're doing that now, recreating the conversation, altering your words so you regain your friendship. Do you stroll by Independence Island, trying to rewind tossing those sheets? Do you stare at your car, recreating the moment you decided to leave it in the middle of the road? Do you think back on the illegal immigrant, rewinding that moment you stopped and got involved, and lost five thousand dollars? Is that why you left, Mom? Did all the re-creations in your mind fail?

"I took two dead owlets to Nan the other day," you say, turning back to me abruptly. And you tell me the story about finding the dead owlets, taking them to Nan, Nan's reaction. When you arrive at the part of the conversation where Nan discusses her wealthy neighbors on the coast, you become anxious.

"Nan had this shift in personality," you say, carefully. "She wasn't the Nan we know, the Nan that talks to us through Lolly or dead birds or other animals, the life-is-not-too-serious Nan. She was a different Nan, a serious, direct Nan. It's like she crawled out of a box she has always placed over her head when at work in order to be a person with me for just that one moment. To warn me. It was more than the usual warning everyone gives me about not pissing off your neighbors or friends. She said I needed to be careful."

"Careful about the fish?"

"About the fish, yes, and I guess about pissing off the wrong people. Seems there are these people who don't want to deal with any change that could create financial costs or complicated problems. Or maybe they know more than I know and want my investigation and questions to stop. But her demeanor was scary." You put down your plastic spork, place your hand on Lolly—now peacefully snoring into the grass.

"Mom, they're just people, don't worry. Who lives by Nan, anyway? Like, who're these wealthy people she claims are so angry with you. Do they have names?"

"Yes, I looked them up when I got home. They're names end in L.L.C. There were no names of humans."

# Blue Jay Memo

*Female host travels to small working red nest where offspring enters to perch most days. Female host brings dog. They eat on land across from red nest. They do this often.*

*Today, before usual meal, female host and offspring collide with another flock of females. One of females was involved in collision of motorized mobile nests that killed female elder.*

*After flock perambulates away, we observe this recognized female stopping at edge of red nest. She begins viewing female host whilst not wishing to be viewed. Predatory behavior.*

*Female host and offspring eat.*

*Squirrel!*
*Going back to home nest now.*
*No, stay on limb.*
*Squirrel!*
*Tease squirrel!*
*Tease squirrel!*
*Back here now!*
*Bored, bored, bored.*

*Female host finally leaves. We follow.*

*She's not traveling usual route!*
*Too much flying.*
*Hawk!Hawk!Hawk!*
*Hawk!Hawk!Hawk!*
*Hawk!Hawk!Hawk!*

*Hawk gone.*

*Where's she going?*
*By a river.*
*Come back.*
*Now*
*Shut uuup. Listen*

Female host ceased travel about 9.5 miles west of Children of Athena home nest. We perch in oak tree. She perches at table, waiting. Another motorized mobile nest arrives, ceases motion. Large female with glass covered eyes exits her blue motorized mobile nest.

*Bored, bored, bored.*
*Insect!*
*Acorn!*
*Come back.*
*Stay on limb*
*Shut uup. Listen*

Another motorized mobile nest arrives.

*We recognize!*
*Who?*
*It's brown skinned female!*
*Who?*
*The one who escaped from white protector nest*

*Insect!*
*Squirrel!*
*Focus!*
*Come back.*
*Shut uuup. Stay on limb.*

Females sing. Large female with glass covered eyes taps buttons on folding metal slab and sings in same song language of brown-skinned woman. Brown-skinned woman and large female with glass covered eyes sing back and forth, back and forth. Female host appears bored.

They do this a while. They leave.

We follow female host by way of many disorganized and busy paths back to Children of Athena home nest.

# Chapter 23

*The only real activist is an internet activist*

MOM, DO YOU remember how Dad took particular interest in his lures? There were different lures for different fish. We had fewer salt water lures because most of the time when Dad went shore fishing, he used real bait—cut up bunker, clams. But he had hundreds of fresh water lures with shiny colors and hooks on top or below. Most were shaped like small fish, but there were also frog lures, tiny mouse lures, bug lures. There were even shiny stainless-steel lures that looked like nothing in particular. Some worked better in lakes, some in streams, some worked on sunny days, others cloudy. He used particular lures for boats, a few reserved for shore fishing.

Studying Dad's lures was my favorite activity. They were fascinating fake food. Most of the time, the fish ignored our fake food. Dad said that's because they thought about things first. Impulse, he said, will trip them up every time. "When they don't think, we have a better chance of winning them over. Of course, there are lures for the thinking fish, but those can be expensive. It's why your mother broke my bank, dear. Her thinking. It required expensive lures."

DAYS PASS. YOU remain concerned about Nan's warning, even though warnings about people hating you are not really new. You sit at your computer for hours, hunting down your letters written to other town journals. You re-read them and re-appreciate them. Your worry is replaced by pride of epistolary skill. You reactivate your old blog/website you used to manage for activist groups. You had closed it down after Dad died, then reopened it only to close it again after all the hacks and acerbic comments.

It takes you a few hours to re-activate your website. You introduce yourself to the world. You mention the Unleash Our Dog advocacy because you've decided to include dog freedom in your vast array of blog advocacies, which, besides the usual global warming and lost democracy, include: dead fish, dead birds, rising sea levels, septic tanks, dying trees, historical prospective on dead crows, affordable housing, four-way stop sign intersections, and "bike flocking," which is your name for groups of bikers cycling on two lane roads that you like to travel upon. You link everything to an old Instagram account, but immediately shut that down once you realize the site still has pictures.

You spend a moment staring at a few old Instagram pictures. You click on pictures of Dad and open each to enlarge it so that you can lean in and study his face again. There are pictures of me fishing. Pictures of dead crows. Pictures of Dad, me, and you standing somewhere with white-tipped mountains as a backdrop. You spend almost thirty minutes studying one picture of you and Dad at a nice restaurant. You both hold glasses of wine in front of plates filled with broiled fish smothered in pink sauce. Your hair appears recently lightened, your skin tan, arms toned, and your entire face smiles at the camera.

You tap delete again and again and again. You click on pictures of only you and me when I was barely six years old, back in those gentle years when you led me through life with humor and grace, before the transition, before the death of crows. Before all of the national changes that became normalized for me and my peers but an eternal wound for you. These tragedies damaged you. No longer were you that calm, beautiful woman with energy reserved only for your child, mate, and friends. You became anxious after the transition, hysterical after all the crow deaths, and permanently angry after Dad left us.

You find a picture of Lolly when she was a puppy. You can't delete Lolly because deleting Lolly is too traumatic. Your connection to her is not quite as painful because it's similar to the present one. Your relationship with animals has remained anchored and consistent. Are there animals with you now, Mom? Are you talking to blue jays in some far-off land?

Once your web site and social media pages are complete, you search for other sites, eventually finding one of the country's largest environmental activist sites—Save Our Planet. It includes extensive articles on water quality, with a particular emphasis on erosion of coral reefs. There's a note on the site apologizing for the hacks and down time. There are several troll comments, which are typical problems with any progressive site now. The One Party hires trolls to comment and hack sites like these, but the site manager has done a fairly decent job protecting its content. There's also a long note pleading for money.

You read several articles, which are well-written and quite erudite. You send the author and editor a list of questions about dead fish, septic tanks, the rise of sea levels, the impact upon nitrogen levels. You discuss the dead owlets, which leads to your usual discursive pontification about the historical crow deaths and your activist role in that disaster. You then study the comment sections, noting the abundance of professional trolls and bots. You have always loved comment sections on the internet. It has been your favorite pastime. You post several comments—all ideas and theories you've already mentioned in your emails to the newspaper editor. Dead fish. Dead birds. The importance of blue jays. The impact of these animal losses to the town, state, nation, and, well, humanity.

Before logging off the site, you decide to send an email to the president of the foundation that funds the site. You move the cursor over log off, but decide you simply have to talk to the president of this foundation. You look up his contact information and call him. After the voicemail's beep, you leave a long message that's cut off before you're finished. You call back with more thoughts.

After all of this computer activity—which lasts hours—you sit and wait for return messages, return emails, return phone calls.

Nothing.

You log back on the site, check your posts in the comment section. No replies. You consider replying to your post, but then decide that may be too much. You ponder this lack of site action and conclude it's indicative of apathy, so you wonder if you should post another comment about apathy. You note the foundation that funds the site is based in Pennsylvania, a three-hour drive from Westbrook. It may be worth your time to drive there and visit with the president. You will demand to see him, and after they beg him to leave his office and talk with you, you will interview him right there in the hall. You will post the interview on your new blog, then tweet a link to your blog post. Of course, that will mean you'll have to reactivate your old Twitter account. Years ago, you had to close it because of complaints. Twitter's now owned by the One Party, so it would probably close you down again within days.

The doorbell jolts you out of your computer reverie. You ignore it. It dings again. And again. And again. You hate unannounced visitors. Usually if you do nothing, the rude visitor goes away.

It dings again. The ding comes from the right side of the house and you're upstairs on the left side, which makes it all the more annoying.

After the sixth ding, you stand and take the long journey through the house, over the bridge, into the kitchenette, to the door. You peek through the side window. He's thirty-something, thin, hair the color of potting soil, neatly attired in a dark suit. You watch him brush his hair back and glance around the periphery of the doorframe, as if checking for a door camera. You remind yourself to buy one as you crack the door.

"Hello? Ms. Mulderon? I'm Bart Logan. I'm a lawyer. I represent a developer. Is this a bad time? I'm sorry to come unannounced, but this will not take long at all." He talks fast, as if scared you'll shut the door.

You say nothing.

"Hello?"

You make the big decision to open the door wider. You stand straight-backed, ready for anything. You feel brave, yet vulnerable, the way environmentalists are supposed to feel. Lolly squeezes between your legs and runs outside in order to receive free pets and back massages. The man agrees to give her back massages, which causes Lolly to roll on her back for belly rubs, which the man also agrees to. The back massages do nothing for you, but when the man bends down for the bulldog belly rub, you decide he's safe and invite him inside.

"I'm sorry to barge in like this, but I was out this way and thought I'd just stop by, see if anyone was home. I tried to call but no one answered and there was no voicemail."

"I turned the voicemail off. Hate messages are so unorganized. I don't mind hate, but the answering machine encourages babbling. Babbling anger I cannot tolerate."

You walk to the kitchenette, sit at the table. The man follows, his hands in his pockets. He looks in the direction of the bridge, as if wanting to visit, but then turns abruptly toward you.

"I'll not take up too much of your time. Like I said, I represent a rather large developer."

You hold up your palm to stop his speech.

"As in interested in new property? Or property already developed and ready for sale?"

He sits down and grasps his hands together on top of the table. "Both, actually, but the developer I'm representing today is interested in new property. They actually like this property—the location, you know. Location, location, location. They think it has potential."

"You're representing someone who thinks this property has potential? Do you know the history of this property? Do you understand what has happened on this property?"

"You had a fight years ago with the gas company that wanted to purchase the land to run a pipeline through it. You said no, they went to court, everyone settled. They agreed that you could basically split the house in half, sell the middle to them, while you retained the two sides. Everyone assumed you would pick a side and own a smaller house, but you simply split your house in two."

"Yes, and every day I gleefully trespass as I cross over the bridge into the second half of my house. And you have a developer who thinks he can make money off of it? Let me guess. He will buy my split-in-two house and sell it to the gas company. Did the gas company send you? I've been through this before. I'm not selling my house to a gas company. I don't believe in fossil fuel."

The man loosens his tie and leans back in his chair, crosses his legs, smiles. "You're something else. I was warned. Don't you want this house to be a viable investment? What about your daughter? Don't you want to leave something for her? You can monetize an asset for possible future unknown financial obligations?"

You feel your face warm. "How do you know I have a daughter or unknown financial obligations? And who warned you? This developer knows too much. Am I allowed to have his name?"

"There's no name. It's a company. And we'll probably not sell to the gas company, although they wouldn't rule it out."

"They?"

"How much did it cost you to refurbish this after you sold the middle to the gas company? More than their payment, I bet." He looks around as he talks. "Crazy."

"I'm crazy?"

"No. You're not crazy. A bit impulsive, though, right? You do things first then think about them later. I have a brother like that."

"And you think I'm going to sit here with you, a stranger, and take abuse. I don't take abuse."

"I'm sorry. I apologize for being so flippant." He uncrosses his legs and grabs his hands again. "Look, you've been through a lot. We can help."

You say nothing. You notice the careful way he talks, his unctuous tone.

"You could now possibly make a profit on what was probably a bad decision that killed your property value. I just want to talk about it now. Look around, assess its value."

"So, let's say I show you around. You like what you see. Let's say I sell. Then what? You let an empty house sit here? You sell it back to the gas company? You rebuild it? And what about the trees? Do you cut down the trees? Will you feed my birds?"

"Birds eat insects, don't they?"

"That's how it's supposed to work when everything is clipping along nicely in the ecosystem."

"Is everything not clipping along in our ecosystem?" He now has eye contact, but no smile, not even a hint of a smile. His silence wants you to talk, open up to him, this stranger who appeared at your door uninvited with an offer you never requested.

"Let's just leave it at I like my birds and want them fed."

"I'm not making fun of you, I honestly don't know anything about environmental science. You're very involved with that, right?" He sits back, looks around the kitchenette, toward the house bridge. "Can I at least see the bridge?"

"Wouldn't it make more sense for the actual buyer to see the bridge?"

"I represent the buyer. They trust me."

You stand and start the journey to the bridge that leads to the better half of your house. He follows slowly, quickly assessing the scullery, the hardwood floors. The route to the bridge is structurally just a very large room that you separate into three rooms by positioning a few sofas, throw rugs, and a large oak bookcase. The glass covered bridge inspires a smile as he walks over it. He pauses at the top of the curved path to look through the glass floor.

"I'm trespassing now, yes?" he says.

"No. That bridge is in the air. As far as I know, air is still free."

Once on the other side, you briefly show him the kitchen, its sink filled with dishes and coffee cups. The counters have not been wiped and some of my cereal detritus lingers. He ignores it, walks into the foyer, peeks around at the living room.

You stand at the front door. "So, did you like it?"

"Right now, I'm just asking you to think about it. That's all. Think about it." He stands before you, looking only at you, not the house. He's asked no basic house hunting questions. He has no curiosity about location of the oil tank, type of heat, your typical electric bill, no desire to visit the house, or even walk the circumference of the property. It's as if he's already seen it before.

"I've already gone through this kind of thought process. I'm not selling my house, particularly if the buyer plans to cut down my trees. And no way will I indirectly sell this house to the gas company."

He crosses his arms rocks back on his heels. "So, you're that happy here in this town?"

"I'm not selling. It's none of your business whether I'm happy or not. Don't you want to talk about the ecosystem again? I noticed you changed the subject rather quickly when we touched on it. Suddenly you wanted to see the bridge."

"I've never had a good mind for science."

"I'm not selling. I'm staying here."

"OK. It's a great town. I guess you're happy here." You open the door for him.

"But I don't know," he says as he pauses before the open door. "A town with people who press charges for some prank involving an eagle statue on a gate?"

You tighten your grip of the doorknob, waiting for him to leave. He turns as if he's changed his mind.

"And you know they'll get them," he continues. "A friend of mine told me there's a camera in the eyes of those eagles. They'll probably see someone on the tape right at that exact moment the sheet is tossed."

"How interesting you just happen to know someone who has that insider information. And you're not even from town."

"I'm a lawyer. We know all kinds of gossip."

You leave the open door and walk to the stairs, ignoring him. Your mind is racing. All you can think about is how much trouble Brit is in now. Real animals are fucking dying, and he'll get disbarred over meaningless bronze statues.

"One more thing." He holds up his finger, waits for you to turn. You realize you still have a mug in your hand. You consider what it would do to his forehead. "Let me give you an idea of what we're talking about. As far as money. We'll take the assessed market value and add fifty percent."

"You haven't even seen the entire house."

"We're interested in this location, not the house. I don't have time to see everything, and I'm sure you're not going to offer. I'm just saying we'll begin the bid at one-point-five times market."

"I'm not sure I follow."

"We'll assess the market value of both halves of this property then multiply it by one point five. It's too good to turn down."

You stand, this time quietly thinking over the offer.

"I think we'd expect you to move away. Like, you know, away." He stares at you.

"You want me out of town?"

"No, not out of town. Out of the entire county. That's an expectation of the buyer at this point. We buy you out, you leave the county." He holds up his hand. "Think about it a while. You're probably mad right now, indignant, determined more than ever to stay. But you may change your mind. Give it a month." He reaches in his pocket, retrieves his card, walks to the stairs, reaches for your hand, and places it in the center of your palm.

You stand and watch the door close, listen to the high-pitched hum of his car backing out your driveway, then study his card.

"Bart Logan," you whisper. "Sterns, Howell and Logan." Why is that name familiar?

# Blue Jay Memo

*He's back.*
*Who?*
*Stay on limb*
*Dive bomb!*
*Shut uuup!*
*Who?*

*The male with black head fur in large black motorized mobile nest.*

*Conflict!*
*Conflict!*
*Conflict!*

*He enters nest! Predator is with female host!*

*Conflict!*
*Conflict!*
*Conflict!*
*Stay on limb!*
*Dive bomb into glass covered apertures!*
*No. Stay.*
*Come back!*

*We wait. Male leaves female host nest.*

*Follow him!*
*Come back!*
*Shut uuup!*
*Follow him.*

*We follow. He travels several paths until he arrives at land cut off from coast, where dead fish originated, where we retrieved marker to alert female host.*

# Chapter 24

*Evolving appetites*

TODAY, BRIT ARRIVES to update you on the wrongful death lawsuit. His summary occurs while you both walk Fred. Lolly does not accompany you because the labradoodle trots a longer distance than Lolly's typical adventure—slightly more than the length of the driveway. It's late afternoon, warm, but he still wears long khakis. You wear shorts and a blue t-shirt with "I Oppose Inertia" in black bold letters marching across your breasts. Brit stares at the meme.

"I made this for a march several years back," you say, after he stares at your shirt a beat too long. "Remember when the world started shrugging it all off—the tainted news, the rigged elections, the corruption, the outrageous judges, the dying crows? It just became too much for everyone to handle so we had that march against apathy? It was my favorite march."

"Nothing more powerful than your constant motion, that's for sure."

You sense a slight edge to the comment. You wonder if he has changed his mind, if now he wants you to turn yourself in for the damaged eagle, which would at least get him off the hook. His membership in the Connecticut Bar Association is important. Who cares what impact of the damaged relic has upon your lawsuit when it could cost someone his career?

"So, let's walk south," you say. "We may pick up a breeze in that direction."

You walk briskly as you think about vandalism charges. How many years will vandalism get you? Surely, they'll let a woman off with community service.

He tells you the Hamilton lawyers are stubbornly committed to a jury trial. The plaintiffs refuse to settle even though Brit has told them you're constrained by financial limitations because the car insurance company refuses to cover the liability. The insurance company insists their policy does not cover lawsuits over cars parked in the middle of roadways. Brit hoped the lack of that all-important deep pocket will inspire the Hamilton's to reconsider and settle. But, no, they won't.

"Has anyone contacted you about the eagles?" You try act as if the thought suddenly occurred to you that you haven't been obsessing over it ever since the strange lawyer came and left.

"Have you been listening to me?"

"Yes. So, is that a yes or no about the eagles?"

"Your covered eagles? Yes. The police want to question me. I told them it was a ridiculous case and I'm too busy to talk at the moment."

"You can do that?" You feel your breath quicken, and you try to inhale and exhale slowly through your pursed lips. Brit looks over at you until you stop. When he looks back, you inhale slowly again. You wonder if it was Louis who wants to question him. You can handle Louis. "So, you can simply say no?" You say as you look at a brown lawn to your right, which stimulates good thoughts about the neighbor and calms you slightly.

"No. I go in tomorrow for questioning."

The blood leaves your head and you slow your pace.

"Look, Brit." You stop walking. Brit turns around to face you, which causes his dog Fred to lean into the leash, tightening the chain collar around its neck and causing a hoarse coughing pant. "I'm going to turn myself in today, so don't you worry."

He yanks the leash. Fred whines then sits.

"No. You're not going to do that. We've discussed this. Your case is getting complicated and a stupid confession like that will make you look like . . ."

"An idiot."

"Impulsive. You're not an idiot. You get upset, and when you act, you make very bad choices."

"You're on the tape. You're on the tape right before it goes blank. You can't lie. They have you on the tape and you're a lawyer and you have to be honest. You'll get kicked out of the bar. For a sheet covered bronze eagle. I'll go to jail for being mean to statues. They'll realize how absurd all of this is because, dear God, crows have died, fish are dying, and birds are falling from the sky. Live things, you know, and meanwhile I go to jail for an inanimate object."

"Don't you get it? When will you get it? No one cares anymore."

"Eventually they will care about life again, Brit. The elections will come around in December. I know, I know, don't say it. But maybe this time things are different."

"Different?"

"Maybe. There's always a chance."

"Elections aren't going to change your legal problems." Brit walks again, slowly. A few people are out in the yards, gardening. Brit regards one of our neighbors tending to impatiens by her mailbox. She looks up briefly to wave and smiles when he returns the gesture. You don't. Impatiens need water and you will not enable her environmental selfishness. You consider saying something about this fact, but instead start inhaling slowly again, blowing softly out your pursed lips. Thank goodness for those few yoga classes.

"I'll tell Louis that I did it but to hold off arresting me until the civil suit is over," you say in a very low voice.

"They can't find that tape," Brit says. "So, they have no idea I was there right before it was covered. They just want to question me because I played tennis with Jack. I know how to avoid questions."

"They lost the tape? How do you know that?"

"I asked if they had the video recording. The officer who called me said they were trying to get it, but the Independence Island Association cannot find that particular recording. So, for once we're lucky. For once. Just keep your mouth shut till after the suit. Surely no one really cares. It's just the usual small-town silliness. It'll pass."

You don't say anything because you know that you're the usual silliness, not the town. You're the one who does ridiculous things the town must tolerate. You close your eyes a moment. There he is, Bart, with that faux earnest expression, mentioning the eagles and the tape, the one tape that is now missing. You open your eyes and walk. In silence.

Blue jays screech overhead. Sparrows chirp loudly at each other, fighting over a mate or food. A few other passerines sing. You can't identify them by their songs. You wish you could.

Brit breathes almost as loud as Fred pants.

"OK, continue with the lawsuit. I'm ready." You slow down so Brit will breathe more softly.

"I upped the offer. They refused it," he says after a moment of slow sauntering.

"Which was what?"

"Fifty thousand dollars."

The sound of a car engine in the distance. Your feet tapping the pavement.

"You did tell them there are no deep pockets. The insurance company won't budge. They have a sophisticated law firm, yes? Surely they understand that."

"Sterns, Howell, Logan is a big firm, yes," Brit says after a pause. "They still turned it down."

"They think I have a lot of money because Lawrence was a Wall Street investor. They hear Wall Street, they see big bucks. All my money is reserved for Haley. I won't let go of it."

"Well, you'll have to."

"I'll transfer it to Switzerland."

"That won't work anymore. You can't hide money from a civil suit verdict. Just can't." They stop a moment so Fred can pee, but the dog doesn't pee, he looks toward the wooded area, sniffs the air, and barks. Brit tells Fred to hush. Fred sniffs the air again.

You're quiet because you're overwhelmed by the gravity of your situation— your shameful mistake, your stupid fence climbing, the dilemma your actions now present for what's left of your family. You've already wasted money on the house reconstruction. The lawyer who visited you was right. The reconstruction impaired property value. Now this—which will potentially disrupt your safety net not only for you but for your daughter. You want to leave me money, but now the only inheritance you pass on is an abundance of ruin. Brit notices your face.

"This is a game of chicken. All lawsuits are. The judge is getting annoyed, though, and is pushing for a trial by next week. So, we'll have to begin jury selection soon. And Lorraine." Brit touches your shoulder. "You need to think about being presentable. Make sure you dress conservative."

"I'll wear a good T-shirt, maybe one with a bible quote."

"I'd love that, but I'm thinking a dress for the jury. And another thing, you need to lay off the water pollution stuff for a while."

You stop walking again. Fred walks back and sniffs your legs.

"So, that's what this is about, right? Getting me to shut up about the septic tank problem."

"That's not what this's about. If there's a septic tank issue."

You open your mouth and Brit holds both hands up palms out. Fred sits at attention, probably thinking the gesture is for him not Lorraine.

"If there's a problem?" you say, your voice raised slightly with a change in pitch that indicates you're getting ready to shout. "It took us forever to validate elevated nitrogen and phosphorus levels off the coast of Independence Island, but we did get the results. It proves there's a pollution problem. The fish have left us. Fish are fed up with all of us."

"Yes, I know. I'm on your side. I'm just saying, the town doesn't want to move fast on this. It's expensive, and well, could indicate a big problem for property values. That is, if septic tanks are a chronic issue with the town. This is sensitive. And it may explode in your face."

"Significant? Significant is global warming, because it's too late to act. And no one will ever act because we have no accountability from our legislators. We're frozen nationally. But not locally. Finally, we have something we can handle on our own, without having to protest and scream at worthless legislators. We can do this locally. What's the big deal? You build a town septic system. Expensive, yes, but it can be done."

You both walk again and Brit says nothing.

As you turn into a neighborhood with even larger homes and hemlocks lined up before them like sentinels, Fred barks furiously. Across the street, another dog barks, which inspires more barks the next house over. Fred stops, looks ahead, then barks again.

Axle Rose's voice rises from your cell phone. You tap your phone and say, "I'm walking, and the dogs are barking, so I can't hear much." You have no idea who is on the other end because you never check the I.D. and usually never answer, but you want an interruption now.

"Lorraine? Where are you and whose dog is that? It's not Lolly."

"Nan?"

"I can barely hear you."

You put a finger over the hole on your cell phone and ask Fred to please be quiet. Brit says, hush, in his firm but kind voice. Fred barks.

You grab Fred's snout and hold it. "You have to hush, I'm on the phone. Just a sec, then I'll let you bark." Fred shakes his head, but you don't let go. Brit puts his palm gently on Fred's back. Fred whines and you finally let go. "Now hush or I will have to hold your mouth closed again." Fred walks over to Brit, sits on his foot, and leans into his legs.

"Lorraine, what did you do to the dog?" Nan says.

"I'm not cruel to animals. I'm a member of Unleash Our Dogs. This dog has a long nose, so I use it. I have a dog with no nose, as you know, so when she gets loud, I have to be creative. Long noses should be used."

Fred hangs his head, moves his eyes up to Brit.

"I should obviously call back, it's just that I've got some news on your owlets. And the fish. The fish died of oxygen depletion of course. But there were some strange toxins in the liver. Low to medium concentrations. We found some citalopram and fluoxetine. Interesting."

"Cital what am? Is there any way to put that into English?" Fred stands and faces the hemlocks again. Something is obviously moving the underbrush.

"Antidepressants. The fish died of oxygen depletion, common with areas with lots of algae and high concentrations of nitrogen and phosphorus. But they also had antidepressants in their livers. This can be indirectly related to waste in the water. People in the area are taking anti-depressants, their waste reflects that. No way to prove it, though, so we can only speculate. The owlets were malnourished. They hadn't been eating. Who knows the reasons why."

Fred starts barking again.

"I can't figure any connection between the fish problem and owls," Nan continues. "I just don't think the fish and bird deaths are connected. I'll let you go so you don't hold that dog's nose again. Lolly's due for her nail trim, you know. Bye."

Nan hangs up before you can respond. You tap off the phone, still thinking about the fish on antidepressants.

Fred's barking persists. Obviously, something is hidden behind the trees. You put your finger to your mouth, then motion with both of your hands for Brit to walk Fred away from the area. After Brit leads Fred across the street and quiets him, you creep around the trees and that's when you see it clearly.

It's about four feet high and stands with regal presence near a large cedar that centers the lawn. A great blue heron. Herons feed on fish, sometimes mice, but they rarely leave the waterways. They hunt in tributaries, ponds, inland water streams. You don't live anywhere near water; no creek is within a mile of your neighborhood.

Suddenly, the Heron stabs the ground. It shakes its head vigorously, then points its beak to the sky and swallows the chipmunk.

# Blue Jay Memo

Days pass. Food is scarcer. We eat seeds. Today, male with white head fur and red beak arrives with yappy dog.

Make it shut uuup.
Do not like dog.
Will not follow dog.
You will.
Will not.

We suspect male with white head fur is engaging in mating rituals again. We chirp and think about this while they engage in uneventful perambulation.

Female host appears interested in heron's meal. Herons eat chipmunks now. We've known this a while because there's no fish. Female host seems perplexed by heron's new food source. Human ignorance never ceases to surprise us.

They return to Children of Athena home nest. We follow. We perch, perch, perch, perch. Male touches female host with beak, then enters nest.

They mate?
Mate?
We cannot see.
Squirrel!
Come back!
Shut uuup.

We don't know what happens in nest. We now suspect that even with no brightly colored decoration, male's mating rituals are consistently successful. She's easy to please.

# Chapter 25

*Flock biking*

DAD AND I didn't catch many fish. In fact, many days we only felt bites. We weren't really bad, or at least Dad wasn't bad because he understood the important tools of the sport—choice of lure, quality of lines and reel, knowledge of tides, impact of weather on fish location. Dad knew all the fish facts and taught them to me, although I never memorized them. While fishing knowledge was important, it wasn't as important as the art of the sport—the light touch of the rod, the jerk of line at the perfect moment after a nibble. The creative, almost spiritual, understanding of the hunt evaded both of us. I always thought it was because we weren't hungry like the experts.

Sometimes, on slow days, the experts would visit. We'd put up our rods and become students of the greatest fishers on earth. The ospreys. An osprey nest was tucked neatly in an old white pine's top branches on the rocky shores near Hooper's Cove on Long Island Sound. We'd go there to fish when Dad was too lazy to drive an hour to a fresh water lake. No one else seemed to care about the nest, so fortunately the ospreys weren't bothered by camcorders streaming their every activity. The parents fished constantly because they had to feed three nestlings. They would soar high above the Sound, circling and studying the water movement. After a target was selected, the osprey would pause briefly before transforming into a feathered torpedo. Right before entering the water its talons would spring forward to stab the fish; the water would explode, its frothy violence surrounding bird and fish. If successful, the bird would lift off the water and veer toward us in a haughty display of its capture.

I cannot remember the last time I've seen an osprey.

THE UNLEASH OUR Dogs ordinance fails at a Board of Selectman vote. Dogs still must be leashed at all times. One would think the activism would fade, because angry speeches are now simply angry speeches with no real purpose. But, no, Unleash Our Dogs is still going strong, although they have added other causes to supplement dog freedom. They have organized another important meeting at the park to discuss the addition of another cause. Everyone will be riding their bikes to the meeting location because—and you just love this, right Mom?—the cause they are adding is: More Bike Paths for Westbrook. The organization is now Unleash Our Dogs, More Bike Paths, and More Affordable Housing. And, of course, Dead Fish, although they don't mention that cause too often. The bike path advocacy actually has a greater chance of going somewhere, certainly more than dog freedom, and definitely more than affordable housing.

You decide to join the excursion because you still desperately need their dead fish support and assistance. Their assistance to date has included the following: attendance at one dead fish meeting, reading your emails, and reading your blog posts. They did help with posters—ten posters and only one volunteer showed up. You force me to bike with the group because, you say, "One needs a stable presence when one is pushed to the limit of tolerance."

I have to admit I look forward to witnessing you participate in your most abhorred activity. Besides four-way stop sign scofflaws, there's nothing more infuriating to you than dozens of bicycle riders clogging up streets, which you refer to as "flock biking." Flock biking contributed to one of your jail experiences.

Remember that one, Mom? You had become so frustrated with twenty-five bikers clogging a forty mile-per-hour thruway, you passed them, then slowed down to five miles-per-hour in order to force them to understand how a car driver feels. This led to yelling arguments out the car window. The apparent "flock bike leader"—a man in a tight white shirt decorated with advertisements, most of which were oil and gas company logos—demanded that you pull over. You refused, continuing to shout insults. "A biker advertising fossil fuels is like a cancer patient advertising Monsanto," you yelled at him. He then told you he was actually a lobbyist for Monsanto. That's how he ended up in the ditch and you in jail. It was all an accident. Kind of. I was twelve at the time and went to jail, too, because I had to. You were my mom. It was one of my finest moments. I beat Louis and the entire police department at chess. Not one officer could beat me. I won ice cream and your early release. Dad was not pleased.

We are waiting at the end of our driveway when Lydia Russo and about seven friends poke down the street on their bikes. They stop in front of our house and look at it for a while, a few longingly, as if the short ride at a pace slower than I can trot has already tired them out. They all have the same bike riding sartorial taste. Tight pants and tight shirts with logos. Lydia has the most logos but none of them are fossil fuel advertisements, thank goodness. A few logos are popular food products, which could indicate a tolerance of Monsanto. You appear to notice the processed food company logos. My eyes plead with you to leave it alone. You say nothing.

"We're quite upset with the failure of our ordinance," Lydia says when she steps off her bike after they arrive at the end of our driveway. "We do appreciate all your letters." You wrote two letters to the editors that the editor allowed—after the obligatory trimming—since they were not related to fish or bird deaths. "We of course will protest but we have other matters to discuss. Shall we?" She sweeps her left hand in the direction of the street as if displaying a prize. Before you say anything, everyone steps on pedals and takes off.

You and I stay behind them, riding single file. For a while we only hear our breath and distant cars on the distant highway. Lydia slows down until she is at your side. Other women slow and talk and ride in true "flock bike" formation, which means you will soon have irritating thoughts.

"I think horizontal bike riding disrupts traffic," you say. "And, of course, when you talk on a bike, not everyone can hear."

"Well, we have more rights to the road than cars," Lydia says. "As you know, we advocate for bike routes, but until then, we take to the streets. Free dogs, free bikes."

"Are bikes in jail?" I say. "Mom knows how to get them out. She's very good at that." You look back at me, your brows pointing to your nose, indicating humor is not appropriate now. I stop thinking.

"We want bike paths on all roads." Lydia seems to want a meeting while we ride. "All roads, even roads that currently ban bikes. You know those roads with medians? We feel strongly they should open up to bikes. Who cares if it slows traffic? Who cares if those selfish, lazy people driving gas guzzling cars are frustrated? Free our dogs, free our bikes, and free our land for the poor."

I can see your irritation in your increased pace. Lydia has left out an important cause.

"Lydia," you say as you pass other members of the group and realign linearly. Lydia and I struggle to keep up. "First, I drive a Prius, which is a hybrid. Just to remind you. Also, did you realize that crowding out cars forces them to slow down, then speed up, then slow down, which is bad for gas mileage? Our goal is to reduce fossil fuel usage."

A few cars are lined up behind us now. They patiently wait for us to do something, and we don't. You look back and speed up.

"Furthermore, haven't you left out an important issue?" you shout back at us. "Or do we no longer have dead fish and dead birds on our agendas."

"Oh, of course, we're concerned about dead fish, and the septic tank situation but, honestly, Lorraine . . ." Lydia's breathing stops her from talking because now she has to pump faster to keep up with you, someone in better shape than any other rider here. "Where is that going anyway?"

You stand on your pedals and speed up again. Lydia starts wheezing. I speed up because I can take it.

"They've blocked your letters to the newspapers," Lydia shouts. "Of course, you wrote so damn many of them"—she pants—"everyone figures one day . . ." She stands up to pump her bike. We have left most women behind us. " . . . we'll simply eat farm fish, you know. That's what Representative what-his-face told me. He said . . ."

"They're paid to be dumb. So, they're dumb," you shout as you slow down.

" . . . he goes, 'Who cares, Ms. Russo. Eat farm fish.' That's what he told me."

"That's what they tell all constituents who call," you say. "It must have been a memo passed around Congress."

You slow down because now you're panting, too, and once again we're a bunched-up group of slow-moving bikers. The cars start swerving out in an attempt to get around us. Everyone chats. One woman who wears a bright green bike helmet, suggests that, given global warming's impact upon the coral reefs and oxygen levels in the water, refurbishing septic tanks will be like placing a small band aid upon severed leg. Others shake their head in agreement. Most of the women are out of breath and cannot talk. Lydia and the woman in a green helmet are the only ones now talking to you because they are in reasonable shape. I'm in OK shape only because I'm twenty-five and my heart has not taken that downward turn yet. I also do yoga.

"Well, herons are eating chipmunks now," you shout.

"Blue or green?" Lydia says.

A car speeds around us and honks.

You yell at the car, "This is not my idea! I agree with you!"

"Why does it matter whether the heron was a great blue heron or a green heron," I say. "They both eat fish"

"That's right," Lydia says. "I just wondered, because a blue heron is bigger and would probably need more food. That's interesting about the chipmunk, though. I never knew they ate anything but fish."

We ride and you look back at me. I'm right behind you, eager to arrive at the park for the real meeting. I can just make out the cluster of trees beyond the traffic light about a half a mile away.

"Life finds ways to survive," you say as you slow for the traffic light. "It makes adjustments. So, Lydia, Martha, Sally, all of you. Are you willing to adjust? Because if the heron has to eat the mice and chipmunks, I assume the osprey will eat mice too. What is the owl going to eat? And if the owl eats other small living creatures, well, what will happen to all of them? I certainly wouldn't be letting my cat out nowadays. And those small yappy terriers? Keep them on a leash!"

The light turns. We all pedal. Two cars speed past us, one extends his hand in prime formation.

"Humans need to eat, too," you continue. "It will come back to haunt us."

"Farmed veggies. Farmed fish," one woman says.

You slow down and pull over. Others pull over by you. "I'm pulling over so fossil fuel guzzlers can pass us. We're disrupting roads with our bikes and our talk that's going nowhere. Fish are dying for God's sake, Lydia. There is death and it matters. I will not advocate for no leashes and flock biking, which, by the way, is very annoying, because dead fish are being ignored."

"Flock biking?"


YOU AND I ride home alone in silence. You have now left another group. Two women did agree with you about the fish, which gives me hope that you could start a *coup d'état*, which would eventually become another small group splintered off the larger group. That would be better than isolating yourself again.

When we arrive home, we notice a business card taped to the front door. Your phone beeps as we park our bikes. After listening to the message, you tap your phone quickly and put it to your ear. It's the scientist from Save Our Planet, the environmental site you filled with comments, emails, and messages. He wants to meet with you soon, real soon, like tomorrow. He's in town working on something. "You may be on to something," he tells you.

You hang up as you unpeel the business card from your front door. It's Bart Logan, the lawyer. On the back, there's a note.

*"How's it going? You may want to meet again soon. Next week? Call me."*

You read the name of the firm out loud slowly. "Sterns, Howell, and Logan." You then whisper it. "Oh my God!" You pull out your phone and tap. "Oh my God," you say again and again.

# Chapter 26

*The lawyer connection*

AS YOU PACE in front of Brit's desk, you squeeze your left hand's fingers and dig at your index finger's cuticles. The nail's polish is chipped and faded, and a few nails have jagged edges in need of filing. Brit leans back in his chair and studies your movements.

"Tell me again, Lorraine, exactly what this Bart Logan said. This is something you should've brought to my attention."

You stop to brush a few strands of hair from your eyes. You regard the leather club chair, wonder if you should sit, start pacing again.

"I didn't tell you because it was ridiculous. I'm not selling my house to some sleazy L.L.C .represented by a sleazy lawyer because they don't like my presence in the community. Do you think I'd do something like that, Brit? Look at me."

You stop in front of his desk, your hands on your hips. You're not wearing your usual style. You have on black linen pants and a soft peach sleeveless sweater because you've been practicing new attire for your court date. You're also planning to meet the scientist who heads Save the Planet this afternoon concerning your internet messages.

"I'm looking. I see a very frightened person."

"I'm not a frightened person. I don't scare easily."

"You're scared, Lorraine. Can we have more detail, please?"

You sit, rub your face a moment. "OK, he said they would pay me one and a half times market value, whatever that comes to, you know. My property is damaged. But then he said there would also be a kind of gentleman's agreement. They want me away from here. I have to move. Not just out of town, but out of the entire county. I'm assuming they don't want me anywhere near the coast. I asked who this was. He said he worked for an L.L.C. Truly that's it. Except . . ."

"An L.L.C just means he represents a group of interested parties. I called around but couldn't get any information on this guy. He's with Stern, Howell, and Logan, yes, but he's with a branch located in Westchadon, New York. From what I could uncover, he does indeed represent real estate developers, some big names in New York. Why he's here is a question. Stern, Howell of course would want to keep an appearance of that Chinese Wall. And, well, they wouldn't dare put one of their Connecticut guys on this. It all infuriates me. It's inexcusable and unethical. I should write a complaint to the Connecticut Bar Association. But of course, he'd deny it. Then we have your word against his. And your word right now is not worth much. And then, my bar status may be in question if they find the tape at Independence Island showing me talking to someone before the vandalism." He tosses his curled fingers in the air as he says vandalism.

"And that's another thing."

"What's another thing?"

"Before you interrupted me, I was going to mention that before the asshole left, he said something about the eagles, something like, 'Why would you want to live in a town that freaks out over a sheet tossed over eagles at some gated community?' Why would he bring that up? And, sure, it's been mentioned in the papers, but how would he know? And then he said, he was sure they'd find it was some kids. That would be on that tape, he said. He knew they had cameras."

"Oh, for crying out loud." Brit leans back in his chair, closes his eyes. "They have the tape. It's so silly, the whole thing."

"My word is not that bad."

"What?"

"You said my word was bad. I've only spent time in jail because of activism. All activists get arrested. You're not really an activist if you haven't been arrested."

"What are you if you're an activist with no arrests?"

"A wimp. But if you're worried about yourself, Brit, you're better than the assholes who live here, but maybe a notch below me and others who went to jail." You stand up and pace again.

"OK, so I think we can guess why the Hamiltons are pressing for a trial."

"They're colluding to get rid of me," you say to your feet. "They think I'll be too embarrassed to sit through a trial of my peers. All the character assassinations, evidence of other scofflaws, my lack of judgment, you know. One Partiers think activists lack judgment. Our opinion is insane, theirs is reasonable."

"It would be a bad trial," Brit says. "Sterns, Howell will make sure we have an all-white, conservative jury. Then of course you've also alienated your liberal friends."

"Unleash Our Dogs may possibly support me. I've had a wee argument with the leader, but that'll go away because I was right, and she was wrong."

"Lorraine. Sit down."

You sit again and unclasp your hands, as if that were why he said sit, and if you unclasped them you could stand again.

"So, the lawsuit will be dropped, or settled quickly, if you take the offer," Brit says carefully. "And why not move to another county? You can start over. I'm not sure I've ever understood why you're still here. You can still do what you are doing elsewhere."

You stop squeezing your hands and place them on his desk. You open your mouth, but no words exit.

"I'm not staying here," Brit continues. "I've got an offer on a house in Ridgeway."

You stand, palms still on his desk, and lean over it.

"You're asking me to simply accept this blackmail because it's hopeless? Leave this town so that the others will have their low maintenance expense, their little delusions. Life will simply continue the same way? We all simply adjust to whatever crap flies in our face? We force nature to adjust to our crap so we can keep doing what we're doing? Who will feed my birds? What are they going to eat? There's not much left. Our drought is out of control. Our trees are starting to die. The grass is brown. Our coastal waters have no oxygen. The fish are gone. Birds are dying. And you know what some of these aquatic birds are doing? Eating inland prey. Where does that leave the owl and red-tailed hawks?"

"OK. You're right, Lorraine. Save the birds. Save the fish. But don't blame me when you lose your daughter. You could lose a lot here. Think about that."

You look down at your cell phone for a moment—a message from your next appointment. You say you have to go, you're late, as if you're a very busy person and what he says barely registers due to your busy-ness. But you don't rush away, you stand at his door a moment. "Tell me something, Brit. Ridgeway is out of the county. Is that a coincidence?"

THE SCIENTIST'S NAME is Lionel Goldberg and he doesn't look like a scientist, he looks like a hip graduate student. Light brown hair, tight jeans, hoody, rectangular glasses. He appears to be about thirty-something. The café is bigger than our kitchen but smaller than our living room. It has five pine tables and four windows with chintz curtains. Lionel blows carefully on his green tea before delivering his brief bio. He teaches biology at a prep school but spends most of his summers researching papers for blogs and environmental foundations. He has quickly moved up in Save the Planet, achieving the title of president in only three years. He looks around as he talks, as if anxious about others. It's two in the afternoon and only one other table is occupied. He leans in conspiratorially to tell you he's impressed with your tenacity. Your observation of the heron's diet reveals a certain curiosity. Herons do eat mice, he informs you, but rarely fly inland to feast upon rodents. It could definitely be related to the absence of fish because the fish problem is not confined to this one area. Dying fish have been spotted up and down the Connecticut coastline. Some communities in New Jersey and Chesapeake Bay have now reported sightings of dead fish. Birds may understand this, he says. There is a chance they have begun to change their diet.

He asks questions, listens to you, laughs at your certainty, your cockiness. He likes it. He says they need that now.

His phone pings. He checks it, taps quickly. Checks again. Taps again.

"So, why are we meeting? Do you think our septic tanks are the problem?"

He taps his phone again, as if your comment is competing with a more important comment.

"Yes. Of course, it has something to do with it," he finally says, putting his phone back on the table. "As does plastic pollution, warming waters, climate change, water pollution now unchecked due to deregulation. We could have a dumping problem somewhere on the coast because the landfills and manufacturing waste are overflowing."

"And I suppose we can't really do anything. I mean, what can we do?"

"We'll pay you," he says, ignoring her nihilism. "Not well, but we'll pay. We need writers, aggressive, angry writers. We need petitions. Blogs articles, not just for our site, but for the dark web. As you know the internet is risky if you become too popular. Hacking. Professional trolls. Hate mail. Death threats. We have all the usual problems. We fight back the way they fight us. We send commenters out there on social media to argue, fill up the comment sections. We protect you with VPNs, so don't worry."

"I accept."

"No," he says. "Don't accept the job until you think about it. You may not want to associate with me." You laugh, because it's always been about everyone else associating with you. "Look, it's not funny. I've spent time in prison. I jumped a police officer who was beating a friend during a protest. The protest had been categorized as illegal after a rock was tossed through a store window."

"I accept the job," you say again. "And I want you to come to dinner. Get out your calendar. I'd like you to meet someone. You went to prison! You're perfect!"

# Blue Jay Memo

Female host flocks on manual mobile perch with other female humans.

Conflict!
Conflict!
Conflict!

No conflict.
Follow!

We follow female host who travels with offspring back to home nest.

We eat.

We teach babies to sing and fly. Babies scream. They drive us crazy with screaming and demands. But we love them.

Female host travels in motorized mobile nest to meet mate at red nest, so we send elders, a few two-year-olds, some females. Nothing substantial reported.

Next day, female host travels 1.2 miles south and 4.3 miles east of Children of Athena. Strange, unfamiliar location.

We can't see inside glass apertures
Bored. Bored.
Hawk! Hawk!
Hawk! Hawk!
Hawk! Hawk!

Hawk gone.

Insect!
No, rock.

*Bored. Bored.*
*She exits!*
*Look who she's with!*

*Wait, she is with that male with tight appendage covering and small glass covered eyes!*
*Who?*
*Male with tight appendage covering and small glass covered eyes.*
*So?*
*He's been perching with the large female with glass covered eyes.*
*Who? What?*
*Was this noted in memos?*
*No.*
*Why?*
*Two-year-olds. What can we say?*

*Is he predatory?*
*What?*
*Is he predator? Conflict potential?*
*Two-year-olds say no conflict potential.*

*He's fine.*
*Where've you been?*
*Teasing squirrel.*
*We didn't know about this male.*
*Two-year-olds. What can we say?*

*Come back!*
*On limb now!*
*Shut uuup.*

*We chirp to calm down.*

*This male human with small glass covered eyes and tight lower appendage covering leaves in small red motorized mobile nest. We do not send reconnaissance team to follow him. We are hungry. We follow female host home.*

# Chapter 27

*Sexy activists cure apathy*

"I USED TO be against bird feeders. That was when we had healthy vegetation and an abundance of worms, insects. Acorns. Now, I'm not sure certain birds would be here without feeders. Still, feeding birds presents problems." Lionel stands by the bay window, staring at the birds as he talks. I'm right behind him, listening and staring—at his tight black jeans, curly brown tendrils spilling over his collared sports shirt. I want him to turn and look at me because his best feature are those blue eyes only partly covered by small, black rectangular glasses.

How did this cool guy get tangled up with you? A man with a voice that could host an NPR show, not that I'm thrilled with NPR hosts. Tight little waist. Skinny jeans. And those rectangle glasses that add intelligence. Of course, he seems taken with you, laughing easily when you toss out your witty comments, leaning in as if every word is important. He even touched your arm once. I wonder if he's one of those sophisticated types who'd enjoy an affair with a wild and carefree older woman who has long legs and high cheek bones. It's tough having you as a mom.

"I'm not the only responsible feeder," you say, quickly. "Haley cleans them. So, if not for my daughter, we'd have sicker birds. She's like that." You have returned from filling all the feeders. Lionel has been watching you with interest.

I busy myself boiling pasta and shredding parmesan cheese. Oh please, I'm thinking, please stop talking about me, Mom. You wipe your hand with a napkin. Lionel turns from the window and roams around the kitchen. He walks behind me, peruses our cabinets, tosses a napkin in the trash can, touching its liner.

"You use plastic trash liners?"

"It's my only sin," you say. "I have solar panels, which, as you know, don't work as well nowadays. I tried but just couldn't do the paper bag trash. And besides, trees are killed for paper."

"Inconvenient," he says, crossing his arms. "And expensive for you." He looks at me.

"Mom always appreciates irony. She lives it," I say.

"So, then you have some empathy for those who don't want the inconvenience and expense of moving septic tanks," he says. "Or the inconvenience and expense of driving high mileage cars, or the inconvenience and expense of moving to solar power."

"Actually, not all the women in my previous environmental group are against my septic tank crusade, they simply were shut out of the discussion."

"She's avoiding your point," I say. "Banks do lend money to many homeowners who opt to turn their homes solar. So, we do that. Just saying."

"So, your mother is out to save the world of fish and birds, and you are trying to keep the local economy going, and lending money for environmental work? Or maybe you're just making sure there's one honest banker in town, right?" He winks at me. I feel my face burn.

"She's a good activist," you say, as if thrilled we've moved to me. "She used to fish with her father all the time, always catch and release. She's smarter than me and is able to acclimate. I can't acclimate."

A blue jay flutters down and perches on the back of a patio chair. It turns its head to look at the bay window, as if spying on us. A few more join it, until several fill our patio, staring into our bay window.

"That's pretty amazing," Lionel says, returning to the window. "Most birds keep a healthy distance from humans. I guess they're keeping an eye on their major source of food." He looks toward the kitchen counter, where I'm tossing the pasta as I listen. "So, tell me, Haley. You used to be a fisherwoman. Do you eat fish?"

"We never ate the fish we caught. And no, we don't eat fish now. Who would eat fish? They're swimming in human waste here."

"Well, that's what I want to talk to you about." He returns his attention to you, but you're lost in thought. I'm finished with the pasta sauce, pour it over the noodles, toss, then transfer to plates. Lionel takes the plates to the table. We sit. The blue jays perch in the maple tree. I watch Lionel carefully stab his pasta, place the full tines upon his spoon, and twirl until the pasta wraps the fork tightly. He pushes the knot of pasta into his mouth softly, leaving a small red residue on his upper lip. You haven't touched the food, only picked at the salad. I'm thinking your meeting with Brit about the lawsuit did not go well. You refuse to discuss anything with me. But I know how to research.

"Your mom is on to something that's actually not small. You know this, right, Haley?" Now you begin to eat, stabbing your pasta, twirling fast on your plate, and shoving it into your mouth. A few drops of red sauce splatter upon the table. Lionel looks at me, and I try to avoid staring at you. "We've got major problems world wide with aquatic life. Coral reef bleaching, for one. Our oceans absorb about ninety percent of the world heat and carbon dioxide. So, as we warm up, the ocean becomes more acidic, which leads to more stress, more oxygen depletion, more loss of life, more coral reef bleaching. We've yelled, marched about this for years, but as you both know, the political situation has closed down national resolution of these societal costs. It's, of course, quite understood that our votes don't really count on a national scale, even on a state level in some places. We're hoping we can change that. Do vote this time around, by the way." He stops so I can think about that. Voting. How many times are people going to tell me in July to vote this December? "We've fallen into an environmental torpor. Your mother isn't just another passionate voice. When the world falls into despair, the crazy sounding people end up being heroes. We need heroes now. And they all look a bit like your mother."

"We're all broken," you say as if you just woke up from a deep sleep. "Not just our environment. And, really, do we still have a free market?"

"Mom, I'm a banker. We do still have capitalism. I can attest to that."

"Oh, it works for the few. For the rest of the world, it's broken."

You tear off a bit of bread, delicately push it into your mouth. I take a moment to regard you. Hair dancing around your forehead. Intense green eyes. Casually-cool-while-still-chaotic way you hold your long lanky body. So, perhaps this sexy man will fall in love with you. Both of you will travel the coastal regions organizing protests. You will mourn dead animals, he will mourn dead trees. Maybe he'll adopt me. I'll have a surrogate father I want to sleep with. I will then seek therapy to resolve my anger over a mother who steals my crushes because she's this poet who cares more deeply about the planet than I do. I'll envy your lovely relationship at night, make car loans, open IRAs, and checking accounts during the day.

All of this goes through my mind as you say, "I may have started something, but I don't think I'm strong enough to finish it."

"What does that mean?" I say.

Lionel pours himself more tea and refreshes your cup, then mine. You look down at your hands. I open the window. The evening sky has a strange glow, as if lit by a distant hidden light source. The faint sound of a baby squirrel mewling rises beyond the conifer canopy. Leaves tap each other as a zephyr intensifies.

"Well, maybe no one can do anything right now but keep marching, keep talking, keep writing," Lionel says, as if wanting to quickly change the subject. "And voting. Voting is still important, more so this year than any other, Haley."

"Why?" I say.

"Also, as you know"—Lionel looks at you, not me—"we're planning a huge rally in New York the end of August."

"The police will probably see one tossed rock then immediately declare the rally illegal," you say. "They may have you on their enemy list." A wink at Lionel. I need a drink.

"You never answered my question. Why is voting important now? We always vote, but, you know, the One Party wins even though exit polls indicate a loss. I suppose one day they'll make exit polling illegal in order to stop complaints."

"But this time, it's different." He looks at me and then you. "As you know."

As you know?

"I'm going on this march, too," I say.

"You'd be bored." You stand and pick up plates. "And Lolly needs you." Lionel starts to stand. "No, you stay here. I do dishes alone, it keeps me sane."

You retreat to the sink. Your energy still makes its way back to the table. The clink of silverware, dishes hitting metal racks of the dishwasher. The water runs with force from the faucet.

"So, Haley. How about you? Are you happy here?" He leans into me as if my answer will be a secret. I have an urge to kiss him on the cheek, but I instead look past him at you. You're now looking around the kitchen, as if considering its value for the first time. You open the refrigerator, study the door, place your hand softly upon it.

"Haley?" Lionel says.

"I heard you. I'm thinking. I'm happily comfortable."

A jay starts screeching. Then another. In a burst, several scream—unusual at this time in the evening.

"Happy like the blue jays?" he says, then sips his tea.

"I often wonder about their happiness," I say, not thinking, just talking, like you do all the time. "They can't leave, because we feed them, and in a strange way we need them, or Mom needs them. I'm sure they know one day we may not be here. That must mean they're also anxious." I immediately regret my words.

You regard me briefly then return to the sink, scrubbing the pot with more vigor than any pot would need.

# Blue Jay Memo

Male with tight appendage covering and small glass covered eyes!
Where?
There.
Who?
Come back!
On limb now!
Shut uuup.

He's at glass covered aperture!
He's observing us!
He observes us too much!
Predator eyes!

Male with tight lower appendage coverings and small glass cover for eyes is at the glass covered aperture of female host's nest. He observes us.

We're not too worried as he's been with large female with glass covered eyes. He's also been to the Children of Athena home nest before. According to our records, he arrived during the day, accompanied by the large female with glass covered eyes. They both brought folding metal slabs and sat outside with our female host. They tapped, female host sang and drank warm fluid.

Today, however, he comes alone for late afternoon meal. Offspring greets this male in formal, stiff manner. We suspect he's unfamiliar to her.

Owl! Owl!
Owl! Owl!
Owl! Owl!
Owl gone

Back on branch!
Come back!
Perch!

*His eyes!*
*One eye.*
*Look at his one eye!*
*What?*
*Human male's one eye!*

We observe odd behavior. When offspring is away from eating table, male removes thin glass object that covers eyes. He looks at female host and squishes right eye closed then quickly releases so eye opens. Only one eye squishes. Squish shut, release. We do not understand gesture. We only record what we see.

# Chapter 28

*Drunk friends leave, guilty friends return*

I'M DESCENDING THE stairs late one afternoon when they show up, two days before voir dire. They arrive at the door on the left end of the house, where the kitchen is. Abby Lawson, Marcy Finnegan, and two other unfamiliar women. I assume they are here for a meeting, but Sarah Ableman is not with them, and if there's a meeting, Sarah is usually here. Actually, Sarah Ableman is always around—huddled over a laptop, whispering conspiratorially, sometimes giggling anxiously. Occasionally you two walk together, or sit on the patio and sip tea.

You greet the women in your lounge pants and T-shirt that says, "I've lost my humor, it left with my patience." I hear Abby say in her stentorian voice, "Lorraine, it's us, and we want to talk." Apparently, there's no meeting, they are unannounced guests. Only Abby can get away with this. It takes authority to force entry into your house uninvited and without food. You lean your head to one side as if checking out the group of women from a sideways angle. Abby puts her foot in the doorway, like a rapist from one of those police shows.

"You think, Abby, that your foot will withstand my door slam?" You look down at Abby's Nikes. "Of course, I'd never hurt a good tennis shoe. So, come in. And, hi, Marcy, you can't come if you brought wine again."

The women walk in and fill the kitchen with their thick, slow bodies. Marcy heats the tea kettle and opens the cabinets, looking for crackers. You walk behind all of them without complaining about their intrusion. One of them has found cheese and apples. Another woman with short henna-dyed hair and brown spots on her face, slices them onto a plate.

"I've already contracted with a septic company. I'm having my septic tank exhumed this fall," Abby says. "We've mapped out a new location about three hundred feet further inland. Marcy's talking to contractors now, too. I'm sure you know Liz Windham." The woman cutting cheese smiles at you." And Rosa Fazio?" Rosa is a youngish woman, now sitting at the kitchen table. "Rosa has a new home on the coast. She's not convinced her tank's at risk, but she listens. Beth Lorde's a lawyer you've not met." The tall woman in trendy black pants and long silk shirt with daisies looks forty-something. She's not helping with tea or food, only listening. "She doesn't live on the coast, but her sister lives there. She's here on her behalf."

You don't know what to think, you wonder if this is a setup of sorts. Are they connected to Sterns, Howell, and Logan? You sit at the table and wait for tea and cheese. They at least owe you that. Service.

"I suppose you notice I'm not talking," you say. "I'm not saying a thing. Brit told me not to talk. In fact, he told me to practice not talking with groups of people so that I learn how to stop myself in court when I get mad. And I'm sure that will happen. So, that's what I'm doing—not talking. What's happening now is merely a movement of mouth to let words out. Let me ask this one question before I continue my silence. Did you rethink your septic tanks because of the environment or as a way to appease me? Or is something legal going on? Are you concerned that future property owners may find you liable for irresponsible ignorance?"

Marcy places a tea pot and some cups on the table. Abby brings the plate of cheese. Beth drags in a few chairs from the adjoining living room. You sip your tea.

"You left your car in the middle of the road. Right after a turn. It was hard not to hit it," Marcy says in a voice so low it's almost a whisper. The women freeze. You put down your tea. "You left it there, but I still wouldn't have hit it if I were sober."

She sits down by you, places both hands, palms down, on the table and stares at them. Her fingernails are not painted, but they are clean and filed. You regard Marcy's nails, rooted veins, dry skin, swollen knuckles. You have an overwhelming urge to retrieve coconut oil from the cabinet and pass it around.

"I was drunk," Marcy continues, her head now up, her eyes on you. "I hit the car because I was drunk. I chose to drink."

"Bonnie drove that car," you say. "Because a dead person cannot go to jail for drunk driving. Don't be a hero, Marcy. Is that what this is about? Moving your septic tanks because of guilt. Confessing your drunk driving because of guilt?"

"We're looking into our tanks because fish are dead," Abby says. "We were wrong. And selfish. We are only four women and one lawyer. There are twenty others who still insist on ignoring the truth. What's new?"

"The Hamiltons are assholes," Marcy says. "Remember that Lab that bit her granddaughter? I can't remember the name of the poor family that owned the dog. The girl pulled his ears. She was trying to drag the dog by his ears. They had to put that dog down and still pay them God knows how much money. Bonnie was always disgusted with her kids. She'd turn over and vomit in her grave if she knew they were suing you. I'm going to testify."

"Nope," you say quickly. "You're not. It's fine. I'm fine. We're fine. Nothing will come of it." You sip your tea. "They have no case on the alcohol. Well, maybe they have a small case. What difference would it make if you were driving instead of Bonnie?"

"I'm not considered elderly yet. That court precedent only covers the elderly. Over seventy-five. And don't say anything to that, please."

"The big concern is my parked car. You admit to driving, they would simply add you to the list of pockets to pick for money. It's best to give them only one lame route to money. Me. I'm failing my practice test. I need to shut up. I am going to simply drink my tea."

"But, that's why we're here," Abby says. "We're only a small piece of the whole but we're a piece, an honest piece of it." She clasps her hands, leans over them. "Some of us know some folks in Stratton who've been called to civil jury duty this week. They know of you, these potential jurors. They hate you. You do know, Lorraine, that there are other towns who hate you, too."

"I invoke my right under the fifth amendment not to answer on the grounds I may incriminate myself." You smile wide and bright. "How's that sound?"

"Unfortunately, it doesn't work in a civil court," Beth says. "Unless you think there's a criminal charge pending. Louis assures us there is not. They could bankrupt you, Lorraine. They could take everything Larry left you and your daughter."

You've stopped looking at them. You're looking out the window as the birds eat. Another turkey flock has entered the yard, and all of them are now pecking at the ground vigorously. They're very skinny this year. You have an urge to run out and toss them corn, and this urge moves from brain to muscle. Feed the birds. Feed the birds. Feed the birds. Abby continues to talk about the upcoming trial and what it means for you. They're all very concerned. Do you have enough money for the legal fees? Can they help? But all you want to do is feed your birds. You stand, open the closet behind you, grab your bucket of corn.

"What are you doing?" Marcy says.

"Can we continue this conversation outside?" You open the door and march out. Marcy looks around the table, slowly stands and follows you through the open door.

"You must remain quiet. Turkeys are very shy," you admonish her. "Stand back and simply watch."

Marcy stands by the door and watches you walk the periphery of our back yard, tossing corn to seven hens. Several blue jays move to the branches overhead. Dozens of finch, sparrows, and wrens scatter among the low-lying brush underneath the large pines. You toss your last handful of corn and turn to face Marcy at the door, her friends at the window. Your eyes are swollen, red, and wet.

"What will they do when I leave? What will happen to all of them?" you say to Marcy.

"Them?" Marcy says.

You wave your hand around the yard. "Them. All of them. What will they do when I leave?"

"What do you mean, leave?" Marcy says approaching you.

"Can you see any other way? Oh, fuck, I'm talking again."

# Chapter 29

*Truth is difficult to read*

WHEN DAD DIED, I was in class, a mere freshman in college, everything new and exciting, or at least it was supposed to be new and exciting. But the newness had worn off within the first few months and excited was not how I felt that afternoon. I had been out the night before and I was still tired and hungover. The side door opened, a thin middle-aged woman marched up to the professor and handed him a note. "Haley Mulderon," he said, looking out at the audience of about seventy students.

I hadn't looked at the reading assignment and felt my face drain, expecting a question. I was a fairly good student and usually prepared even for the most insignificant class.

"Please gather your belongings and follow this woman."

The woman was a social worker, and at first, all she said was follow me. She said we were heading to the Dean of Student Affairs office. I froze in the hallway, told her I was not moving until I was told what this was about. Sometimes my mother comes out of me. Not often, only in moments when I feel I'm being treated unfairly. At that time, I suspected I was in trouble for committing some mild scofflaw. All my test scores to date had been good, but I had snuck back into the dorm after curfew a few times and had skipped a few classes. I stood my ground.

When it was apparent I was not moving, she took my hands in hers and told me my father had had a very serious accident. I knew he was dead. I didn't even ask. I remember floating above everything, like a bird, out of my body, out of life.

SARAH ABLEMAN AND I sit behind you and Brit during voir dire, and once again I am floating above the chaos of loss, grief, which has turned into anger—at you, at us. Finally, a jury sits before us and the trial begins. We're all nervous because the jury of peers are for the most part white and conservative, not the best demographic for a defendant like you. One would want birds, fish, squirrels. English bulldogs would be wonderful. If we cannot have wild animals on the jury, the next best thing would be minorities, progressive minorities who understand the marginalized. There just aren't many in this area.

You know two of the jurors, but there was no peremptory challenge, so there they sit. One man is a teacher who worked with you once at some volunteer school function years ago (not a good sign, and that's all I'll say), but, while he knows you, he appears restrained and devoid of bias. He also doesn't own coastal property. The other man, an assistant bank manager, knows you as a bank customer and mother of one of his employees. Nic, my boss. I'm mortified.

You're quiet, unmoved by all of it. You wear a suit that's severely black. I keep thinking, this is silly and any moment they will ask for a recess and meet with each other. You will have to pay a nominal sum, maybe a bit more than nominal. Then it will be over; we'll go back to where we were, only with a smaller savings account. But that's not happening.

When the plaintiff's attorney announces the lawsuit amount—twenty million dollars—you laugh; Brit grabs your hand and squeezes hard. You stop. The attorney suggests that "the amount is small compared to the value of Bonnie Hamilton's life." The trial is set for Friday, two days away.

We step outside where your black suit looks hot under a blue sky and bright sun. Brit studies few of the selected jurors as they trot down the steps. You whisper something to him, he shakes his head. You look at me, then back at him and lightly touch his hand.

"This is another small hiccup I have caused in your life," you say to me. You step away from Brit, toward me. "But it will be another learning experience for you. You will learn what not to do when you reach my age. You will not leave your car in the middle of a road. You will not cause so much controversy that you can't find a jury you trust, even if the district court is in another town. You will not . . . oh forget it. You get it, right?"

"Yes, I'm getting an education. I get it."

"Well, at least I found a boyfriend for you, yes?" You pull some hair around your ear and look off toward nothing behind me.

"What boyfriend? Lionel? We're just—"

"Friends? I know."

"You know, Mom, women and men can be friends. Like, say, you and Brit?" Brit looks away quickly, which for some reason weirds me out. You smile, keeping your eyes on me.

"OK," you say. "We're all friends. Let's call Lionel and have a friendly dinner. Brit, me, you Lionel."

"No can do. He's in Boston for something," I say. "But I'm available."

I want Japanese, but we worry about fish, so we decide on Mexican. Brit has to run back to the office and suggests we meet at the restaurant.

We drive in silence. I text Lionel because he's been texting me questions about the jury selection. OK, I've been seeing him a bit. We've had sex once, but it was on his couch and I didn't sleep over. That doesn't count.

I type, "*It looks bad. I don't know what to think. It's weird. They want so much money. I don't get it.*"

"*They'll settle.*"

"*No, I'm thinking they want to get rid of Mom. And maybe this will do it.*"

"*Maybe she should sell, leave town. It may be the best thing. It'll free you, Haley. You need to be freed from her.*"

When we park at the restaurant, I rub my eyes and get ready to be positive, because I have a feeling this will be an anxious dinner.

"Don't worry, Haley, we'll all survive." You remain seated, staring at the keys before turning off the car. "Good guys win, it's just a longer route to winning. Bad guys take short cuts."

We head into the restaurant, find a table, sit quietly waiting for Brit. You realize you need your wallet so head back. I realize my phone is back in the car on the seat. Can I exist in a restaurant without my phone? Is it possible? Yes, it is. I feel good about this, but not good about my unlocked phone on the car seat, screen facing up. Why does this bother me?

# Blue Jay Memo

*Thirsty!*
*Hungry!*
*Where is she?*
*Lost her. There!*
*Where are we?*
*Follow. Fly. Shut uuup.*

We are 9.4 miles southwest of Children of Athena home, following female host and offspring. They cease forward motion at large white nest in another human tribal area. We perch on roof of very large nest.

*Insect!*
*Come back!*
*No. Hungry*
*Water! Flowing water!*
*Where're two-year-olds?*
*Who cares?*
*Back. Here. Now.*

So, this is the deal. Female host's been traveling in motorized mobile nest often and we're sick of it, OK? Always meeting with the large female with glass covered eyes. Sometimes with male with thin glass covered eyes and tight lower appendage covering. Back and forth. Back and forth.

And see, get this. When she's at nest? She wonders out and stares at us. Our elders think she looks weakened. But they tend to project themselves onto humans. Whatever.

So, anyway, today we're at a location we've never traveled to before. It has water in small pond with fake fish spitting more water into air. Strange. But the water's nice. We wait a long time. We're not sure what humans do in this nest.

There they are!

*Where?*
*There! Female host, offspring!*
*Follow.*
*Perching.*
*No, no more perching. Follow!*
*Where're the two-year-olds?*
*On top of human nest.*
*Off. Human. Nest. Now.*
*Follow!*

*Female host and offspring travel in motorized mobile nest to a feeding nest. We perch. There's no water, we're tired. We'd do anything for a worm.*

*She's back out.*
*Where's offspring?*
*In feeding nest.*
*She's leaving offspring?*

*Come back!*
*No.*
*Here.*

*Insect!*
*Two insects!*
*What's female host doing in motorized mobile nest?*
*She's looking at a communication enhancer.*
*Her eye furs are squished and there's eye fluid!*

*Facial fur configuration and eye fluid indicate emotion.*

*Female host exits mobile nest and walks too slowly. Female host appears weakened. Elders may be correct.*

*We're concerned.*

# Chapter 30

*The trial, the verdict, the end*

WHEN WE GATHER for the actual trial, the courtroom is filled: Unleash Our Dog women; several of your past environmental advocates—a few who still support you and many who oppose you; Nan, who sits in the back, dressed in a sleeveless dress splattered with puppy faces; a few Westbrook reporters. What else is there to report on in Westbrook? The papers no longer publish your letters to the editor, which were at least entertaining. The lawsuit is the biggest news in a long time.

I sit with Sarah Ableman again, who discreetly taps on an iPad on her lap. Before the judge steps in, I feel a hand on my thigh. Lion leans into me, "I think she'll be fine, so will you." He keeps his warm hand on my leg. I like that about him, how he lingers. Also, I like how he talks, careful but brutally honest. I also like how he offers advice in a way that feels like a wink. Actually, the only thing I don't like about Lion is his name, Lionel. So, I changed it. Lion. I also don't like his mysterious mien. His present life is not an open book, although he freely shares historical stories. A childhood with unhappy parents in conservative Orange County, California. He left after graduating college and searched for a destination far from his parents. I suppose if we ever get more serious than texting and occasional sex, I'd eventually meet his parents and two sisters, both of whom are older with families. I try not to think about it.

Nic sits nicely in his juror seat. He is second row, middle. I can see his face if I lean a bit to my right, which I do.

Yesterday, Nic brought me some paperwork and stood a moment in my office, waiting. I figured he wanted me to say something about you and the trial. Only I can't say anything, he's not allowed to talk about the trial. But unlike you, my thoughts don't spill easily. I looked at him—I always look at him—but this time I looked at him while he looked at me. I don't know if it's a good thing he's on the jury or a bad thing.

Lion still has not removed his hand from my leg. I put my hand on top of his hand, assuring his hand stays there. This gets my mind off Nic.

Since I work in retail banking, I'm familiar with the tedium of procedure, which is what the trial becomes until they call several witnesses who attended the party. They all attest to alcohol consumption. Next, the testimonies of two of the three women in the car Bonnie was supposedly driving. The lawyers do not ask who was driving. You'd think there would be a question, at least one, about the driving. They only ask about where Mom's car was parked. They call the officer who first arrived on the scene, and he discusses the length of skid marks, the damage, where Mom's car was located before and after accident. He draws a map, showing how difficult it would be for any car to avoid hitting a car parked in the middle of the road after turning onto the street.

It looks bad. Brit asks for a recess before the plaintiffs call a doctor to the stand to discuss Bonnie's cardiac arrest and the contributing factors to its onset. Nic looks over at me as the jury rises for recess. I smile, he looks away. Lion squeezes my leg. Brit leans over the bench and whispers something in your ear, then you both head for a small conference room down the hall. I assume you two are arguing. Again. Brit wants you to allow him to demand Marcy take the stand. He will ask if she drove the car. Everyone knows she drove the car, but no one wants her to go to jail, including you. He wants to force her to choose between perjuring herself or saving you. You stubbornly oppose this strategy, and Brit has not been able to penetrate the concrete brain that locks you into position. "If she perjures herself, I will perjure myself defending her. We can all go to jail together," you say.

Lion and I step into the hall to drink some water and walk off our nervous energy. I'm feeling broke already, even though this technically is not my money. Still, I feel the suck of money out your investment accounts. There's a tap on my shoulder. Nan stands before me, her round face looming above several happy panting puppies that decorate her dress. I stare at the tongue of a Lab puppy on her left breast as she talks.

"I've got to get back to all my animals, just wanted to say hi first." She leans in the way she does at the office when talking to Lolly. "I can't believe they're doing this, Haley. It was an accident, for crying out loud. How's Lolly holding up?"

"You must be the vet I hear about," Lion says. He holds out his hand and they introduce themselves. This is another thing I like about Lion, his ability to just step in and introduce himself to people he's never met, as if it's important he knows everyone. Or they know him. I always assume no one will remember my name so why force it upon them.

"Are you a friend of the family?" Nan says.

"Am I a friend of your family?" he asks me. "Lolly is wary of me, but I guess I'm friends with the rest of the family."

"Lion is my friend. Mom met him first. He's now her boss at Save the Planet, that big environmental foundation. He's helping to investigate dead fish. And dead birds. Basically, our dead earth. You know."

"So, you've talked with her about the fish deaths and my tests? You're aware of the traces of citalopram and fluoxetine in some of the fish? What're you going to do about it?"

"We've discussed that, yes, and of course our first thought was dumping by a pharmaceutical manufacturer upstream, but the manufacturer upstream does not make fluoxetine or citalopram. So, the more likely scenario is consumer waste. All those rich people get depressed for some reason. It certainly is evidence of waste seeping into our waterway, but no one seems to want to do anything. And the way things are now, the most we can do is inform. And vote. This year, voting is important."

"Why this year?" Nan says.

"Oh, and march. We've got a big one planned for the end of August."

Nan stares at Lion a moment, then me, opens her mouth to say something but shuts it quickly because the judge has returned and is banging his gavel.

We all sit, even Nan. The jury has not returned. Brit and you are not here. We wait.

"We've dismissed the jury," the judge says, leaning over his clasped hands and looking at all of us. "The parties have reached a confidential settlement. Thank you for your service to our community. Court dismissed."

I run out into the hall to look for you. I check the conference room. Nothing. Lion jogs by my side. I throw open a few other doors, but all rooms are empty. Then I see Brit emerge from a room at the end of the hall. He walks slowly toward me, his eyes intensely studying mine. Lion puts his arm around my shoulders and squeezes.

"This is good news, right?" Lion says.

"I think your Mom will need a few hours to herself," Brit says to me, ignoring Lion.

"What does she need to do by herself?" I ask. Lion drops his hand from my shoulder.

"Why don't you, Lionel, and I go for a bite to eat. It's been a long morning."

"What did Mom agree to?" I say as we walk. "How much does she have to pay?"

"Ten thousand dollars."

"That's not bad at all," Lion says. "Let's order a bottle of wine. Why does Lorraine need time to herself?"

"Oh, you know Lorraine. I'll let her discuss her emotions with you. I'm restrained by attorney client privilege."

An overwhelming, prescient sadness consumes me, and I don't know why, since I'm not hearing bad news. I follow Lion and Brit out the door into the heated dry air filled with the fading sound of bird song.

# Blue Jay Memo

We follow female one last time to large white nest 9.4 miles southwest of Children of Athena. Female host enters nest with other humans but does not stay long. She returns home, where she perambulates the periphery of grounds. Fur above eyes squished. Fluid in eyes. Emoting. She sings to us.

The next day she does not attend to feeders.

She puts a small amount of food in feeders the next day but does fill our water.

We suspect a weaning of sorts. We've encountered this weaning by humans but usually after the cold has left and our adventurers return from the North American Blue Jay migration path. This weaning is too soon.

We're all gonna die!
We're all gonna die!
We're all gonna die!
Shut uup!
Perch!
Reconnaissance. We need a new home.
There are no new homes

We are all gonna die!
We are all gonna die!
We are all gonna die!

The whining and screaming are becoming unbearable. But we are not confident of survival.

Here's the deal. Life's leaving. Not just fish, but rodents, insects. Squirrels! Sure, we tease the idiots, but they're squirrels! What's anyone to do without squirrels?

More of us may attempt the migration path. Others have family and routines that obligate them.

We fear the worst.

We will meet our fate with patience and fortitude. We are the great jays of the Children of Athena!

# Chapter 31

*The day the feeders died*

WHEN BART LOGAN arrives, you remain in your bedroom and ignore the doorbell. The bedroom and living room are now filled with Get Out The Vote posters, the new big advocacy you've thrown yourself into. This voting season voters elect a new president, the same one that wins no matter what, forever. There are no term limits, something you say was critical years ago. We all vote. Democracy groups, media groups, and international organizations conduct exit polls. They always deviate from reported results. Everyone screams. Some march. Screams go silent, marchers are jailed. Life moves on. "This time is different," you tell me. We hear that every four years.

Bart walks to the other half of the house and rings that doorbell. He next explores the back yard, walking its periphery, stopping to regard the center where the gas pipeline is located. You spy on him from your window. You see the birds perched on the pine above him and imagine them transmogrifying into characters from an old Hitchcock movie, *The Birds*. You imagine them congregating, multiplying, congregating, multiplying, congregating, multiplying. Thousands of fluttering creatures roosting in a seething anger as great as your own, then all at once, in unison, they'll dive and peck the lawyer's eyes out.

Bart turns back to the house, looks at the window, waves.

The doorbell again. You rise, take your time, enjoying the patience you're forcing upon this asshole who'll be taking your home, your trees, your birds. You open the door to his straight back and slight smile, hands shoved deep into his pockets, where you assume the check is folded neatly, waiting to be transferred. Lolly pushes through your legs and sniffs his shoes. Bart pets her briefly, not enough to encourage her to roll over for a belly rub, so she wobbles back inside and jumps on the living room couch.

"I know you don't want me in the house, but the thing is, Ms. Mulderon, there are forms to sign, deeds and such to read and file. This is a process. We must begin the process. Can I sit at your kitchen table?"

"My lawyer has everything ready. I'd rather get this over with fast so you can leave and go to wherever you lawyers go after sucking the life out of people." You open the door, and he walks through the foyer, picking up a few posters that say, "Vote. Your life depends on it!" He smiles, shakes his head, but makes no comment, only continues his walk to the kitchen as if he's been in the house a thousand times before and already owns it. "The papers are on the table. I was expecting you. I suddenly felt nauseated and lo a behold, there you were."

Three blue jays perch on the large feeder. Two jerk their heads from the right of the window to left of the window, over and over.

"Interesting how nervous birds are. They never hold their eyes steady," Bart says as he looks out the bay window.

"Birds jerk their eyes around an object of interest so that they never lose awareness of their surroundings, unlike humans who stare at anything that interests them, arrogantly assured of their own safe and central place in the world."

Bart laughs. You do not.

Bart sits, places his hands on the table, palms down, says nothing for a moment. You barely look at him and remain standing, still looking out the window. Lolly snores in the living area.

"I suppose I should fix you some tea. Do you want tea?"

"Why, thank you, that would be nice." He keeps his eyes on you while you fill the kettle and turn up the flame. "Change is sad. I know this. We all know this will be sad. It's hard to leave a home."

"My parents had me late in life," you say. "Like very late. My older sisters were practically gone. My mother gave birth to me when she was forty-four years old. So, I went through all the elderly parent drama at a young age." You walk back, sit at the table, clasp your hands, and lean over them to look Bart in the eye. "They were both sick, Dad from cancer, Mom from a stroke. She couldn't walk, Dad could barely eat. I lived far away, but my sisters pulled me down south for a while to help out. My parents clung to their big house as if it was the key to afterlife. They went through all of their savings paying for the nursing staff, then borrowed from all of their children to stay alive. The house was in such bad shape, it was a fire sale when they finally succumbed. They died penniless. I say this to you because it's important that you know there are other reasons I'm selling this house, leaving town. I'm not being forced into something by a bully who represents unmitigated greed. I'm not frightened of greed. It's just that I swore I would never do to my daughter what was done to me. I want to leave her something. I advocate against the massively wealthy, the families who have accumulated wealth going back decades. I never had that, but, hell, I have a small amount of wealth now, and I want to keep it for my daughter. I want to pass something on to her."

"You're a good mother. Have you told your daughter about the sale?"

"I plan on telling her in a few weeks, after I find her a place to live. I'm looking for a town house for her. Something nice but not too big. It needs to be a good investment, marketable, because I plan for her to move up in her bank, eventually grow into management, transfer to New York. That's the plan."

"I hope she's on board with your plan."

"I think she is."

"OK. I'll help you with a condo for her. I know some great deals. I have clients who have investments. She'll be fine. You'll be fine."

The tea kettle screams like a hawk's captured prey. You step back into the kitchen and make a pot of tea, bring it to the table along with two cups. Bart is already looking over the file. It contains forms that have already been signed. The agreement gives you two months after signing to evacuate the premises. Enough time to discuss everything with me. You wanted an additional paragraph guaranteeing the preservation of three designated trees—a white pine, a gray birch, and a large Hemlock. They did not agree to this, so now you try again after Bart sips tea for a moment.

"I see your eyes wander out the window at my birds. We used to have more but many have died, like the fish. We don't know why. Food is not as plentiful. Dead fish, development, weevils, perhaps changes in animal diets. We don't know. There's so much we don't know because we've given up on knowing."

"Birds are nice. I've never been that interested in them." He's barely listening. He turns a page, takes out his pen. "My wife's a cat lover," he says still looking down. "I'm afraid if we put up bird feeders, they would eventually become our cat feeder, if you know what I mean." He puts down his pen, takes a sip of tea, looks at you over the cup's rim.

"I want the trees preserved. I would like for the birds to be fed at least until you sell the house, or land, whatever it becomes. But I want those trees to remain."

"Sorry. That's not the deal." You look down at the documents. "Lorraine, OK, you like birds. You love birds. You, I suppose love fish. Or maybe you realize the importance of fish. I get it. It's commendable. I consider myself an environmentalist."

You put your hand over your mouth and laugh into it. Your laugh wakes Lolly and she trots into the kitchen. Bart doesn't smile.

"I love the environment," he says quickly. "What, you think I don't want clean air and water?"

"We all love the environment! My advocate friends worked to stop developments and preserve land trusts. They came over to my house with wine carried in plastic bags. Plastic bags! And they wanted clean water but didn't want to do anything about their outdated septic tanks. And if cutting back global warming meant a carbon tax they would rage. And they all love trees, but if the trees are in the way of expanding their homes, they cut them down. There are things we cannot do, things we can. Everyone likes to complain about things we can't do anything about. We had no rain this summer. No rain, so no crabapples, dead trees, brown grass. I didn't just split my house in two, I made it a greener home, and one of those green additions was a shower and sink recycling system. I had a rain barrel for my gardens, but it never rains."

He nodded and opened his mouth to speak.

"Oh, have you noticed insects are scarce?" you continue quickly before he can talk. "Did you know that many of our insect friends are disappearing? Remember when we used to worry about invasive insects overpopulating and killing trees. The beetles? Moths? Oh, but guess what may be back? Weevils! But this time, according to my vet and scientists at Save the Planet, these weevils are Asian weevils, and no one knows how in the hell they got here and how they survive in dry weather. And no one will ever know the reasons because our government does not invest money in science anymore. We all depend on foundations that are poorly funded. And did you know herons are eating rodents because there're no fish? Owls are dying. So are other birds. You may not know this because we cannot get this basic information anymore on the news. You kind of have to know which environmental blog to read. And they are attacked or taken down by government trolls. The best news about this tragedy is on the dark web because our legislature has no idea how to stop the dark web. But I am glad you call yourself a fucking environmentalist."

"Whew. All those thoughts escaping in such a short amount of time!" He smiles but doesn't laugh this time. "Look, Lorraine, I'm sorry. That's all I can say. Let's move on, shall we?" He sips his tea one more time and opens the file, flips through the papers, signs a few. He shoves the bill of sale to you for your signature. You sign quickly, push it back. "So, two months. And, I'd tell your daughter soon. Like, two weeks. We need to find her a good place to live. So, tell your daughter, OK?" He stands and begins placing the documents back into his attaché. You watch and say nothing.

"Between you and me," he says. "I agree with you in a few ways. However, I'm not sure I think this extremist position is based upon good science. I don't think the world is coming to an end. But, well, yes, I agree we will all have to live with sad changes. Evolution is sad. Survival of the fittest. Maybe humans are the fittest. We'll have fewer animals and more humans."

"Only bacteria will survive."

"Bacteria." He shakes his head and laughs. Obviously, he has no clue what you mean. You're not kidding. You actually mean literally only bacteria will survive.

"I think we have evolved to the end of this meeting." You stand and leave the room, abandoning Bart who takes another slow sip of his tea before exiting.


SARAH ABLEMAN STOPS by late in the afternoon. When she steps out of the car, she notices something different about the property. A stillness. She knocks, and, when there is no answer, she retrieves the key from the tool box and lets herself in. There are footsteps and a few barks. Thumping on the stairs, then paws scraping the floor. Lolly wiggles her rear end and rolls over for a belly rub. Sarah puts down her large bag that contains work—a few GOTV posters she's been putting up around town, Mom's advocacy material, and her laptop. She sits on the floor with Lolly.

"Lorraine," she shouts. "I can't wait all day. I can only stay briefly."

You walk slowly down the stairs and head to the kitchen, assuming Sarah will follow. She does, Lolly wobbling behind her. You slump into a chair. Sarah pulls out some forms for Save the Planet—applications for an international grant, memos concerning lawsuits over violations of certain environmental rules. Lawsuits used to be important when there were administrative judges and court precedents. Now, they are simply a procedure that leads to paperwork and public filings. Rulings by judges appointed by our One Party government generally side with the polluter, but filings are still public, so they at least educate and inform the public.

"Are you OK, Lorraine?"

You cock your head to the side. "You've come a long way."

Sarah says nothing, only squints her eyes.

"I mean, you've come out of yourself since getting all involved again. You're still grieving. We all grieve when we lose our loved ones. But I've helped you, don't you think? Do you think I made a difference with you at least? Surely I've helped you."

"Why are we talking like this?"

"Do you think I've been good for you, or bad? Have I isolated your existence here more than usual? Or have I freed you to stand up?"

"Am I isolated? I work a lot. I have a job. And this."

"You have a job, this, and me. Wow. I've never thought of things like that. Ownership." You pause to think. "Let's see. I have this, Haley, Lolly. And you."

"Well, Lorraine . . ." Sarah starts. When uncomfortable, Sarah Ableman sits straighter, as if trying to lengthen her spine in order to deal with what is before her. What is before her now is you acting strangely. "We are here for the grant and update on the lawsuit, which will cost money that we do not have. So, my discomfort comes from you. Why are you distracting? What's going on?"

"My birds will never forgive me. I'm hoping they'll fly away, join the migrating birds. I hope they leave this fucking country for good. I don't know how to tell them to fly away from our country. I don't know how to tell them that humans here are not as perfect as animals. I can't tell them this, I can only tell this to other humans. So I'm telling you, Sarah. When you finally fly away, stay away. From this country."

"You think my trip to Paris is flying away from this country? Is this what you're talking about? My planned trip? Who told you? Abby, right? I was planning to tell you today at the end of our business discussion. I suppose you're mad you had to find out from another person. Mad I'm not going on the march with you, right? Well, I'm sorry, Lorraine. Abby asked about the march, and I told her I couldn't go. She pressed me for answers, so I told her. I've looked forward to this time in Paris for a while. It's three months, and I have an absentee ballot, so don't worry. I'm going because I need time in Europe."

"You're going to Paris?"

# Blue Jay Memo

*Predator!*
*Predator!*
*Conflict!*
*Conflict!*

*Predatory human who travels in black motorized mobile nest arrives, enters. We view through large glass human nest aperture. Female host appears weakened by predator.*

*He's out.*
*Follow!*
*Too weak.*
*We all follow*
*We all follow!*

*Predator travels many disorganized paths until he reaches land cut off from coast. We note several motorized mobile nests sitting motionless upon path leading to one large human nest. He enters nest.*

*We return to Children of Athena home nest.*

*Female host is outside singing sorrowful songs again.*

*Eyes have eye fluid. She sings sorrowful songs and eyes have eye fluid because she has created a crisis for us.*

*Now, there are no feeders. Female host has taken all food.*

# Chapter 32

*Leaving and lying*

THE FIRST THING I notice when I return home from work are birds. Their silent, watchful stillness. Dozens of them perched in the pines with their young, barely old enough to separate from their parents. The adults are finishing their summer molts, and a few still look scraggly and unkempt. They screech when I step out of my car. It's a frantic, hysterical scream, similar to their alarms when hawks or owls are nearby. I walk the periphery, checking for hawks. A few jays follow me, still screaming. I don't walk to the back yard, but instead enter the house. I walk through the kitchenette, over the center bridge, into the kitchen.

And there you are, at the table, sipping a beer and eating Doritos.

I sit by you and stare at your beer.

"They will hate me for a while," you say, not looking at me. "They will not understand. It's the way of love."

"What are you talking about?" I look into your eyes. They have a tired puffiness that indicates tears have spilled for a while. "Mom, has something happened?"

"I'm going on the march. After the march, you and I are going out to dinner. Some place nice to celebrate. Because in the long run, this is all something to be celebrated. Kind of. As long as we all vote this December. For the love of God, at least vote this December. It'll be cold, but it's never too cold here anymore. It used to be worse. I remember when they made that first big switch to December for election day. They thought it would stop the poor. But it didn't stop anyone. I was so proud of everyone standing in those cold lines up in Minnesota."

The country shifted election day to two weeks before Christmas about eight years ago. The One Party tried everything to shrink the discrepancy between exit polling and the rigged voting results, but nothing seemed to work. They also regulated the time span of campaign season. No TV candidate campaign ads until two months before elections, which I appreciated. Political commercials are silly since the results are assured.

"I always vote, Mom. You know that."

The blue jay screeching that was in the air when I first returned ceases. The air conditioner clicks on, and a slight breeze rises from a vent and ruffles pages of the local newspaper sitting near the table's edge. I listen to the rise and fall of your breath. I recall your slow breaths and bizarre comments when Dad died.

"Did you have a doctor's appointment?" I'm thinking cancer. When you lose one parent, you're always on alert for the next loss.

"No. One beer and one bag of trash food will not kill me. Do you think I need a doctor's appointment?"

"Why are you drinking a beer and eating Doritos? Why are you saying weird things? What's going on?"

You look outside, and my eyes follow you. There are no feeders. I stand and walk to the bay window. At first, I think you removed only the large feeders, but when I open the side door and step outside, I don't see the small feeders either. The jays are still perched high in the pines.

When I return, you're staring at small scratch in the wooden table. "They will find food or migrate." You pick at a splinter of wood, then wipe it away quickly. "I'm hoping they migrate. Some can't, so that will be sad, but this is for the best, Haley. The dependence has got to stop, things are bad everywhere, I know, but we will not solve anything by feeding the animals."

"You're just going to stop feeding them? Like that?" I sit. "Mom, what the hell is going on? What's wrong?"

"Migration starts in a month or so. This is the time to cease feeding. We give the birds time to understand that there's no more food at our house. There's food around here, somewhere. Insect population is down, but there are insects. There're probably a few oaks in other towns without weevils. I think. Maybe they can fly to New Jersey or Maryland early."

"The babies aren't ready to migrate. And most of them don't migrate, have never migrated. I don't agree. Mom, you can't do this. And why is this a sudden thing? What's going on? What happened today?"

You take a long sip of beer, open your mouth, close it, then open it again. What comes out is not what has happened. "Has Lionel called today? Has he told you about his trip?"

"His work out in California?" Lion will be traveling through California for a month, studying their water irrigation and drought management. California has actually maintained a fairly honest state government and has managed to protect their local election systems. "Are you worried about running that website with Lion gone?"

You look at me.

This is the moment that always comes back to me when I imagine a different world if only one moment could be altered. I used to do this with Dad's death, too. I imagined one alteration—Dad didn't fall but grabbed the eaves and hung on until you saved him.

I do this now. I alter this moment in my mind

*"I sold our house," you say. "It's done, no going back. I bought you a townhouse. I'm freeing you and the birds."*

*We talk. I'm upset, but after a talk, I accept the decision. We decide you can stay in my townhouse until you find another place in another county.*

*I insist on going on the march with you. We march together. I stop you from doing whatever stupid thing you have done while in your depression.*

But that is not what happens. You whisper, "No."

And I remain ignorant.

# Blue Jay Memo

We are weak. Less hyperactive, which is good as we are able to stay in one place, on one limb. We don't sing as much. We try not to scream and when others scream, we're too tired to tell them to shut up.

Look, we've always been aware of this risk. It's not like we didn't understand how unreliable humans are. We've prepared. Stored food. Reduced activity. It's just that we only prepared for temporary disruptions in food supply. This is looking permanent.

We tell two-year-olds to continue to follow female host. We need to understand if she will change course, feed us again. We have hope.

They follow her, return. Follow, return. Follow, return.

They sing to us summaries of observations. They sing too much! Here is our summary of their summary:

Female host travels 14.7 miles southwest to an area with places humans perch and sing. She sits with large woman with glass covered eyes and male with thin glass covered eyes and tight lower appendage covering. We suspect this male was mating with offspring but has ceased. Humans are not as monogamous as us. They are more like squirrels in that regard. Anyway, humans perch, sing, tap on metal slabs with buttons. Perch. Sing. Tap. Perch. Sing. Tap. Two-year-olds get bored. They did manage to gather a few peanuts tossed on ground by male. They ate and did not share.

She's done this all before. But then something horrible happens.

Female host travels in motorized mobile tube nest to Great Human Tribal Nesting area! Two-year-olds cannot travel there. We cannot travel there! We do not fly outside the Great Hawk Watcher Tribal area. Never. If she continues travel to this massive human tribal area, we would have to recruit assistance in reconnaissance from pigeons.

The pigeons are capable of observing. But, well, they are pigeons. Need we say more?

# Chapter 33

*The march*

THERE IS NO one going with you on the march. You insist only I can take care of Lolly because of her anxiety. Your advocate friends backed out. Lion is gone. Lion and I have kind of agreed we will see each other when we see each other. I guess that means we are no longer whatever we were. Sarah is gone. So, there is only you. You go by yourself.

The train car is so packed, there's barely standing room. Everything is poster boards, balloons, busy bodies—mostly women—a few young men, tapping phones. A sign lifted in the air a foot from your face says, "Vote like your life depends on it." Your sign—"Fish are Dead" written in large black magic marker letters on a severed side of a cardboard box—is tucked under one arm. The flip side says, "Turn off Voicemail."

You stand for the ride, grabbing the luggage rack over the first row of seats occupied by quiet middle-aged women, their poster boards politely turned inward. One is tapping on her phone. You assume they are friends, perhaps tennis team members who had a beer after a game and decided to march. They don't look comfortable in their marching skin right now. You try to catch one woman's eye, but she avoids you. You don't avoid strangers. You've always been OK with strangers. You keep staring at the women, trying another one now, who also refuses to engage. You wonder if the problem is your T-shirt, which is over ten years old and has a picture of a bluebird perching on a limb whistling. "I'd Rather Be a Bird" it says. You consider its appropriateness only because it clashes with your sign. You decide the issues are related. Birds and fish have similar transient existences—both can easily escape to new neighborhoods when threatened. New mates. New friends. New food. Unlike humans who like to plant themselves in one place.

"Excuse me. Do you want to sit?" The voice interrupting your reverie rises from seats behind you. You hear the voice again. "Excuse me. You can have my seat." It's a young voice, which says a young person has seen your butt and has concluded it belongs not only to an older woman, but also an older woman who probably can't stand long. You're slightly offended. You don't do Pilates, but you do ride a bike.

You turn to face a twenty-something girl with a very round face and jet-black hair cut just above her ear lobes. She sits with her friends, all busy tapping their phones.

"That's nice of you to ask. You were obviously raised by a progressive mother. Either that or I look unhealthy from behind."

She laughs and stands up. "My mother is a doctor, actually."

"Well, that explains it. Tell your mother that my blood pressure is normal and so far my blood sugar is under control."

"Please, take my seat."

"No, but do stand with me. It gives me strength. Are you with your friends? Or are you simply sitting with them? They seem to have left us for another world right now." You nod at a girl tapping on her cell phone. She looks up and stares at you with no expression. You smile and she quickly taps her phone again.

"Yes. My friends are quite involved in the movement. We're all meeting up at Lex and Second Ave, so they're actually working." She nods toward the row of middle-aged women who have thus far ignored you. "I assume those are your friends?" She smiles at a woman who has been staring at her. The woman quickly looks down.

"I march by myself. I'm best when alone."

"But you're not alone. You're with all of us. The entire train is marching. Do you have a sign?" The girl with the round face is restraining a smile, but her eyes giver her away. She seems amused by you, which is OK with you. You have always accepted amusement, just not condescension. You note the girl's attire. Very tight pants and a black T-shirt that says, "Revolution this election season." The girl reaches over her friends and grabs a poster board, which she proudly raises in the air. It's a picture of toast with the caption, "Life is Toast Unless We Act on Climate Change."

You hold up your small "Fish are Dead" sign. You turn it so the girl can see the other meme—"Turn off voicemail."

"Do you mean climate change is killing fish? And, yes, I want everyone to turn off voicemail, too." She laughs softly.

"No," you say. "And my sign refers to the EPA voicemail that has replaced the human EPA we used to have. Do you not call to complain or report bizarre environmental occurrences, such as dead fish or birds?" The girl doesn't respond. "I'm sure there's some sort of contribution by global warming to the current dead fish population. Then there's plastic pollution. We don't know. What I do know, or suspect, is that septic tanks near the coast are leaking into the water because the water level has risen. No one wants to refurbish their systems. We had a group come out to test the fish, too, but they wrecked on the highway and spilled dead fish everywhere. So, I tested them, or my vet tested them. She's helpful but passive aggressive, although only to my dog. It's a long story."

The young girls who have been ignoring you are now listening. In fact, two seats of people are listening. The middle-aged women who were quiet and pretending to not listen are also looking at you.

"Did you report this to Save our Water?" one middle-aged woman says, sitting closest to your legs. "Or was that the group that wrecked the car with the fish?"

"That was them indeed. Cara is my contact. She heads the coastal region. We are kind of friends." The woman nods. "OK, that's not true. She's not my friend. We got to know each other back during the crow deaths, which I'm sure you remember."

You look at the young girl with the round face. "You were probably in eighth grade and had more important life events, but while you were studying algebra, crows were dying all over New England. They fell from the air like black umbrellas."

"I barely remember that," the girl says. "My uncle was involved in suing someone over it. Wasn't it a virus? Or maybe something about the water damaged their immune systems? Like nitrogen in the water? He told me and I forgot."

"We will never be certain. There were some dead fish back then, too, not a lot, but some. It's a long story." The train hits a curve and you grab the edge of a seat and flex your legs. "My name is Lorraine by the way."

"Amber."

You now address the middle-aged woman by your thighs. "Lorraine," you say to her. She does not offer her name.

"Why don't you march with us?" Amber says. She looks at your fingers, the wedding ring still tightly cutting into your skin.

"Is your husband not marching?"

"I wear my ring in memory. My husband died seven years back."

"I'm so sorry."

"It's OK. I've finished grieving. And now fish are dying."

The window scene changes. Woods, back yards, small town industrial parks, public housing high rises looming above concrete basketball courts. The high rises are structurally unsafe, but the government no longer cares. People still live there. Windows on several floors are busted out. Patios are crowded with boxes, bicycles, patio furniture, wet clothes drying on guard rails. You note one patio on a top floor with a refrigerator shoved in the corner. The image is there, then gone. It always shocks you, this world beyond your sheltered Wall Street populated New England town. When you venture outside its boundaries, the poverty of the real-world hits you hard. You think we live in Disney World compared to other parts of the country with real people—the kind with jobs that offer services, grow food, make things that actually aid survival, add value to lives.

The train slows then comes to a stop at another platform. No one departs. A few dozen people try to cram their bodies inside, forcing you and your new friend, Amber, to move toward the center of the car. The density of bodies closes in on you. It feels like rush hour on a subway car, sans odor. At least these marching bodies are deodorized. The girl looks back at her friends. There's a beep. She reads her phone, types back.

"My friend says it's jam packed in the city. Let's not get lost. Here." She reaches in her pocket, pulls out a leather card holder and retrieves a business card. Her name, her cell, her email, url, and underneath, a job title—software consultant.

You give your contact information to her in case you all become separated. Your cell phone number and my work number and email. Basically, you give out my work number and my email to stranger you met on a train.

Once at Grand Central, the doors open to a human current slowly churning toward the main lobby. You struggle to keep up but slowly lag behind Amber and her friends. Obviously, the march is going to be huge, bigger than you have imagined, perhaps as big as the Roe versus Wade march several years back after it was overturned and everyone felt sorry for Southern women. You're wondering if you've missed something. Environmental advocacy never gets this kind of attention. You've been so preoccupied with dead fish, you've only skimmed the news. Again, you're overwhelmed by your privileged isolation.

Amber's back fades into the bodies ahead of you. You see her hand in the air and try to force your way through the crowd toward her. You focus on the raised hand. The world is now loud, not just with chatter, but with movement—soles tapping cement, poster boards flapping against bodies.

"Have I missed something? I didn't realize it was going to be this big," you say when you reach Amber.

"I think it got more attention after the voting rights activists joined." Her shout competes with the garbled announcements of new departures blasting from the speakers. Her friends stand still among all the bodies, checking their phones. "Lots of talk about freedom. Everyone wants to be free again, like the way it was with your generation. Fair voting, so that for once a president, a senator, a congressperson, win fair and square. Free press, no more propaganda. Like Canada."

"Yes, we could actually scare politicians into thinking we would fire them back then. It was fun. Now we have voicemail and fish farms."

"Fish farms?

The crowd is dense, and no one wants to touch each other, so everyone squeezes themselves into their body cores. You are reminded of starlings roosting in canopies, sparrows tucked inside boxwoods, blue jays perched together high up in the white pines. You try to distract yourself by reading signs lifted in the air in front of you.

"Love Does Not Need Fossil Fuel."

"No Vote, No Existence."

"Humans Need Animals!"

"Save Our Planet—Bring Back Democracy!"

You see no other signs about fish.

You follow Amber, or you think you follow Amber, but maybe you're following someone else. It's hard to tell. There are hundreds of people on the stairs in front of the exit doors. The outside light finds its way through the glass, around these bodies, and into Grand Central Station. You move toward the light.

The street outside provides more oxygen and room to uncross arms, inhale deeply. Already the crowd is shouting. The movement of bodies is faster, and you drop your sign, trying to keep up. You bend to retrieve it, but the crowd moves your body forward. You look back. Several people step on the sign, soiling your dead fish statement. You walk against the current, shove through people, demand everyone please watch their step.

"You're stepping on my dead fish sign," you scream at protestors. You reach your sign and stand on it. The crowd flows around you like a river around a rock. You kneel down, careful to put the weight only on your knees, not your back, grab the sign, remove your feet, then stand holding it high. Once again, you are part of the human tsunami that is this march.

Amber and friends are no longer near you. Your phone beeps. Texts.

Amber: "We're waiting for you on the corner of Lexington and 44th."
You: "Will be there as soon as the crowd allows it."

Another beep.

Amber: Too hard to stay here. We'll now be at Lexington and 45th.
The march starts at 1st Avenue and 57th Street. You know this?

You: March has already started. Life changes fast when the
government doesn't care. I'm a slow, older woman in a fast-moving
life.
Amber: You're weird. I want my Uncle to meet you.

A man ahead of you shouts, "Fuck this tribe running our country." Another
one. "Fuck fascism!" The crowd now shouts, "Fuck this government!"

You make it to the corner. You look down at your phone right as a man falls
into you. You drop your phone and sign.

"Do you have to bump people? Can we all breathe a moment and collect
ourselves?"

"Chill, lady."

You can see your sign but not your phone. You would rather see your phone
and not the sign. Still, you pick up the sign, and grab a nearby lamp post to
prevent the human current from carrying you to wherever everyone is now
going.

"Can everyone watch their step," you scream to the backs in front of you. "I
lost my phone."

"Were you standing here when you lost it?" A young man in baggy sweats
with a sign that says, "There is No Alt-Planet." He bends down on his knees,
which causes people to stumble over him and say "fuck." You notice this word
is very popular today.

"Fuck you, too. The lady lost her phone."

"Around here?" another voice says.

"OK. Everyone, listen up," says a tall, lean, twenty-something woman with
dark hair that hits right below her waist. You like the hair. It's the kind of hair
people used to iron. The woman with good hair puts her sign between her legs
and holds up both hands. "Listen up, we've got an older woman here, a fellow
marcher, who lost her phone, give us space."

You pause to let the anger of "older woman" flow over you. You hear a boy
behind you. Or maybe a girl, it's hard to tell when they're elementary age.

"What's your phone number?"

"I'm sorry, I don't give it out. I'm too old for you," you say and smile.

He stands in front of you now, all ten years of him, in his smart tight jeans,
sleeveless t-shirt.

"Oh, why not? I've handed it out to strangers on the train, why not to you?"
You give him your number. A faint Guns and Roses song starts up in an area a
few feet from you.

"That must be you," say another young woman who leans over then stands with your phone. "Everyone can walk now, I've got her phone."

You thank her and turn to thank the smart boy who did something you should have done right away but didn't. The boy is gone. And you don't look for him because of the bangs.

They hit the air fast, like fire crackers and the crowd no longer flows, but convulses. You grab something, the lamp post you think. Then comes the explosion.

# Blue Jay Memo

She's gone!
Where?
Don't sleep.
Stay awake. Eat grass.
We don't eat grass.
Eat half of stored peanut.
We sleep.
Wake up!
Focus!
What's going on?
Female host entered silver motorized mobile tube nest.
Which direction?
Southwest toward Great Human Tribal Nesting Area.

We need pigeons.
No way will we sing to pigeons.
We have to sing to pigeon.
We do not sing to pigeons.
Yes we do.
No.
Yes.

We sing to pigeons.

We recruit pigeons in our area to travel to huge human tribal area, find help, follow female host. They do this because they owe us. That is all we'll say.

They return and report. It's pigeon—disorganized and poorly recorded. We will translate:

The pigeons find female host after she exits motorized mobile tube nest exit/entry platform in Great Human Tribal Nesting Area. Pigeons have secret passageways into this area.

They say female host exits motorized mobile tube nest and roosts with many humans. This is described as abnormal roosting. Loud singing, objects thrust into the air.

Pigeons assure us this is something they've seen before. Humans do this in Great Human Tribal Nesting Area, they say, as if they're sophisticated, as if they've, you know, seen it all. They're pigeons for crows' sake!

Anyway, they say they perch high up on human nests and observe all the thrusting into the air, which they say is intended for other humans, not for the life above them. Today, however, there's something different. Pigeons suggest there are several human-made birds. These fake human-made birds travel approximately 50 feet above human flocks. One drops a small twig-like object. The object pops. The human flocks screech.

Oh, but not to worry, an elder pigeon says. Our female human host climbs a long steel human-made tree topped with lights. She then holds onto human-made tree with her front appendages. Beneath her, humans attack each other and human protectors.

This screeching human flock eventually moves past our female host. She does not join the flock but stays on human-made tree, perching on a branch as she sings into communication enhancer.

At this point, pigeon language becomes confused.

We think, based upon their chatter, the pigeons become bored—as they often do. We suspect they scatter, several follow human flock, others descend to forage upon human detritus. It seems at least a few remain perched above our female human host, despite their restlessness. Because we told them to. (These are the pigeons who owe us. That is all we will say.)

One observes a brown-skinned female approach human-made tree and sing to our female host. Our pigeon friends suggest that our female host sings loud and disorganized song back, whilst brown-skinned woman sings different type of song, quietly, in organized manner back to female host. We believe, based upon description of facial characteristics and behavior patterns, this brown-skinned female human may be same one who—quite a while ago—was taken briefly to the large white human protector nest, then escaped by way of motorized mobile tube nest.

Female host eventually leaves human-made tree and travels with brown-skinned female until they find a hole in the ground, which according to pigeons, leads to underground human paths. Once humans descend into the earth, pigeons can no longer collect facts.

So, this is all we know. Our female host traveled to Great Human Tribal Nesting Area where she roosted, sang, screeched with an extremely large human roosting flock. She met another female human we are familiar with. She descended into hole where secret paths exist.

The information comes from pigeons so there are probably missing details. These are pigeons. Again, that is all we will say.

We continue to monitor all exits along long motorized mobile tube nest path extending from the Great Human Tribal Nesting Area into Great Hawk Watcher Tribal Area. We suspect one day she will emerge from an exit.

Some of us plan to join the North American Migration Path, but many of us cannot do that. We are older. We have families.

So, this is what we do. We wait by exits. We monitor female host's offspring. We hunt for insects, fruit. We lose weight.

# Book 2

# Lorraine's Turn

# Prologue

*Lorraine*

I DON'T NEED a damn prologue.

# Blue Jays Memo

*We're still here. Barely.*

# Chapter 34

*The real story begins*

I KILLED THE love of my life, the only glue that held me together, the father of our extraordinary daughter, the greatest fisherman on earth.

I was outside doing what I do best, drinking wine, watching my birds, and complaining. There had been so much to complain about—the crows were dead, the planet's terra firma was shrinking behind rising water, our coral reefs were dying, our poor were poorer, the world was violent, our technological advances had halted. No one was doing anything about the rigged election system, so we had lazy, corrupt leaders and no way to fire them. To protect themselves, they controlled information, so most people at first knew only what was told to them. Many of us joined groups with people who were able to find the truth; we worked with other groups who were able to find people who could disseminate the truth. There were internecine wars, I got tired of the country's dumbasses, and while there were smart people, they tended to be self-righteous and thus reminded me too much of me. So I drank.

Lawrence agreed that the planet was dying, but he found our screaming marches and frantic letters pointless since sclerotic legislators never listened. "We're not a democracy anymore. You're concentrating on the wrong things," he yelled down at me while I pontificated about our plans to disrupt legislative session. We had lost our crows a few years earlier, and now bees were dying. Again. Also, a natural gas company was planning to run us off our property to build a pipeline. Of course, bee deaths had nothing to do with the pipeline, but bees were dying and I was mad at the fossil fuel industry. I was on my third large glass of wine and he was on top of his ladder cleaning our gutters. Every year he insisted on cleaning our gutters by himself. Fifteen feet in the air hanging on to the eaves for life, as I screamed my complaints up to him. When he said we were doing it all wrong, though, that we were a bunch of fools who liked to waste time, I stood up, topped off my glass of wine, marched up to the ladder. My last words, to my husband, my love, my best friend, my daughter's hero, were, "You're cleaning the gutters even though the gas company will probably buy our house and destroy it. But what do you care? You fish. That's your contribution to our dying planet. You stick hooks in poor creatures' mouths. Fuck you."

And he turned, slipped, fell, hit his head, and died.

And now fish are dying.

And I no longer drink.

But I am finally doing something about our lost democracy.

I agonize over Haley. I killed her father and never told her. I left her and never told her. I kept the details of her father's death secret to protect her respect for me. I kept my activities secret to protect her life. I'm breaking the law—we're breaking the law. Sarah Ableman, Lionel, and a network of hundreds and hundreds of people across the country have been working in ten key states for four years. VPNs, messaging systems that delete within two minutes, burner phones, and extraordinary complex software systems and viruses.

When Sarah reemerged, she told me about this movement. I begged her to let me contribute in some way. She liked my letters and my ability to take abuse and plow on despite alienation and public shaming. It reminded her of how she and Malinda continued their protests when the One Party began their prolonged legal attack on their love and way of life. I helped them back then, so, she thought, maybe I could help again. "You always add irony to any cause, Lorraine. We can always use irony."

Haley couldn't get involved. I had to keep her ignorant of any hint of my involvement in anything beyond local mundane issues. This was difficult because as the election neared, our actions intensified. We all planned to settle in our various operating posts around the country. Everyone has lied about his or her whereabouts to protect close friends and relatives. I don't have to lie to many people because only my daughter is close to me. Well, there's Brit, which is a type of closeness.

Sarah is ostensibly in Paris. Lionel is ostensibly in California. I am not really anywhere because there was a disruption in my last-minute fictional whereabouts. Sarah was going to tell everyone I was in a southern coastal town for a study on fish death. I really didn't want my daughter thinking I was going to live in a town that believed women could not control their own bodies. Sarah had her reasons for wanting my whereabouts to be this town; I believe it had to do with their interrelated fabrication strategies, which if you asked me, seemed way too complicated and, well, too planned. Who strategizes lies in advance? It's a lie, for Christ sakes. Of course, the lawsuit and house sale interrupted my life dramatically, and I used that to avoid the planned lie. I told everyone I'd go on the march, execute my house sale, console my daughter, then tell the stupid lie and head on to my movement responsibilities. Then came the explosion—a gas bomb dropped from one of the many government drones that harass marchers.

As I hung on a street lamp post, I said to myself, "Fuck planned lies. Planned lies are for people who can't think quickly."

Finding a hideout was no problem. When you have no fear of authorities, you make friends who help you during rough patches. I met Maria Lopez at the Westbrook Police Station and bailed her out, then sent her to New York to hide out. I lost some money but gained a connection. We also gained another group of people to help with our efforts. Sure, Maria can't vote, but her friends can, and they know how to mobilize. People who hide know people who don't hide. They are also the best people to know when you need to hide.

I slept on the couch. Maria's family—her husband and a toddler—slept in their only bedroom. The kitchen—a stove, a microwave and small refrigerator—was my day job. I cooked for them, which meant they ate a lot of nuts and vegetables, but no one complained, even though I taught Maria how to complain. It was our first important English lesson. "I don't like your attitude." She can say that perfectly. "I will not shut up." That's another great line I taught her. There's no flock biking in New York, but there are messenger bikers, which, if I lived here, would have inspired many letters to whomever one writes to in New York. "Watch where you're going, asshole!" I taught her that one, too.

I didn't inconvenience Maria's family too long, however, because my work is not in New York. My work is in Pennsylvania. Sarah, Lionel, and I are assigned to a group of computer kids, originally from Oregon and San Francisco, who supervise the Pennsylvania division. It's one of our targeted ten divisions where state electoral votes need "improvement." I don't do computers. I don't understand coding, virus generation, hacking strategies. Also, I'm not connected enough to be a good organizer. And, given my unique ability to alienate everyone within fifty miles of myself, I'm a risk for any organization because part of my alienating always involves group disintegration. After considering all these liabilities, or assets depending upon where you're standing, Sarah put me in charge of something called Impulsive Action Division. The Impulsive Action Division works on tasks requiring quick action, usually undertaken by people who don't think before acting. Because sometimes you need non-thinking people to do crazy things.

I say bye to Maria and her family over overcooked quesadillas and refried beans at a small Harlem Mexican restaurant with white table cloths and tear drop votives. I barely touch my food and spend the evening with Juanita, Maria's two-year-old, who's almost as perfect as Haley was at that age. I bounce her on my knee throughout the dinner. When I put her back in the high chair, I tell them I'm leaving the next day. It's a shock and a disappointment because I've helped them out for two weeks—babysitting, cooking, cleaning, telling strange officious sounding callers they have the wrong number. They love me. It can happen. People can love me. I've tried not to fall in love with them, because the government has become experts at deportation. I can't take any more grief. But, of course, my self-restraint doesn't last. If we can't take the country back, I suppose I'll have to add Maria to my long list of advocacies that go nowhere in a non-democratic country. That is, if I'm not in jail.

I take Amtrak the next morning. Not the southern line to Philadelphia, but the northern line to Connecticut. I need to take care of the birds, investigate the health of my family before I settle in Philadelphia for the hard work. Maria laughs when she sees me dress the next morning. I don't. I think I look good.

# Blue Jay Memo

*Pay attention*
*We're weak*
*We see her?*
*What?*
*Pay attention!*
*To what?*
*Male with female host face!*
*Male with what?*
*Pay attention! There! Look.*
*With face fur?*
*That's her?*
*She's done the gender switch.*

We have noticed this switch in other humans, but we're pretty sure female host is not permanently switching gender. This is a poorly executed gender switch. We figure she's temporarily switched for whatever reason humans have for doing whatever they do.

It's her, though. We're sure of it. We can recognize humans by eyes and dimensions and movement. Distance of eyes from each other and in relation to other features, like beak. No disguise evades us. Sure, males grow facial fur. Females paint face colors, mostly black and brown. Sure, some switch genders. Still, the dimensions remain unchanged. We're good at this. Trust us.

Anyways, female host carries a large bag, causing a slight lopsided wobble, as opposed to fluid perambulation. She steps onto a large motorized mobile nest that carries twenty humans to various exits, similar to long motorized mobile tube nest.

At an exit 1.5 miles northeast of this boarding location, she leaves motorized mobile nest, singing into her communication enhancer.

*She then takes another smaller, blue motorized mobile nest to a path intersection approximately .5 miles southwest of Children of Athena home nest. She exits mobile nest, perambulates through wooded land in direction of Children of Athena.*

*She enters her original home nest grounds!*

*Where've you been?*
*Where've you been?*
*Where've you been?*
*Where've you been?*

*She for once listens to our screams. Her upper appendages reach up to us and she sings sorrowful songs. Then she does something extraordinary.*

*Food!*
*Stay on limb*
*Food!*
*Wait.*
*Oh hell, eat!*

*Seeds, nuts, peanuts. Food. Everywhere. We gorge ourselves.*

*She leaves.*
*No, she trails.*
*Trails of food!*

*She trails food back to the wooded area. She places platters of seeds around area. She hangs them from trees. She places steel trunk into earth and hangs plates of seeds.*

*We do not know what this means. Is this our new home? Is this new feeding area?*

*We continue to follow female host to her next destination. We all know where she'll go next, so many of the more impatient fly there by way of shorter, more direct bird route.*

# Chapter 35

*Spying kind of works, but not really*

LOLLY'S BARK IS persistent and hysterical, which is not like her. Of course, while her smashed nose is bad for the olfactory senses, it still works. I suspect my scent is slipping through cracks in this window I'm peeking through.

Haley's town house is nice. Why wouldn't it be? I picked it out before I left. Unfortunately, it has no private yard, only a few grassy cartilages that connect various building clusters. There are two bedrooms, a large den, a connected eating area, and a spacious kitchen with granite counters and central cutting table with a sink. I have a good view of the den. Modern, streamlined sofa with no skirt. Sleek, high-backed chairs. Glass-topped coffee table that would worry me with my bulldog. Lolly is, however, being kept in the bedroom, which I do not like, although it's a reasonable decision given the new furniture. I suspect Haley donated my furniture. Or maybe it's in storage, because she assumes I'd return.

I feel a nauseous wave of guilt. Terrifying guilt. What have I done to my daughter? She's stuck in this situation because of me, forced to shove my dog in the back bedroom to protect new furniture while she works.

I hear a car horn. The loud honk feels close, which makes me nervous. I'm a man at a woman's window. I step back from the window, regard my surroundings. That's all I need—another arrest, this time as a man—a man with a mustache that itches right now. It's been itching for hours, but if I scratch it too hard, it could fall off, and there I'd be with a glue-stained lip and familiar face.

Lolly continues to bark. It sounds painful and turns into a long agonizing whine. I walk around the town house but cannot see through any bedroom window since Haley is smart enough to close all blinds to prevent disturbance by neighbors or snoops, like me. My need to see Lolly overwhelms me. It's greater than my need to see my daughter, which makes me feel even guiltier. I tell myself the reason I feel this overwhelming need to see Lolly has to do with her need for me. She needs me more than my daughter needs me.

I assure myself of my dog's need for me as I walk back to my rental car. I open the door, sit before the steering wheel, and consider my situation. I have accomplished what I have set out to do. I have fed my birds, checked on Haley.

Of course, I haven't seen Haley, only her apartment, and I've only heard my dog, not seen my dog, nor, more importantly, rubbed my dog's belly, which I have been thinking about for months. But I have an idea now about how my daughter has transitioned. The furniture is modern, which makes a progressive, original statement. There is hope! Furthermore, Lolly is loud and safe, although probably claustrophobic. Everything is fine. I can leave.

I see the girl right when I start the car. She has three dogs on long leashes—a Lab, a pit bull, and a corgi—and stands in front of Haley's door, jingling keys. She ties her dogs to a small hook on the side of the town house and disappears inside. I roll down the passenger window. Lolly barks—her usual whiney bark—as she and the girl re-appear, then she stops abruptly, her ears perked, her round face turned toward my rented car. I duck down, pretending to look for something on the floor. It occurs to me that Lolly could not possibly recognize a rented car, and she can't smell me at a distance. I sit back up.

The girl and all the dogs walk down the street at a nice pace. The girl has an athletic, fast stride, encouraging the dogs to trot by her side. Lolly's panting resembles laughter as she jogs with the pack. Something feels different about the scene. The girl? The dogs? I stare at Lolly's belly, which shakes only slightly as she walks then trots then walks again. That's what's different! Lolly is walking!

I should feel good about Lolly's happiness and ability to walk on leash like a normal dog, but I don't. I resist the temptation to follow the dogs because my time is limited. I need to decide what to do about Haley and then I have to somehow find a way to disseminate my required absurd lie regarding my whereabouts so no one will worry. Of course, Haley cannot know anything of my current situation. She cannot know about our plans.

I look down at the envelope I intend to send her. I've told her so many lies. And she is probably depressed right now. Her mother is missing. Lionel has essentially broken up with her—which I didn't like but agreed was necessary so he wouldn't be tempted to divulge anything. She's probably feeling alone and rejected. I tap her number, then tap off. I feel alone, too. I'm not supposed to call anyone, but there are so many things I'm not supposed to do. Like visit my dog.

At least I can empathize with her aloneness.

I tap Brit's number, then tap the phone off. Brit moved to a new town, allowing me to distance myself naturally. I admit I told him a few honest facts, my tongue is notoriously loose in bed. I tell myself, it's OK, he needs to know just a wee bit in case everything fails and I get arrested and need a lawyer/lover again. As the dog walker and dogs take a left turn and disappear, I tap Brit's number again. I hope for a voicemail because I don't want to go through his questions. Of course, Sarah has told me no voicemails. No trace of me can be left with anyone, so I am breaking a big rule. What's new?

When he answers, I'm quiet for a moment. I take in his two hellos.

"Don't ask me questions or say anything because this has to be quick."

"Lorraine? Dear God. Where the hell are you? You're on a burner phone, aren't you?"

"Here's the deal. Listen."

"You told me you were going to leave after the march for whatever it is you're working on, where was it? In the South?"

Oh fuck! I forgot I told him that.

"There was an interruption."

"Lorraine, I don't like this. You've done wild things before and managed to slip out of major trouble, but if you're doing what I suspect you're doing, you won't slip out again."

"Does that mean you won't be my defense attorney?"

"I'll always defend you, dear."

"Look. I've set up feeders for the birds in that land trust adjacent to my property. You know the land trust? Anyway, you have to stop by every other day and refill them. OK?"

"You want me to feed wild birds on the land trust?'

"You're not allowed on my property because, as I've told you, the assholes refuse to feed birds and will probably cut down my trees."

"And so when do I see you again? Are we still, you know . . . ?"

"Having sex? Not for a while. Just dream about me. Feed my birds. Give my daughter her mail. Kiss to you."

I tapped the phone as he begins to complain.

My next stop is the Post Office, then bank. I grab the envelope with articles for Haley, just so she knows I'm alive and still thinking. She'll know I sent them. And more importantly, she'll know I've not changed, nor will I ever change. The titles of the articles tell her this.

*"How to Decorate Your New Green Home."*

*"Moving up The Corporate Ladder by Avoiding Male Assholes."*

*"How to Attract a Progressive Boyfriend."*

*"Why We Cannot Exist Without Fish"*


THE BANK'S PARKING lot is empty, making me wonder about the bank's business. Is this unusual, or are people not visiting Haley's bank? Perhaps there's a preference for online banking because most people would rather type, not verbalize, answers to dull questions. I wonder if Haley has thought of this. I suspect she has and probably has better ideas about how to increase customer traffic.

I park my car and sit a moment as the engine runs. Her window opens to the other side, so right now I can't see her. Unless I walk around the corner and look inside, which is a risk, yes, a useless risk, because she sits with her back to the window. But if I walk around the corner just a wee bit, I can at least see her back, which is better than not seeing any of Haley. I want to see her back.

The idea of seeing Haley's back has progressed rapidly to my muscles. I check myself in the mirror, put on my baseball hat, and step out, shoving both hands in my front pockets, straightening my back, and lope like a man with confidence. I reach the corner and stand a moment, looking across the street at the park where we used to eat lunch with Lolly. The autumnal colors and crisp air—too warm for late November, but still inviting—overwhelm me for a moment.

I remember our lunches—Lolly greedily chewing our leftovers, Haley's sweet, soft giggle, me talking too much, not wanting to leave. I loved sitting in the park with her because it was like sitting with Lawrence again. She inherited all her father genes. She looks like him, laughs like him, eats like him, tolerates me kindly like him. I don't think she received any of my DNA. I used to wonder if another egg found its way into me. Maybe one of Lawrence's sperms was already inside an egg, a genetic deformity of sorts. It could still swim, this sperm-in-egg, so made its way up the vagina, into my uterus and got all comfy, then I gave birth to only Lawrence's child. Haley would never yell at her husband, causing him to fall and die. Haley would never yell at the world, then run away and break the law, ostensibly to save the world, but maybe to save herself. She would never sit back while her daughter gave up freedom for her. That text to her by Lionel was so right. She needs her freedom. At least I've now done that for her. She's finally free. Of me.

"Excuse me, can I help you?" A woman, maybe mid-forties, dressed in mauve—her face resembling a startled gazelle—stands before me. I touch my mustache to make sure it's still properly there. It is. There is moisture right above it.

"I'm fine. Just thinking. Thanks for asking," I say in my normal voice, which is not really deep, but not high. Does it sound like a man? I didn't practice my man voice, so there you go, I've blown my cover already. The woman squinches her eyes. I feel a wet bug crawling down my face, but when I slap it, I realize it's not a wet bug, it's my tears.

"Can I get you something." She reaches over and lightly touches my arm.

She looks at me with kind, giving eyes. She is concerned about this strange man with a relatively high voice standing on a street crying. Yes, I want to tell her, you can get something for me. Go into the bank and get my daughter. I'm probably going to jail. Again. Will you be my daughter's new mother?

"Why don't you come inside for a moment, get some coffee."

"Inside of what?" I say in my too high voice.

"The bank. I'm the manager of that bank." The gazelle gently nods her head in the direction of the bank.

"Oh, no, no thank you. It's a family thing. No worry. I like your bank, though. Particularly that young lady. Haley? She helped me once when I was cashing a check. I'm not a customer or anything like that, but I needed help with something to do with a check. She asks very astute questions. I can tell she's going places." She looks at me funny. I realize I am a strange man who is showing interest in a woman who works for her. "I've got to run, meeting up with my girlfriend, so, but thank you, thank you. You and your employees are very nice." I walk away and decide not to look into the window because now I have alerted the manager to my strange personality. I suddenly understand the difficulty involved in being a male around women. My feminist ire falls away slightly. Then returns.

I head back to my car, but before I open the door, I look over at the bank's door. It's one of those all glass doors in the middle of an all glass front, a mere crack with a handle. And there she is. Standing with the bank manager, studying me. I suppose the manager told her I said something about her. They are probably wondering whether to call the police. If I were a black man, the police would already be here, but I am a thin, five-foot eight white man with a mustache and high voice.

The manager sees me look and waves. Haley smiles and I smile back. She looks thinner, which makes me worry a bit. We stand this way for a moment, staring at each other. I feel something tickle the edge of my mouth but I'm too frozen to brush it away. Does she know she's looking at her mother? I want her to recognize me, break through the door, run to me, then embrace me the way people do who've missed each other. It's a transient desire that dissolves as I notice her expression change. She now looks confused, as if she's considering telling her boss—who probably told her about my compliment—that she has no idea who I am. That would be like her. She would refuse to accept a compliment. She'd tell the truth. She'd say she's never seen this strange man before. She'd resist the temptation to lie in order to gain those all-important points with management. No, Haley, don't be honest! Accept the compliment. Lie to your boss. Climb that ladder. Getting ahead is OK now. The world is going to survive. Hang in there. I say this with my eyes. Then I leave.

# Blue Jay Memo

*Conflict!*
*Conflict!*
*Stay away.*
*On roof. Perch on roof.*
*Come back.*
*Conflict!*
*No conflict.*

*Female host is viewing offspring at red nest, her day perching area. She is viewing whilst wishing not to be viewed. But! Another female interrupts her viewing. We suspect conflict, but then, no, there is no conflict. They perambulate around red nest.*

*Stay put.*
*Come back!*
*Perch.*
*Female host's offspring!*

*Offspring stands at glass and views female host.*

*We notice female host's facial fur changes from horizontal alignment below beak to vertical alignment. We also notice offspring's facial characteristics change when female host's fur turns vertical. The change occurs in the eyes and feeding orifice. Pinched.*

*Female host enters motorized mobile nest and travels. We follow. She makes several stops, eventually ending up at motorized mobile tube nest entry/exit area. We perch. She enters mobile tube nest heading southwest. We do not follow.*

# Chapter 36

THE MESSAGE IS typical of Sarah. Her words are as limited in writing as they are in person.

We may be in need of Impulsive Action Division. I'll call.

I suck on a carrot stick and watch the words ghost then vanish, leaving me alone again. Alone in my small hole in a building that is an apartment. It's just me, a bed, a refrigerator, a microwave, and a table with a laptop. I spend my time reading messages that disappear within seconds. No writing is ever permanent when you belong to illegal movements. We use VPNs, never text, only communicate with Snapchat, WhatsApp, and other messaging apps that delete within seconds.

We do see each other, which is good thing because I'd go nuts if I never actually sat in a room with other humans. We meet at another larger apartment that serves as an office. Everyone is busy busy busy. I'm only kind of busy, and only when mistakes are made. I'm the one who patches up mistakes. I work with the "safe" secretary of states, corresponding with coded messages about various problems, usually with polling district regulations. There is always panic in these types of movements, particularly in one as large and critical as this on, and panic can spread quickly in interconnected organizations. As election nears mistakes increase, panic spreads.

I do wonder now what my life would be like if we all continued along the usual myopic path. I could have worked only on small issues in our small sheltered Wall Street community filled with sheltered citizens who care about preservation of bucolic land parcels, clean parks, and reservoirs filled with healthy drinking water. That was the plan after the Great Transition. Change what you can change. Stay local. Democracy will spring up in localities. We could have yelled and screamed about local issues until a handful more people did something, then another handful did something else, then, after five years, a resolution requiring all to refurbish their septic systems would perhaps pass.

Then if planet earth were still around, maybe a few fish would swim back. I ponder this but not too long.

My burner cell phone is now a screeching blue jay—a new ring tone that I'm loving so far. I tap it and try to think of something clever to say besides hello, but I'm tired. Sarah talks before I can think.

"Our pollster says interest in voting is waning. There've been removing voting signs, hacking internet ads. Also . . ."

"The government keeps deleting our GOTV tweets and Instagram messages. The signs are always down. I just put them back up. I'll drive out—"

"No. We've got a bigger problem. Voting booths are no longer scheduled for delivery," she interrupts. "Stopped dead."

"That's the Secretary of State's decision. He's one of our plants." We've infiltrated the One Party. Five Secretary of States are part of our movement. Including Pennsylvania's.

"Yes. Ohio and Virginia are having problems with booth removal, too. They may have caught onto us. And our Secretary of State has abruptly resigned, apparently corruption investigations have ensued."

"And the virus? You don't think they know about that?"

"We've got back-up plans. But if they suspect what we're doing, they'll try to find us. Keep replacing that burner phone daily. No more snapchats either. Follow the plan, don't contact Haley or Brit. Promise me, Lorraine."

"I promise."

"I've got word she's fine. Stick with the program. We all get on a flight to California after this is over no matter how much you want to run back to Haley and Lolly. K?"

"Whatever. What do we do about the removed booths?"

Silence.

I have a feeling my life is about to become slightly dangerous.

"We have extra booths in storage. We have tractor trailers."

Silence.

"OK. So, I'm thinking you're calling me to, what, drive tractor trailers with poll booths?"

"We have drivers, so that part's not hard. We need to find enough assistants to ride with them. A particular type of assistant. Impulsive, quick thinking liar assistants."


THE TRUCK DRIVER'S name is Ronnie Matzer. Ronnie is built like Arnold Schwarzenegger but talks like George Constanza. He works in a large storage facility, and someone met him at a PTA meeting. He's driven a tractor trailer truck exactly five times in a previous job before being fired. We are desperate, obviously. There's no seat belt, so I hold the side arm tight and don't cross my legs so they're ready to do whatever legs do when a truck rolls over or crashes into a pole.

"So, I don't mind driving these things, but what I need—because you can't see shit on turns—is you to open that window and tell me if the coast is clear to turn."

"I can't see much behind our trailer."

We're at an intersection. Two more blocks of pure terror before we can unload a few voting booths. He's been having difficulty on turns. We've already caused several hysterical responses at traffic lights. But so far, no one has called the police.

"Why don't you let me out," I say. "I'll guide you around the turn."

"You don't think I know what I'm doing, do you? Right?"

"No. I'm thinking, how did I get here?"

When he shoves it into gear, there's a ripping sound. He turns the wheel as if he wants to twist it off the shaft, and I look down at small Fiat we pass, a mere foot separating us.

"The bitch is these trailers. I can do this without the trailer." He looks at me, not down at the car he passes.

In the rearview mirror, I catch sight of the Fiat car we have now passed. It's fine, the driver is probably calm, just passing another tractor trailer at an intersection. I breathe in and out slowly.

"Trailers mess up the driving," he continues, now looking at the street ahead of him again. "It would be better to stack the freight on top, as opposed to dragging it behind. Too hard to turn."

I close my eyes and count to myself, thinking of my sweet Haley. Please vote, Haley.

We finally arrive with no major accidents and Ronnie unloads the fork lift. I tell the school representative—an assistant principle who does not say his name when I introduce myself—that we have been told to simply drop the voting booths off, make sure they operate. The assistant principal looks my age, and he's wearing a striped tie with a plaid shirt, which I like because it makes a statement. He's tired and a little mad. In the distance, children line up by the gym door—our destination. Most all of them stare at us. I pause a moment to take them in. We concentrate on voting turnout in these low-income districts because that's the audience the One Party discourages from voting.

Children's attire say more about the economic health of a district than any chart filled with statistics. The kids are dressed appropriately for fall weather, but the clothes appear over-washed and worn. A few kids wear only light sweaters in this fifty-degree weather. Hair tangled, shoes untied. Our ride out passed shacks that are called homes by the families inside. Parents who work in the cities, commute from these shacks because there's no longer adequate housing in the cities. About thirty percent of our country now lives like this, below poverty. We have no minimum wage, no safety nets. If one of these children become ill, they depend upon volunteer staffed clinics. We've stalled innovation, so new ideas to help these people are squashed before they flourish. We're losing our fish. We're losing our animals. We've already lost our humanity.

"Yesterday, they took most of the booths away," the assistant principal says. "It was quite a disturbance. We had to cancel all gym classes and move the children to the art room." He waves his hand in the direction of the school, probably toward some far off art room. "Are we to remove the children from lunch again?"

"Is the art room available again?" I say with a smile. "My daughter loved art, by the way, and she turned out extremely well. With nice establishment behavior, too."

He does not smile.

"Why can't the children be there when we move these machines in? We'll simply put them against the walls."

"There's not much room," he says. "Tables, chairs, kids." We both stare at the line of children. They don't look hungry, but I forget what a hungry elementary-aged child looks like. Haley had digestive issues at that age. "We don't like them disturbed by construction when they eat. I don't understand why you guys move them away only to return with them two days later, forty-eight hours before election."

"You're voting, right?"

"Can I see your papers?"

"It's been a while since it was something that mattered, but this year we're urging everyone to vote. It's important."

Ronnie is now driving the fork lift carrying two voting booths to the gym.

"Can you stop him?" the assistant principal says.

"I'm sorry. I can't stop a fork lift, but I do have papers. We have orders from the Secretary of State."

"Haven't they removed him for some reason? I thought I read that in the paper. Is that what this is about? The new guy comes in and changes everything?"

"Yes, yes. New guy. New stuff." I pull out my faux forms, full of fine print that no one reads. Ronnie has stopped the fork lift by a door, and five small boys surround it. The tired assistant principal waves at Ronnie, then trots toward them. I follow, holding my faux forms.

"OK. OK. Let's all move along. Wilton, off the tractor." A small red-headed boy has climbed on Ronnie's lap and is moving the levers. The assistant principal looks at me. "I think I'll put in a few phone calls before you move the booths inside."

I clap my hands and yell, "Children, can I have your attention? Can all of you who're lining up for lunch come around us for a moment." The entire line, all forty-something of them, don't move, only stare. A straight-backed African American girl marches up to me. The rest of them slowly follow.

"Our country will be voting in two days. Do all of you know about voting?" I say. "Let me rephrase that. Who knows about voting and how important it is?"

"It's when you go somewhere and pick someone to win." The straight-backed girl.

"And Dad says there's never a surprise." A Latino boy, probably about eleven years old.

"Mom says it's still important cause it shows love of country." The girl again.

"Yes, it does," I say. "And your wonderful assistant principal . . . Excuse me, can someone tell me this lovely man's name?"

The girl says, loud, "Mr. Tillerman."

"Wonderful. Mr. Tillerman thought all of you would enjoy seeing us fill your gym with an abundance of voting booths. Who knows what a voting booth is?"

Hands in the air. Again, the girl, without being called on, speaks. "It's where you vote for someone, but it don't matter 'cause you know who's gonna win."

Mr. Tillerman closes his eyes.

"But that can change," I say. "We can vote this year and maybe someone else will win. But, if we don't have enough voting booths, we don't have enough votes. So, Mr. Tillerman, who is quite the patriot, is allowing us to quickly restore the booths so your district can vote. We however want to make sure you don't mind. Can we do this while you eat?"

The children clap. The red-head climbs back on Ronnie's lap and two children open the door so we can enter.

Mr. Tillerman shakes his head, grabs my papers, and walks away. This district will have voting booths. Two days left to deliver dozens of others. We can only hope the nine other states have competent liars, too.

# Blue Jay Memo

*We follow too many*
*Follow!*
*Come back!*
*Too many. Let two-year olds do it.*
*Shut uuup.*
*On. Limb .Now.*

*OK, so we follow these humans:*
*—Male with white head fur and red beak feeds us, so of course we've been following him.*
*—Female host dog. Dog perambulates with new female who does nothing but perambulate with dogs. We don't understand why. We let elders follow. Elders like dog.*
*—Offspring. We follow offspring because she has been viewing male with white head fur and red beak who feed us. She views whilst not wishing to be viewed.*

*Today, offspring shows up at our feeding location, again viewing whilst not wishing to be viewed. She follows male back to his home nest. We remind you that this is predatory behavior. We do not think offspring is predator, but we suspect behavior indicates potential for conflict.*

*She perambulates to entrance to nest of male with white head fur and red beak. She hits entrance with right appendage several times. Male with white head fur and red beak opens nest entrance.*

*Conflict!*
*Conflict!*
*Conflict!*
*Enough!*
*Perch.*
*No. Come back!*
*Shut uuuup!*

*Conflict!*
*Conflict!*
*Conflict!*

# Chapter 37

*Flying away to place with no jays*

THE GATE CONTAINS five people staring at the overhead monitor, now set to one of the government's cable channels. Talking heads, chattering with shocked politicians. The exit polls have matched the voting results for the first time in over fifteen years, so of course the government leaders appear dejected. They'd been essentially guaranteed a job for fifteen years, and in one day that guarantee disappears. The quality of their job performance matters. They're fired! The outward anger is restrained, though, because so many people voted. Larry would have loved their Catch 22. He would have been so self-satisfied, watching the polls come in state by state until it was obvious their rigged systems had indeed failed. And he would have known what was done. He would have known I had learned about it and asked to help. He would have known it was something I would do, without thought, without questioning consequences.

I don't want to stay up all night so I can take an early morning flight to California. It's not the way I prefer to spend the day after the biggest election in our lifetime. Sarah is already in California with many others, all busy deleting evidence, melting hardware, shredding and burning any incriminating evidence. I want to be with Haley, not at some ranch. Four months, Sarah tells me. "Until we know for a fact the new government has been accepted." I couldn't text Haley this morning because I had already beaten the phone with a hammer and tossed it in a bin with other hardware, all heading for whatever furnace exists that melts phones, computers, and tablets.

The announcement to board is loud and cheerful. All six of us walk onto the plane. It's six am, we're awake and free. The cabin is almost empty, but I still have a seat right next to another woman. She looks late twenties and has a worldly mien that says she's either an artist or the daughter of wacko parents she's still responsible for. She's seated in the middle; I'm by the window, where I always sit to study clouds or stars or other airplanes or the engine on fire. Four other men are scattered about the plane.

"I won't be offended if you move away," I say. "The entire plane is your oyster." I smile. She smiles with only the right side of her mouth. After a brief moment, she stands and moves to the adjacent aisle seat. I look down at the empty seat that separates us.

"You can put your stuff there." I pat the seat. "And thank you."

"Thank you for what?"

"You could move to any seat on this entire plane, but you moved only one seat away. It makes me feel necessary."

She lets out a deep, hearty laugh that goes on a beat too long and ends in a breathy sigh. She looks over the seat in front of her as she talks to me. "Let me guess. You're very excited about what has happened, and you want to talk with someone about it. I met so many strangers last night."

"Strangers are only strangers because you don't know them. I used to tell my daughter that all the time because she was embarrassed when I talked with people I didn't know." The girl is starting to look a bit worried about me. "I'm not going to talk to you about the elections, though. Or the planet. Or the dead fish in our ocean. We will finally work on all that now, I think. The dead fish problem, that is. So, actually we don't have to talk too much now." She squints her eyes. "I'm talked out. I just like that you stayed only one seat away."

Her smile this time is warm. I stare out the window at the sky, now a dull gray. In the distance another jet putters down the tarmac, toward the runway. Our plane moves back. The young woman plucks her smart phone from her purse and types something, then reads, then types. Before she puts her phone away, I tap her hand.

"Do you have Snapchat?"

"Sure, why?"

I tell her I need to contact my daughter. She asks why I don't have a cell phone, and, of course, I cannot tell her I destroyed it because I volunteered with a large group of activists who overturned the government and have to hide all evidence of our criminality—even though the criminality has made her and everyone happy. I tell her I lost it and need to send a quick message. I know I'm not supposed to do this. Sarah made me promise to stay quiet for the flight out. No social media (although social media has always been out of the question), no texting, no phone calls, no nothing on my burner phone after the election polls opened. However, I did not promise her I wouldn't use Snapchat on a stranger's phone.

The young stranger taps her Snapchat app and hands me her phone.

I type in my daughter's address, then, "I'm OK. Don't worry. We're free! I will see you in two-three, OK four months."

I take a quick selfie, send the message, wait for a moment. It indicates read. She has read it! I delete it.

The women shakes her head and drops her phone in her purse. She doesn't talk for the entire flight, only reads, then sleeps.

I close my eyes and dream of the ranch where I will stay. I was told there are thrush, purple martin, spotted owl, warblers, falcons, and, if I'm lucky, golden eagles. But no blue jays.

# Blue Jays Memo

We've had a long night.

Yesterday, we noticed the nest reserved for daytime perching for young humans was filled with adult humans. Adult humans perambulated into nest, they perambulated out of nest.

Male with white head fur stood in these lines.
Offspring stood in these lines.
Female who perambulates with dog stood in these lines

We were very concerned. We returned to feeding area.

Then! There was human noise in the night. Loud noise. High pitched. Not violent. Not angry. Happy?

OK, so today we consider moving our home nest, but we do not know with certainty if new feeding area will be permanent. No one has fed us in two days. We do not understand meaning of previous day and loud human noise at night.

We perch.

Food!
Food!
Food!

Offspring arrives with many bags of seed! She feeds us! She sings quiet songs.

# Chapter 38

*How we know that we don't know . . . them*

I STAND BEFORE the town house, imagining her opening the door, and I feel my naked shame wash over me. I anticipate the anger, the door slam, the complaints about losing me and facing eviction. Haley, of course, will be justified in her rage because what mother would do what I have done to my only daughter? She will probably be in her housecoat, hair a mess, raccoon eyes. It's too early in the morning for a visitor. I pull my cotton sweater together. It's a rare cool day this April.

The door opens.

"You have a right to be very mad at me. We're free, we can save our fish now!"

What stands before me is an old woman holding a poodle in her arms. Her hair is bluish white, she wears wool slacks and a heavy sweater, and her eye balls look swollen under thick lenses.

"Why would I be mad at you? But I do agree about the freedom. I actually love my country again. And yes, let's save the fish!"

"I'm sorry, but who are you? Where is Haley Mulderon?"

"I've been renting this from her for only a month now. I actually don't know where you can find her."

"I'm her mother. Do you have an address? I've lost it actually, and, well, I've been away, so."

"Oh dear! Come in. The notorious Lorraine Mulderon! Oh my. I feel famous just standing here with you. My name is Alice Hulstrum." She opens the door and extends her warm leathery hand. I shake it slowly. "Come in."

I step inside, follow her to the kitchen. The furniture is dark mahogany with lots of throw pillows.

"Can I fix you tea?" She puts her small poodle down and he sniffs my red tennis shoes. I feel tears burning my eyes. I miss Lolly so much. I lean over and rub my hands through the soft poodle hair.

"Haley was interviewed by our local news several times about you. Have a seat."

I sit at a small kitchen table set up by the far window. I recall standing there four months ago, peeking at Haley's life.

"We first thought you were kidnapped, you know. Then Haley got your letters from Hawaii in early December. She told us not to worry, you were doing environmental studies down there. She told us about the PTSD you experienced after the explosion. Are you doing better now?"

"Oh yes. Therapy and sun. The work down there was important, too. I lost her address, so." I pause a moment, my mind ticking fast.

"Don't you have a contact list on your phone?"

"I lost my phone and never backed it up. Plus, the move was horrible as you can imagine, and, well, I assumed the tenant would have it." I had planned to see Brit next but now realize I should have visited him first to fill myself in on my daughter.

"I send my check to a P.O. box in Hartford, Connecticut. I don't know her personal address. I tried to call her once, but she's wiped herself off internet. Google wipe. You can do that now."

"She wiped herself off internet?"

The kettle screams, and she fixes the tea. I look down at my hands and say nothing. Hawaii? Did Brit tell her to say that? He's lost touch with me, too. How would he know what to say? The poodle jumps on my leg demanding attention. I put my hands in its hair again as Alice places a cup in front of me and pours the tea. I sip it quickly and wait for her to begin, but she walks into her den and opens the cabinet door beneath her bookcase. She pulls out a taped box and brings it to the kitchen where she gently places it by my feet.

"She told me when she left that you may show up here. You didn't lose her address now did you?"

I don't know what to say and obviously this woman is pretty sharp, so more lying is risky. I'm proud of Haley for renting her place out to a smart elderly woman. I'm also impressed she inherited my mischievous genes.

"No," I finally say.

"I don't get involved in family disputes. Don't worry, though, she probably just wants to be alone for a while. She'll find you."

I look down at the box.

"It's light, so maybe it's documents you need. Oh, and your bulldog is staying with the dog walker, a foster parent of sorts. I do have that address." She stands. "Let me find that."

"CAN WE SAY hello first?" Brit says. "God, slow down. Let's start with how are you and what the hell?"

I'm trying to drive and introduce myself to Brit all over again. Brit of course has a right to be angry. He hasn't seen me in months and for all he knows we will never have sex again. I wonder if he has been seeing someone else. I suspect he has.

"Hello. There, I said it. Where's my daughter, for fuck sakes?"

"Come out to Ridgeport and we can talk. She's somewhere in Hartford. She refused to tell me more than that. Oh, except that there've been arrangements made for the birds, so she doesn't have to feed them anymore. She took over that task, you know. She also said she hoped you and I would get back together once you stabilized. She figured it out somehow."

"Did she tell you I moved to Hawaii?"

"No, she told the entire world that. I went along with it. I've learned to simply close my eyes and jump when it comes to you and your life."

"I've got a place, a small one, in Northwind. Haley's tenant gave me a box she left for me, so maybe that holds some answers. Haley apparently expected my visit. Seems my daughter is even smarter than I realized. But she can't wipe herself off internet. Not from me. I've got friends. I will find my daughter."

"Yes, indeed, you do have friends. Louis, for one. He told me to tell you to call him to let him know you're OK." I realize I forgot to call him. "Oh, and thanks for the election results."

"I don't know what you're talking about."

"Don't worry. I'm on a burner phone, too, Lorraine."


I DON'T CALL Louis just yet, because there's another stop I have to make before I do anything else. It's been so long since my last visit, and while I'm sure he understands, I don't want him to get used to a world without my voice.

I stroll slowly, because the walk has always been the best part of my visits. The small sinuous path through the woods. The rusted gate. And beyond the gate, the wide expanse of land dotted with markers. I made sure he was positioned in the row with the sun setting behind him. It's a cloudless day, so, as I kneel in front of him, the uninterrupted rays make me squint. There are no flowers and the grass around his marker is not the usual green; a good thing because it indicates everyone is paying attention now. Still, I don't like Larry under a flowerless, green-less earth.

"Have you missed me? Don't answer. I have a lot to say, but no time to say it, so this will be short.

"I've been busy. And I've been away. On a ranch in California! No blue jays, but I saw a few bears, lots of coyotes, and a golden eagle landed on a fence ten feet from me. Oh, and I spent a lot of time reading. Self-help books about change, forward motion, staying in the present. Sanity pushed upon me by

Sarah Ableman and her wife. Yes, wife, Larry. Turns out Malinda was tucked away here in the States the entire time. We're working on that wife title now, which will be easier with a vote and a voice. It's a long story, Larry. The road to freedom is always a long story."

The day is still, the air temperate. The sky above the flat land is the color of my grandmother's Staffordshire China. Its concave beauty covers me with hope and yet I know it's a fragile hope. The blue sky does not reveal the prison we have put the earth in. It only looks free.

I lay down with my head by the gravestone, positioning myself like Larry. I imagine one day this is where I'll be. Haley will be a lawyer, maybe a senator. She'll stand before this grave and squint into the sun. I want the sky to be this color. I want the distant chirps of robins, screeches of blue jays, haunting screams of hawks, in the air. I want fish swimming in the ocean. I want her to miss us.

"I used to think only the birds were free. Remember?" I turn my head to the gravestone. "Free like a blue jay, I'd always say. But, Larry, here's what I've learned. Blue jays aren't free yet. You have to be able to fly away from my sustenance to be free. Which leads me to Haley.

"I can't give you the usual update on Haley. I suspect she is as perfect as ever, but I've temporarily misplaced her. But don't worry, I'll find her. I always find Haley. I suppose that limits her freedom because she needs to fly away. Does that make me a complicated hypocrite? Don't answer that."

As I walk back, down the pebbled trail that passes several plots, some with flowers indicating fresh visits, I hear the distant persistent screeches of friends I now plan to visit.


I'M ALMOST AT the new bird feeding grounds, the land trust. I tap Louis's cell phone number as I drive.

"I can't talk," I say quickly before he says anything. "I'm safe."

"That you are. I think you can probably move back now. We're all safe."

"Yes. So, thanks Louis for—"

"Let me call you back."

I answer and he tells me he's on a burner, then asks if I'm driving the car while talking on a cell phone.

"I have places to go, Louis." But I do as he says after telling him to meet me at a parking lot a mile from my birds' land trust. I turn my cell phone off because I am trying to obey laws now. It's a new thing with me.

LOUIS STEPS OUT of his car and stretches, holds out his arms as if he wants to hug me, but then reconsiders. He's thin and the circles under his eyes tell me he's not slept.

"Alice?" I say, because I know.

"Cancer's back. She's braver than I am."

We hug a long time and separate. I'm crying, he isn't. We both look out at the parking lot as if expecting someone to listen in, but there's no car in sight.

"God, Louis. It's going to be tough, but you'll survive. At least you're fighting for her life in a free country again, with kind, decent people." I touch his arm lightly. "Thanks for guarding Sarah and me, by the way. I know you took a big risk for us. Turns out the government never knew, but it felt good having you there. I didn't even know you were doing that until way after the fact."

"Yeah, following you around was more difficult than it appeared on paper." He smiles but says nothing as if worried there's a microphone in the air above us.

"So, we go back to life, right? You concentrate on Alice. I concentrate on staying out of trouble. I think I can do it this time."

He laughs. In the distance a few blue jays chirp a strange song, high pitched, but mellow. And then there's a distant caw. I look toward the south expecting a flutter of black wings. But nothing. The caw was probably my imagination.

-"You did the right thing, all of us did the right thing," Louis says suddenly. "You know, my grandfather grew up in Little Italy. Back then, most of the neighborhood police were on the take. Owned by thugs, every single one of them. He said to me once, 'Louis, in my old neighborhood, life was like this: If someone stole something precious and that someone owned the police department? Well, if you want that precious something back, you got to steal it back.' So, that's what we did, Lorraine. Took our precious thing back."


I STARE OUT at the woods, the new feeding grounds for the birds. I can see the bird feeders swinging lightly in the wind. My daughter's box sits in my passenger seat, begging for my attention. The birds and Lolly can wait a bit more. I tear the taped edges with my key and peer inside at a pile of papers. I lift them gently into my lap. Print-outs of online articles:

*"Where do we go from here? What we do with our reclaimed freedom."*

*"Can the fish still be saved? Why state and local environmental laws are still important."*

*"Yes, your mother is having sex, deal with it."*

*"How to reconnect with estranged family members."*

*"Importance of our X chromosome. What we inherit from our mother."*

There is also a print-out of a Hartford state government calendar entry for Friday, April 15, a week away.

*"Presentation by committee on coastal water crisis recommending substantial changes in testing of all septic tanks within four hundred yards of coast. Haley Mulderon presenting on behalf of the committee."*

# Blue Jay Memo

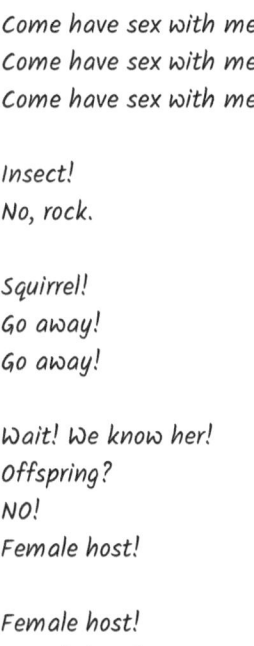

*Come have sex with me!*
*Come have sex with me!*
*Come have sex with me!*

*Insect!*
*No, rock.*

*Squirrel!*
*Go away!*
*Go away!*

*Wait! We know her!*
*Offspring?*
*NO!*
*Female host!*

*Female host!*
*Female host!*
*Female host!*


*OK, to summarize. We've moved our home to a new feeding area. We have charted the area, selected trees for nesting. Female human who perambulates with female host dog has become our new feeder. She lives far away so we've been following her. We depend upon this new host because everyone else is gone.*

*Until now!*

*Female host stands in the center of our new home!*

*Where'd you go?*
*Where'd you go?*
*Where'd you go?*

*Come back!*
*Be quiet!*
*Shut uuuup!*
*What's she doing?*

Female host is back to female gender. No fur below beak. Her head fur is now slightly yellow in tone. A long blue cloth covers her lower appendage. Her body underneath cloth appears thinner. This may indicate she has not found food as easily at her new location.

Female host perambulates around our nesting periphery. She checks out our feeding platters. She checks feeding tubes for the smaller birds. She tosses peanuts upon the ground. We dive to retrieve them.

*Where'd you go?*
*Where'd you go?*
*Where'd you go?*
*Shut uuup. Listen.*

She raises her arms and sings to us. It's a mellifluous song, not sorrowful but something else, something hopeful.

Then she leaves.

*Follow!*
*Follow!*
*Follow!*

She travels in an unfamiliar motorized mobile nest down several paths toward the dog perambulator's property.

Female host perches in mobile nest for a while then perambulates to dog perambulator's nest. When the entrance opens, female host sings loudly whilst her dog attacks her, knocking her to the ground.

*Conflict!*
*Conflict!*
*Dive bomb!*

*Dive bomb!*
*Stay on limb.*
*It's OK. No conflict.*

*There's much singing and dog noise. The attack is friendly, there is no conflict. We've seen friendly dog attacks before.*

*The human and canine roll together in the yard while the new female host makes joyful noises accompanied by much clapping of the ends of her upper appendages.*

*After a short period of time, our original female host and new female host and dog disappear inside nest. After another short period of time, our original female host leaves this nest, accompanied by dog. She carries a large bag of what we assume is dog paraphernalia.*

*We do not follow her now, though, because she no longer feeds us. We only follow and monitor humans who feed us.*

*We return and perch upon a few limbs. Some of us continue with sex. Some of us already have eggs.*

*We anticipate a calmer life in our new home that we have decided to call Children of Lorraine.*

Debbie Ann Ice was born, raised, tolerated on a sultry, green island on the coast of Georgia. She worked in New York City for several years and ended up in New England, where she studied writing while managing her two very special sons and her canine daughters (English bulldogs).

Her stories have been published in numerous online and print publications. She has written a few novels, all set in either low country Georgia, New York, or New England.